WILD SCOTTISH KNIGHT

THE ENCHANTED HIGHLANDS
BOOK ONE

TRICIA O'MALLEY

To Blazing Griffin –
Sparkle on!
xx,
Tricia O'Malley

LOVEWRITE PUBLISHING

- Hen – woman, female
- "It's a dreich day" – cold; damp; miserable
- Mad wi' it – drunk
- Och – used to express many emotions, typically surprise, regret, or disbelief
- On you go then – be on your way; get on with it
- Scunner – nuisance, pain in the neck
- Shoogly – unsteady; wobbly
- Spitting chips – angry, furious
- Tatties – potatoes
- Tetchy – crabby, cranky, moody
- Tea – in Scotland, having tea is often used to refer to the dinner-time meal
- Wee – small, little
- Wheesht (haud your wheesht) – be quiet, hush, shut up

CHAPTER ONE

SOPHIE

What was it about death that brought out the worst in people? Most of those in attendance at the celebration of life event today hadn't spoken to my uncle in years, and now I was being showered with rabid curiosity dressed up as forced condolences. Let's be honest. Uncle Arthur had been filthy rich, and everybody was here for the READING OF THE WILL. Yes, I heard it like that in all caps whenever someone asked me about the READING OF THE WILL. I barely suppressed a hysterical giggle as I envisioned a small man with a heralding trumpet, standing on the balcony and unfurling a long roll of paper, reading off the terms of THE WILL like Oprah during her Christmas specials. *And you get a car...and you get a boat...*

I was currently winning the bet on how many times my uncle's ex-wives would try to console me, a fact which simultaneously cheered and annoyed me. There were seven wives in total, having multiplied like Gremlins being exposed to water, before his last, and my favorite, had cured my uncle of his marrying hastily habit.

Bagpipes sounded behind me, and though I wasn't usually a nervous sort, my drink went flying. Turning, I glared at the bagpiper who had the gall to wink at me. Cheeky bastard, I thought, narrowing my eyes as he confidently strode past, parting the crowd like a hot knife through butter. Suitably impressed, because the bagpipe was the type of instrument that demanded attention, my eyes followed the man as he crossed the lawn, kilt billowing in the wind.

"Dammit, Sophie." Wife Number Two glared at me and dabbed at her tweed jacket in sharp motions. "This is Chanel." The only thing tighter than the woman's severe bun was her grasp on my uncle's alimony. Before I could apologize, Number Two strode off, snapping her finger at a caterer, her lips no doubt pursed in disapproval. Only my uncle would plan and cater his own funeral. I grabbed another glass of champagne from the tray of a passing server.

Arthur MacKnight of Knight's Protective Services, leader in home and commercial security systems worldwide, did not leave anything to chance. His attention to detail, pragmatic attitude, and strong code of ethics had rocketed his company to the top of the list. On the personal side? Arthur had been a known eccentric, disgustingly wealthy, and one of my favorite people. With a ten-figure company on the line, I guess I couldn't blame people for wanting to know the contents of THE WILL. But not me. I didn't care about the money. I just wanted my uncle back.

"Prissy old scarecrow," Lottie MacKnight whispered in my ear. As the proud owner of the title of Wife Number Seven, Lottie had withstood the test of time and had made Arthur very happy in his later years. She was creative, quirky, and the most down to earth of all the wives, and I had bonded with her instantly over our shared hatred of fancy restaurants. I still remembered giggling over a plate that had been delivered with much finesse but carried little more than a sliver of carrot with a puff of foam. Arthur had looked on, amusement dancing in his eyes, as his new wife and only niece had tried to maintain their composure in front of the stuffy maître d'.

When I was twelve, I had come home one day to the contents of my bedroom being placed in boxes by our very apologetic housekeeper. Much to my horror, my parents had informed me—via a note on the kitchen counter, mind you—that I was leaving for boarding school that same evening. Somehow, Lottie had caught wind of it and rescued me, bringing me back home to live with her and Arthur. I'd happily settled into a life of contradictions—business lessons at breakfast, fencing lessons at lunch, and magick studies after dinner. Well, not magick per se, but Arthur had nourished an insatiable love for myths, legends, and the unexplainable.

Once a year, I dutifully endured a phone call with my parents from whatever far-flung destination they were visiting. As an afterthought, I would occasionally receive inappropriate birthday gifts that would leave me blinking in confusion. A few we kept for the sheer madness of it all, like the gold-plated two-foot penguin statue. Lottie had promptly named it Mooshy, set him in the front hall, and put little hats or bows on him, depending on the occasion. Because of them, my tender teenage years had gone from stilted and awkward to vibrant and fulfilled, and I would forever be grateful.

Arthur's loss numbed me, like someone had cut out the part of me where my feelings were supposed to reside, and now I was just shambling about making awkward small talk with people who were suddenly very interested in speaking with me. Even the Old Wives Club, as Lottie and I referred to the other six wives, had made weak attempts at mothering me. Hence the bet I'd made with Lottie. Upon arrival at the funeral, the wives had besieged me, like a murder of crows dressed in couture, angry in the way of perpetually hungry people. Lottie, being Lottie, had swooped forward in her colorful caftan and flower fascinator, rescuing me from the wives by cheerfully suggesting they look for the attorney who carried THE WILL. The Old Wives Club had pivoted as one, like a squadron of fighter planes, and narrowed in on the beleaguered attorney with ruthless efficiency.

The funeral was being held on the back lawn of Arthur's estate in California, his castle towering over the proceedings. Yes, *castle*. Arthur had built his house to remind him of the castles in Scotland, much to the chagrin of the neighborhood. His neighbors, their houses all sleek lines and modern angles, had hated Arthur's castle. I *loved* it. What was the point of earning all that money if you couldn't have fun with it? Arthur had nourished a deep affection for his Scottish roots, often traveling there several times a year, and had spent many a night trying to convince me to enjoy what he claimed were the finest of Scottish whiskies. As far as I was concerned, if that was the best Scotland could do, then I was not impressed.

It was one of those perpetually cheerful California days, and the sun threatened to burn my fair skin. Arthur had always joked that he could get a sunburn walking to the mailbox and back. He wasn't far off. I'd already wished I had brought a hat with me. Instead, I slid my bargain-bin sunglasses on my nose to dull the light. Designer sunglasses were a no-go for me. At the rate I sat on my sunglasses and broke them, it was far more economical for me to grab some from the rack on the way out of the gas station.

"Nice glasses. Dior?" Wife Number Three drifted up, her knuckles tight on the martini glass she held.

"No, um, BP." I nodded. I pronounced it as Bay-Pay, skewing the name of the gas station.

"Hmm, I haven't heard of them. I'll be sure to look for their show this spring in Paris. Darlings!" Number Three fluttered her fingers at a fancy couple and left to air-kiss her way into an invitation to a yacht party.

"Break another pair of sunglasses?" Lottie asked, biting into a cube of cheese. There was cheese? I looked around for the server who carried that coveted tray and grinned.

"Third this week."

"That's a lot for you." Lottie turned to me, her eyes searching my face. "You okay, sweetie? This is a tough time for us. I loved Arthur, and I'll miss him like crazy, but it's different for you. He was like..."

"My father," I whispered, spying my own parents across the lawn, who had arrived over an hour ago and still hadn't bothered to greet their only daughter. Their indifference to my existence still shouldn't sting...*yet*. Here we were. I tried to frame it in my head like they were just people who I used to room with back in the day.

"And as your mother"—Lottie waved a jewel-encrusted hand at my parents—"I don't care that those two idiots are here. *I'm* claiming Mama rights. So as your stand-in mother, I want to make sure you'll be able to grieve properly. I'm here for you, you know."

"I know, I know." I pressed a kiss to Lottie's cheek, catching the faint scent of soap and turpentine. Lottie must have been painting her moods again. She was a world-renowned painter in her own right and worked through her emotions on her canvasses. All of Arthur's and my spreadsheets and business talk had made her eyes glaze over with boredom. "I don't really know yet how to think or feel. I'm numb, if I'm being honest."

"Numb is just fine. As Pink Floyd would attest to...it's a comfortable place to be. Just live in that space for a little bit, and we'll handle what comes. What about Chad? Or is it Chet?" Lottie affected a confused expression, though I knew very well she knew my boyfriend's name.

My boyfriend, Chad, was good-looking in a polished private school kind of way, and at first, I'd just been drawn to someone who'd paid careful attention to me. Now, as I watched him schmooze my parents—*not that he knew they were my parents*—I felt an odd sort of detachment from him. Perhaps that was grief numbing my feelings. Or maybe I liked the idea of a Chad more than an actual Chad himself.

"He's been very supportive," I told Lottie. Which was

true. Chad had doted on me constantly since Arthur had died, but so had all my new besties who had crawled out of the woodwork upon the news of Arthur's death. Lottie patted my arm and turned as the celebrant began speaking.

The words flowed over me, intertwining and blurring together, as my own memories of Arthur flashed through my mind. Our heated fencing battles—a sport Arthur had insisted I learn—his quirky obsession with all things Scottish, his willingness to always listen to any new ideas I had for the company, and the way he'd always called me his wee lassie. No, I wasn't ready to say goodbye.

"Oh, shit." Lottie gripped my arm, her fingers digging into the soft flesh, and I pulled myself from my thoughts to see what had distracted Lottie.

The bagpiper had returned to the back of the crowd, having circled the lawn, and now stood waiting for the celebrant's signal. Behind him, Arthur's five Scottish Terriers tumbled about.

"Did you let the dogs out?" I whispered, horror filling me. Arthur's Scotty dogs, while decidedly adorable, were quite simply put—terrors.

"No, I didn't. But the lawyer had asked where they were..." Understanding dawned, and we turned to each other.

"Arthur," I said, shaking my head.

"That *crazy* man. God, I loved him." Lottie brushed at a tear as the wail of bagpipes began again, and the kilted man once more strode forward.

"Amazing Grace." For one haunting moment, the music transported me to another time where I could just imagine a Scottish warrior crossing the land in search of his

love. Romantic thoughts which had no place here, I reminded myself, fixated on the bagpiper. The dogs bounced after the man like he was a Scottish Pied Piper, and only then did I see that one of them carried a large stuffed Highland cow. *Coo*, I automatically corrected myself. A heiland coo had been one of Arthur's favorite things to photograph on his travels to Scotland, and he'd even talked of developing a Coo-finder app so that the tourists could more easily get their own photographs.

"You don't think..." A thought occurred to me, but it was so ridiculous I couldn't bring myself to say it.

"Nothing that man did surprised me." Lottie chuckled. We watched with horrified fascination as the dogs reached the front of the funeral gathering. The Old Wives Club shifted in unison, likely due to the possibility of getting dog hair on their Chanel, and I couldn't look away from the impending doom. It was like watching a couple fight in public—I knew it was bad to eavesdrop, but I always wanted to listen and pick whose side I was on. Spoiler alert. I usually sided with the woman.

"Tavish and Bruce always fight over toys," I hissed as two of the dogs separated themselves from the pack, their ears flattening.

"Arthur knows...*knew* that," Lottie said, her hand still gripping my arm. I winced as it tightened. A gasp escaped me when the dogs leapt at each other. Houston, we have a problem.

A flurry of barking exploded as the last notes of "*Amazing Grace*" faded into the sun, and the bagpiper strolled away seemingly unconcerned with the chaos he left in his wake. Maybe he was used to it, for the Scots *could* be unruly at times, and this was just another day's work for him. I grimaced as Tavish and Bruce got ahold of the coo, each gripping a leg, and pulled with all their might. The celebrant, uncertain what to do, walked forward and made shooing gestures with his hands.

The dogs ignored him, turning in a manic circle, whipping their heads back and forth as they enjoyed a fabulous game of tug. Growls and playful barks carried over the stunned silence of the gathering, with everyone at a loss of how to proceed.

With one giant rip, Bruce won the toy from Tavish and streaked through the horrified crowd. A fine white powder exploded from the coo, coating the Old Wives Club and spraying the front line.

"His ashes," I breathed. My heart skipped a beat.

"Indeed," Lottie murmured.

Bruce broke from the crowd and tore across the lawn toward the cliffs, the rest of the dogs in hot pursuit, a doggy version of Braveheart. Tavish threw his head back and howled, and I was certain I could just make out the cry for "freeeeedom" on the wind.

The wind that now carried a cloud of ashes back to the funeral gathering.

Pandemonium broke out as the crowd raced for the castle, trying to beat the ash cloud, while Lottie and I stood upwind to observe the chaos from afar. A muffled snort had me turning my head.

"You can't possibly be..." I trailed off as Lottie pressed her lips together in vain, another snort escaping. To my deep surprise, the numb space inside me unlocked long enough for amusement to trickle in. In moments, we were bent at the waist, howling with laughter, while the Old Wives Club shot us death glares from across the lawn.

"Oh." Lottie straightened and wiped tears from her eyes. "Arthur would've loved that."

I wrapped an arm around Lottie and watched Wife Number Three vomit into a bush.

"It's almost like he planned it." As soon as I said the words, I *knew* he had. Raising my champagne glass to the sky in acknowledgment, I felt the first bands of grief unknot inside me. He'd wanted us to laugh, as his last parting gift, to remember that in the face of it all...the ridiculous was worth celebrating.

CHAPTER TWO

Lachlan

"Och, now, it's a dreich day," I grumbled, shaking my coat off as I came in through the side entrance of our castle. Well, I used the term "our" loosely. Technically, ownership of the castle had recently changed hands from the collective trust of the Village of Loren Brae and had passed over to private ownership. Which meant I now had a new boss that I'd yet to meet. The thought rankled, and I'd spent many a night cursing the stupid American who'd purchased the property months ago and hadn't bothered to once step foot in it. For years now, our people had looked at me as the unofficial laird of Loren Brae, and now our village suffered.

MacAlpine Castle, situated on the bonnie banks of Loch Mirren, reminded me of a dowager countess, stately and majestic, yet showing her years if you looked closely.

With four wings, an abundance of historical features, and an area open to the public for tours, MacAlpine Castle was one of the main tourist attractions for Loren Brae. It was also my home, which was why I'd somehow stepped into the role of village patriarch. On weekends, I'd don my kilt and greet tourists, posing for photos and answering questions, while Hilda and Archie, the castle keepers, managed everything else.

The three of us lived in two wings of the castle that had been converted to residential apartments several decades back, and it suited us just fine. Even if the tours had virtually dried up these days. Just the bad weather, I assured myself, running a hand over my hair to shake off any water droplets. Summer would bring more visitors—it always did. An excited yip greeted me, the only response to my grumbling, and I bent over to greet Sir Buster Campbell, one very skittish, loving, and cantankerous chihuahua.

Was it odd that I had a dog that was no longer than the span of both my palms fitted together? Yes. Did Hilda insist on putting him in a tweed vest and kilt and parade him about for the visitors? Also yes. Had he grown his own following on social media through the years, and did I sometimes wonder if people were more excited to visit the castle or meet Buster? Yes, and yes.

I bent to pet Buster, and he bared his teeth at me, emitting a low growl that had me shaking my head.

"All right, you crabbit beast. On you go then. I'll feed you and then maybe you'll be taking the time of day to have a wee cuddle with me." I couldn't blame Sir Buster. Much like myself, I often was cranky when I was hungry. I noted the time on the grandfather clock in the expansive hallway.

It seemed I was fifteen minutes late for Sir Buster's dinner, and he expressed his displeasure as he trotted through the hallway toward our shared kitchen and lounge. My own private apartment consisted of a bedroom, en suite, my study, and a small kitchenette if I wasn't feeling like socializing with my meals. Most nights, I took my dinner downstairs and relaxed by the fire in the main lounge.

"You're late for tea," Hilda said, Sir Buster's annoyed grumblings alerting her to my arrival. A round woman with lively bright blue eyes and hair just edging to silver, Hilda acted as my de facto mum. Having lost my own mother at the tender age of eleven, and my father disappearing into his work shortly thereafter, Hilda had assumed care of me as part of her duties as castle keeper. Since I resided in said castle, I'd fallen under Hilda's domain, and it was only natural that she'd taken to mothering me. While I may be the unofficial laird of the town, Hilda was the queen of the castle and nobody, including Sir Buster, forgot it. He cut off his growls upon seeing her, and I swear that dog softened his eyes and gave Hilda a smile, flirting with her.

"Oh, sure. You were spitting chips moments ago and now you're having a flirt, are you then?" I whispered to Sir Buster, who whipped his head around and bared his teeth at me. No growl, *of course*, as he knew Hilda would chastise him. Smart dog, that one.

"Don't antagonize Sir Buster. He's having a bad day." Hilda pressed a kiss to my cheek before bustling back to the kitchen. Could dogs even have bad days? What could possibly have happened that would put a dog in a mood?

"Is that right? Do tell," I said, my curiosity piqued. I crossed to the cabinet by the crackling fire, nodding to

13

Archie, who snapped his newspaper pages in response, and poured myself a wee dram of Edradour.

"Well, now, I can't be embarrassing the wee one, can I now?" Hilda shot me a chiding look, and I glanced back at where Sir Buster stared at her in adoration.

"This is a dog that has no shame," I said, crossing to the table where Hilda had placed bowls of creamy potato leek soup and crusty bread. "Can I help with anything?"

"Och, no, it's a bit of soup to warm your bones on a blustery night. And chicken for you, Sir Buster. Yes, sir, nothing but the best for my baby," Hilda cooed, bustling through the door into the kitchen and returning promptly with a small dish for the dog. So the dog ate chicken and I got tatties? Roundly put in my place, I pulled out my chair and sat. Archie folded his paper and rose. A limber man with a shock of silver hair, glinting brown eyes, and a terse way with words, Archie preferred to spend his time among the gardens where social skills were not required. Nevertheless, when he did speak, he often made a fair point.

"He had a disagreement with a hedgehog this morning before the rain came on. Seemed the hedgie had the right of it, and Sir Buster wasn't pleased," Archie said as he joined the table.

"Took on more than you can handle, did ya, wee man?" I laughed when Sir Buster paused from his dinner to glare at me.

"That's enough out of the two of you," Hilda said, sitting down with her glass of wine. "We've got bigger things to worry about than Sir Buster's battles."

"What now?" I took another sip of my whisky, the liquid trailing heat to my stomach, and braced myself for more bad news. We'd had a string of it of late, with more businesses closing, tourism drying up, and the people of the village talking of ancient curses. I'd tried my best to assure the town that it was just an economic slump, but even I was beginning to have a hard time explaining a few odd occurrences lately.

"The last of the Order has died," Archie said, and I brought my glass to the table with a resounding thump.

"We've been over this..." I began, frustration rankling in my gut.

"Aye, we have, yet you refuse to listen. What's it going to take, boyo? A Kelpie hurting one of your own before you believe?" Archie slapped his hand on the table. This, from Archie, was akin to him skewering me with one of the ancient swords that hung in our weapons room.

"Lachlan," Hilda said, her tone serious. "The Order of Caledonia is *real*. You can bury your head in the sand all you want, but it won't make it go away. The last of the Order has died, and the Clach na Fìrinn lies unprotected. The last line of defense has been triggered. The village is no longer safe unless we restore the Order."

"The Stone of Truth..." I shook my head and cursed, softly though so Hilda couldn't quite make out the words, and crossed my arms over my chest. "Och, that's nothing but a myth, Hilda."

"It's not," Archie said, sweeping his spoon into his bowl of soup. It was the angriest I'd seen him in ages. "And your stubbornness will have good people getting hurt."

At that, I paused. Archie was rarely adamant about something that didn't truly matter unless it was fly fishing, and his words stung.

"I understand this is sensitive for you, what with the way you lost your mum, but..." Hilda winced as I burst out of my seat and strode to the bar to pour another dram of whisky. There, I stood, memories of my mum's death swirling around me as I stared at the dancing flames.

She drowned, Lachlan.

It wasn't an accident.

The Kelpies, Lachlan.

She was too close to the island.

As a child, I hadn't wanted to hear about the myths and legends that had supposedly stolen my mum from me. No, I had wanted a solid answer that I could make sense of. She'd been swimming, as she did most days of the year in a wetsuit to keep her warm, when she'd developed a cramp and drowned. It was a human, and normal, way to die. That was it. That was all it had to be. It was the truth I'd clung to for all these years and had refused to let anyone tell me differently. If it wasn't the truth, then I'd have to avenge her death against mythological water horses and, well, the thought of that was just crazy enough to make me take another long sip of my whisky.

"I'll listen," I finally said, as much to my surprise as theirs. My hand tightened on my glass, and I stayed where I was, staring into the fire. How many times through the years had another man stared into this same fireplace while contemplating difficult decisions?

"We need to restore the Order if we want to keep the stone protected. Per legend, it starts with the knight. I finally found the last Knight of the Order. Arthur MacKnight is his name. He, well, he was receptive at the time. Enthused, even. I'd hoped he could be the start of a new

Order of Caledonia, but he's just passed this week," Hilda explained.

"MacKnight?" I stared at her. MacKnight was the surname of the new owner of MacAlpine Castle. "The one and the same who bought the castle?"

"Aye," Hilda said softly.

I turned and looked at her over my shoulder. I didn't need her to elaborate who the family was. The MacKnight family, owners of this castle, and much of the town along with it. Owners that had abandoned their people and took seemingly no pride in the care of their castle or village.

I reminded myself, once again, that my mum had loved MacAlpine Castle, though, as well as Loren Brae. Everything I did for the people now, I did for her. Even if it meant entertaining this nonsense.

"What, exactly, does this Order entail again?" I asked. Hilda had tried to tell me more than once through the years, but I'd always stopped the conversation.

"The Order of Caledonia was created to protect the Clach na Fìrinn from falling into the wrong hands. Well, any hands, really. Traditionally, the first of the Order is a knight, and he recruits others to the Order who meet the criteria to protect the stone. Without the Order intact, the Kelpies in the loch will rise and protect the stone themselves. They are the last line of defense and do not discriminate over friend or foe who draws too near to the island," Hilda explained.

Sir Buster trotted over, his belly now full, and turned circles on the little tartan bed in front of the fire. With a small sigh, he settled in, his reign of terror concluded for the

17

night. Did I need to take a tip from Sir Buster about letting go?

"If this is true..." I said carefully, my stomach turning at what this might mean. "Then you're thinking that our people are in danger. And that this is why we've been seeing less tourism lately? Fear?"

"Aye," Archie said. "Just because *you* don't believe doesn't mean that others don't."

And there you had it, I realized. I could fight this whole ridiculous Order of Caledonia protection story as much as I wanted, but if other people believed it, then I had to take it seriously. It was hurting our town, and our people needed the tourism industry to view us as a lovely place to visit, not a haunted village of empty shops where the locals lived in fear of mythological beasts.

"So what now?" I asked, hardly believing the words that came out of my mouth.

"I've contacted the solicitor for the estate," Hilda said, her words falling like a blade on my shoulders. "The next of kin will be notified that they are the knight and are needed to restore the Order."

"And you think he'll just up and fly here? From..."

"California," Hilda said.

Archie hissed, and I pressed my lips together. The likelihood that this supposed Knight we needed would leave his cushy life in sunny California and come save a moody Scottish castle was slim.

Outside, an unearthly shriek split the night, rattling the windows of the castle, and dread entwined its cold fingers around me.

"The Kelpies," Hilda whispered, her gaze on the dark window where the flames danced in perfect reflection.

"It's just the wind," I said. Filling my glass, I left the lounge without another word, the disapproving looks of Archie and Hilda following me the whole way to my apartment.

What this village needed was a stiff kick in the arse, not some tanned Californian Knight, desperate for attention. My lip curled in distaste as I entered my apartment and kicked the door closed behind me. No, *I* was going to save the village, no matter what came next.

It had been the promise I'd made on my mum's grave.

CHAPTER THREE

SOPHIE

The time had arrived.

The READING OF THE WILL was upon us, and it began with less fanfare than I had hoped for. Where were the trumpets? And the songs? Instead, we were gathered in the formal dining room at a table that sat forty people. I'd never once seen Arthur use this room in all his years, but Lottie and I had taken high tea here once a month on Lottie's insistence that we make use of each room in this sprawling castle. Despite our disdain for fancy restaurants, we'd been quite taken with the concept of high tea and enjoyed the little sandwiches and biscuits that the cook took delight in making. Of course, Lottie had insisted the cook join us for tea as well, and after her initial hesitation, it had become routine for the three of us to gossip away a Sunday afternoon at the massive table.

I shifted in my dining chair, grateful they were cushioned, and Lottie squeezed my hand under the table. She'd insisted I sit next to her, promptly kicking Chad out of the room when he'd followed me in, and now stared daggers at my parents who had taken up prominent seats bookending the attorney who sat at the head of the table. Lottie should have sat closest, but she had never been one to stand on ceremony, so why start now?

The attorney, a slim man with a narrow nose, shuffled the papers in front of him. This was the third time he'd done so, and I was tempted to reach over and grab the papers myself to get this show on the road. The ravenous excitement of those around me, all expecting lavish gifts, was almost suffocating. I just wanted to go home, curl up in my fuzzy pants, and get back to my routine. Assuming I still had a job, of course. As brand manager for MacKnight Security, it was my job to protect the company's image. And, right now, we had to ensure a smooth transition after the loss of my uncle. Worry for the future gnawed at me, and I had to sit on my other hand to stop myself from banging it on the table and insisting we get on with things.

"Thank you all for being here today. My name is Harold Stevenson, and I have enjoyed working with Arthur for many years now. He was an unusual and highly entertaining man, and I must express my condolences for your loss." Harold looked around the table as everyone put on their best sad expressions, though I didn't miss the gleam in my father's eyes.

Just to be clear, it wasn't a gleam from the light glinting off tears. That would require the man to have emotional depth, and the only emotion I'd ever seen him exhibit was anger. My father was constantly annoyed, as though the world would run better if everything was done his way, and a child hadn't fit into his idea of how life should be. Children were messy and unpredictable, you see. No, Robert MacKnight preferred order and blind obedience. We'd never gotten along, and now I watched him with barely concealed disdain, wondering how I'd managed to find my voice amid his bid for total control. The biggest disappointment of my life sat across from him, her fingers twisting a large diamond serpent ring on her finger, and I wondered why she'd chosen that ring today. Did she know that in Scottish mythology, a beithir was a fearsome snake-like creature that formed if a snake was killed but not beheaded?

Separate the head from the body, I thought, staring at my mother, and wondered why she'd never been able to stand up for me—or herself—against the tyrannical reign of my father. If I was feeling generous, I'd say her service to him filled some deep-rooted insecurity to always be needed. When I wasn't, like today, I'd just say she was weak.

"As I'm sure you all know, Arthur was a very generous man, and that generosity has continued after his death," Harold continued, and a relieved sigh went up through the room. "Let's get started, shall we?"

I waited, wanting this to be over, not caring who scored or didn't when it came to the considerable assets that Arthur had compiled. I didn't want change in my life, not when I'd finally gotten things just the way I liked. Well, close enough, I supposed, my eyes flitting to the door where Chad presumably waited outside.

Harold cleared his throat and peered down through his glasses.

"The following are Arthur's words, and his wishes," Harold began, looking up to make sure we understood. Yes, Harold. We've got it. Pick up the pace so I can go home and stuff my face with ice cream and grieve in private.

"'Welcome, my loved and not-so-loved ones. If I'm guessing correctly, this is the moment that all of you are waiting for. While I'm sure some of you are genuinely grieving my loss, Lottie and Sophie I'm looking at you, I suspect the rest of you are here to see if I've left you any of my riches. I suppose I can't blame you. I would be curious as well, considering we all know I've amassed considerable assets during my tenure on Earth. It's only natural for you to wonder where those assets will go.'"

I bit back a smile, knowing that Arthur had loved a good build-up and was just doing this to annoy people.

"'Let's start with the Old Wives Club, shall we?'" Harold looked around at the ex-wives, a faint blush tingeing his cheeks. The women grimaced, as one, at the name we'd given their group. "'While I've had no problem being generous through the years, I regret to inform you that the meal ticket ends with my death. Not that any of you actually eat. Not like my Lottie does. A man should be able to sit down and enjoy a good meal with his wife. But I digress. Upon further reflection, I don't regret cutting you all off. I spent far too many years paying for Botox, fillers, cosmetic surgery, and fake implants. Yes, Stassia, I'm looking at you.'" All eyes went to Wife Number Three, who looked dangerously close to vomiting again. "'Suffice to say, your free ride stops here. I've given you plenty in my lifetime, and I hope you've invested it wisely. If not, might I suggest you use your surgical enhancements to land yourself another ailing and overly kind sugar daddy.'"

My eyes widened, and I had to press my lips together to stop myself from bursting into laughter as the wives stood up, again with that eerie synchronicity, and as one stormed from the room.

"They're like their own built-in support group," Lottie whispered to me, and this time, I did chuckle. I couldn't help it, but I was pleased that Arthur had made that decision.

I've never liked any of those women, and I'd always had a hard time understanding why Arthur had continued to pay them alimony even for the briefest of marriages. "Hush money," Lottie had called it. And what she meant by that was the payments kept the women from calling Arthur and harassing him.

"'To my brother, Robert MacKnight, I leave my collection of antique toys and my prized fire engine toy truck. I still remember playing with those toys together when we were boys. I think it was the last time I saw you smile in an open and carefree manner. You've grown cold, calculated, and controlling, and I'm sorry to see the man that you've become. I'm hoping the gift of these toys will bring back a sense of childhood wonderment to your life, and maybe it will help you to realize that life isn't just about acquiring more.'"

I jumped in my seat as my father slammed his fist on the table and stood. Shaking with rage, he pointed at Harold. "I'm going to contest this will. Expect to hear from my attorney. Let's go." The last part Robert snapped at my mother, who immediately started to rise.

"'To Robert's wife, Drea MacKnight, I leave you five million dollars on the condition that you divorce Robert and become the woman and the mother to Sophie that I suspect you're capable of being.'" My mother froze in an awkward crouched position, half out of her chair, her eyes darting between Harold and Robert. My heart stilled, and the tiniest bit of hope bloomed inside me. I don't know why I was hopeful because, at this point, I wasn't sure that a forced effort to try to be my mother would erase years of hurt, but still... I waited, wondering what would be more enticing to her—a chance at freedom and the opportunity to have a relationship with her daughter or staying in the comfort of what she knew with a man who made all the decisions in her life. Robert snapped his fingers again like he was beckoning his prize show dog, and I already knew the answer before my mother's eyes darted to mine and then away. She straightened and cleared her throat. The room was dead silent.

"I, um, will be joining my husband." She started to turn, but Harold stopped her.

"The terms of the will are very clear. If you leave now, the offer is off the table."

I gulped, and Lottie reached over to put an arm around my shoulders. We both knew that the wound of my parents' abandonment was one that would never fully heal, even though I had somewhat made peace with it. Now their rejection reared its ugly head again, and I tried not to feel like a little girl wishing her parents would love her. My father reached over and grabbed my mother's hand, dragging her across the room. At the doorway he turned, not sparing me a glance, and pointed a finger at

Harold. "Five million is nothing. You'll be hearing from my attorney."

With their departure, the room remained uncomfortably silent. I looked down at the table, unable to accept the sympathetic looks of everyone who had just witnessed my mother refusing to put her only child first.

"Your love is worth more than five million. Arthur knew that, and *I* know that. Don't let them decide your worth," Lottie whispered fiercely in my ear. I nodded, though it was impossible for me to speak past the lump in my throat.

"'To my enchanting wife, Lottie, I leave everything else.'" At that, Harold looked up and around the room. "And at this juncture, he's asked that everybody leave except for Sophie and Lottie." Harold waited patiently while the rest of the disgruntled attendees filed from the room. In moments, the doors were closed, leaving us to look across the table at Harold. Poor Harold, I thought as he pulled a handkerchief out of his pocket and dabbed the sweat from his brow. Looking up, he surprised us both with a grin that transformed his face from boring to roguish. Well, then, Harold. I hadn't seen that coming. Perhaps that was why my uncle had employed him? I suspected Harold was often underestimated, which probably made him killer during negotiations.

"Well, that wasn't fun, now was it? Anyone up for a bit of whisky?" Harold stood and helped himself to a glass from the sidebar. Though I still hadn't acquired the taste for whisky, I nodded in agreement. Lottie stood and pulled me to sit closer to Harold at the end of the table. "Sláinte."

We held our glasses in the air and each took a sip. Nope,

whisky was still not my favorite. I grimaced and put my glass down.

"'Now that Robert has punched something and the rest of the gold diggers have stormed off, I have a few other last wishes.'" Harold looked up from the papers and gave another charming smile. "'Lot-Lot, I want to thank you for being the best of all my wives. I only wish that I had met you first, but I can't ever express to you how much I valued every day that we did have together. You brought incredible joy and light to my life, and it was a gift that I will forever be grateful for. I love you, my sweet Lot-Lot, and I trust that you will make good decisions with my business and my investments. That being said, I do have a proposal for some of my land that I would like for you to turn into a protected nature reserve. I hope that you will take joy in establishing a beautiful and natural outdoor creative space. Perhaps even an animal sanctuary? I want you to build a space that will continue to give joy back to the world long after I'm gone.'" Lottie was openly crying now, and tears filled my eyes. I'd known just how much the two had loved each other, but this was a testament to the strength of their bond. Arthur had zero reservations about giving everything to Lottie, knowing she'd do right by him and his company. Complete and total trust. If I knew anything about Lottie, she would likely pour all her money into creating the best nature reserve she could.

"'And to you, my dear, darling Sophie. What a joy you were in my life. I'm sorry about the stunt with your mother. While I do hold some hope that she'll make the right choice, I suspect she won't. If that's the case, let me explain my reasoning for putting you on display like that. I want you to fully understand that your mother's choices are her own. She had an opportunity for freedom from Robert, along with a cushy paycheck to pad the loss of your father's income. If millions of dollars won't change her mind, neither will you. It's time to close that door and accept that your parents will never change. It is one hundred percent her loss, and when she's lying on her deathbed, she will deeply regret that she bowed down to your father instead of standing up for her daughter. It's a shameful thing, this mother turning away from her child, but, oh my, what a wonderful gift it was to me. You, my dear, have been, aside from Lottie, of course, one of the best things that ever happened to me in my life. And I've had a lot of cool things happen because, well—I'm rich. We get to do a lot of cool shit.'"

Harold smiled when Lottie narrowed her eyes at him.

"His words," Harold said, brandishing the papers. "'That being said, my last bequest is an unusual one, and I'd like for you to listen without judgment.'"

"Here we go," Lottie said, taking a sip of her whisky.

"'Sophie, I have set up a trust in your name that can be accessed after several conditions are met. Additionally, there will be some rules for the use of money from the trust during the grace period and until such conditions are met.'" Harold's serious face was back, and he looked at me to make sure that I understood.

"Okay, that makes sense. I have a general grasp on how trusts work," I said. I tried another sip of the whisky, hoping I'd warm to it, but still it just tasted bitter to me.

"'Immediately, I am putting you on a one-year leave

from the company,'" Harold began and my mouth dropped open in surprise.

"What? But...I've worked so hard," I sputtered. It was the truth. Nothing had been handed to me just because I was Arthur's niece. Not only did I love my job, but I was good at it, too. I cared deeply about the company, and our turnover was quite low for the size and global reach we had. It spoke to the fact that Arthur had created a space where people were valued.

"'You may have your job back, after a year, if you want it. However, first you must do the following,'" Harold continued. He looked up at me from the papers, where I just stared at him, my mouth hanging open like a goby. "'You are now the new owner of MacAlpine Castle in Scotland. It's your job, and your birthright, to restore the Order. Harold will arrange your flight on the private plane, but you must go at once. You're needed, desperately.'"

"Wait, what...Scotland? Why? What do I know about castle upkeep?" I asked, raising my hand weakly into the air. "I'm a brand manager. Not a...castle manager. I'm sure Arthur could have found a far more qualified individual for this endeavor."

"'During the time of your stay, you may access your trust for improvements to the castle and the village as needed, as well as a generous stipend for you to live on. When you arrive, ask for Hilda. And Agnes. They'll know what to do.'"

I waited after Harold finished, certain there would be more, and when nothing else came, I turned to Lottie.

"Had...Arthur been drinking more in his last days?" I

asked, desperately hoping this was some sort of mistake. I couldn't just uproot my life and move to Scotland for a year. I had a job here. An apartment. A boyfriend. Lottie was here. This was...this was...*my life.* How could Arthur make such a call? First that stunt with my mother, and now this? He'd known how much I resented people trying to control my life and then he'd swooped in and done just that. For the first time ever, bitterness swelled on my tongue for Arthur.

"No, he hadn't been. This was something he wanted," Lottie said, her tone gentle.

"You knew?" I gasped, my voice rising at least an octave.

"I did. Though very little of the details. I...well, I agreed with him."

"You what? But how? I don't..." I stuttered, rising to my feet. I began to pace, just like I did in my office when I was mulling over a new ad campaign for the company.

"You're not happy here, Sophie." Lottie smiled gently at me, the ridiculous flower fascinator on her head tilting sideways. The truth of her words hit like an arrow to my gut, though my brain refused to accept them.

"But I *love* my job. I'm good at my job," I insisted.

"Life is about more than just your job. Yes, you're an asset to the company. Which you've proven, relentlessly, through the years. I'm, *we*, were worried you'll burn out. You barely socialize as it is. How you managed to find time to date, I don't know..." Lottie sneered slightly when she referenced my boyfriend. A boyfriend, that I, admittedly, didn't have much time for. Either way, I didn't want *this.* I didn't like when Starbucks ran out of my favorite cinnamon syrup, let alone when they stopped serving pumpkin spice lattes each year. Why can't they just serve a fan favorite year-round? It was annoying. So moving to Scotland? Yeah, that was too much change for me.

"'If you spend the year in Scotland and restore the Order, the trust will be yours. To the tune of thirty million dollars,'" Harold said, enunciating clearly so I could understand just what was at stake. At the staggering amount of money, I dropped back into my chair and downed the rest of the whisky, not even feeling the burn as it raced down my throat.

"I can't just...*start* over. My life is arranged just so," I insisted, looking at Lottie. Even the thought of all that money scared me because then it would mean I'd have to make decisions with it. Nobody would expect me to keep working as a brand manager if I had *that* kind of money at my disposal.

"And maybe that's the problem," Lottie said.

"I...I need to think," I said. "Am I allowed that? Or is there a stipulation that I have to decide right now?" I looked at Harold.

"You have twenty-four hours." Harold gave me a wry smile. "Your uncle remarked upon a tendency to overthink and resist impulsive decisions."

"Oh, he's really cornered you on this one." Lottie laughed, and I threw my hands up in the air.

"Seriously? You're laughing?"

"Well, darling, it's not necessarily a bad problem to have. A year in Scotland away from work and the promise of thirty million dollars on the line? I'm sure every last person milling about in the hallway out there would jump at this opportunity," Lottie said.

"I'm not that person." I was dangerously close to

stamping my foot. I didn't want to go to Scotland, and I certainly didn't want to leave my job.

"Which is exactly why he's left this to you." Lottie left her seat and rounded the table, pulling me into a hug. I stood rigidly, not wanting to give in, as my thoughts tangled. "This was important to him, Sophie. He wouldn't ask this of you if it didn't matter. Give it a chance."

Torn, I pulled from her embrace and left the room, closing the door quietly behind me. I wasn't one for dramatic exits and door slams anyway.

"Hey, Soph. I've been waiting for you."

I looked up to see Chad sauntering over to me, his bright smile at odds with his spray tan. He should have gone a level lighter. I almost sneered at his perfectly coiffed hair. I always wanted to ruffle it up, pushing those perfect strands out of place, and he always shoved my hand away and went to check the mirror. I suppose that was what I got for dating a handsome man. I wouldn't know, I guess. Chad was the first truly good-looking man that I'd been with. Before that, I'd dabbled in the nerdy pond, a pond I was very comfortable in, mind you, until Chad had nipped me from the lily pads and dropped me at a private pool where I blinked in confusion at all the beautiful plastic people.

"Hi," I said, accepting his kiss.

"So what happened? Did you get anything good?" Chad asked, searching my face, and that was when it hit me. He'd never once asked if *I* was okay. Sure, he'd doted on me since Arthur had died, but bringing me wine and asking me if I knew the contents of the will did not in fact equal asking after my feelings.

"What do you mean?" I played dumb, tilting my head at him.

"You know...the will? Did you get anything good? Everyone's certain he left you something good, which is why you were in there alone." Chad's face lit with excitement. I could feel it, this visceral thing between us, and I realized at that moment that he didn't actually care about me. Just like my parents. Just like all of Arthur's ex-wives. I stared hollowly up at Chad.

"Nope, nothing good. Nothing but a heap of bricks in Scotland. It was more of a charming memory for Arthur than anything. I'll visit it one day and take a picture there."

"He left you a ruin? What's the point? What about this place?" Chad looked around at the well-appointed lounge area.

"Did I stutter, Chad? Was I not clear?" I asked, being sharp with him for the first time ever. He took a step back, raising his hands in the air.

"Whoa, Soph. I was just curious."

"Curious to see if he left me loads of money? And now that he hasn't? What will you do?" I asked, crossing my arms over my chest, not caring if I was using my loud voice. In fact, my loud voice felt pretty good right about now. "Well, Chad? Is that what you wanted to know? Do you have your answers now? He left me nothing except my job as a brand manager. Do you still want me now?" The room had gone silent at my outburst, and I heard the creak of the dining room door opening behind me.

"I don't like this side of you, Sophie. Here I've been supportive of you at your uncle's funeral, and you treat me like this? I've got better places to be." Chad sneered, his mask dropping, his disdain clear. Without another word, he turned and stomped away.

Without looking back, though I knew Lottie was right behind me, I spoke.

"Tell Harold to arrange the flight."

CHAPTER FOUR

SOPHIE

"I never pictured you with Chad anyway." Matthew, my best friend, pursed his lips as he studied a broken cuticle. Matthew had recently taken a sabbatical from his professor duties at UCLA to work on his book, as well as to accompany his boyfriend on an archeological dig. As luck would have it—depending how you looked at it—Matthew's boyfriend had found new love amidst the dirt and ruins in Israel, and I suddenly found myself with a traveling companion. The timing couldn't have been more perfect, and when I had confided about Arthur's will, Matthew had happily packed a bag and joined me on the private plane across the Atlantic. We'd arrived in Edinburgh more refreshed than if I had flown economy like normal, and I had to admit I was beginning to see some upside to this whole millionaire lifestyle. That may sound ridiculous, but prior to this, I had just existed *adjacent* to a millionaire. While there had certainly been some perks along the way, like a free vacation here and there, for the most part, I lived within my means and enjoyed my simple one-bedroom apartment in a mixed-level neighborhood.

"Why? Was he too pretty for me?"

"Oh, hush. I've told you time and again, you're a classic beauty. It's just not what's in fashion right now." Matthew gave me a look that I knew meant he wasn't going to put up with any self-criticism. Luckily, I'd forced myself out of that habit years ago and had learned to embrace my looks—a well-padded body that meant I'd be the last to starve in a famine, fair skin that set off my blue eyes, and my crowning achievement...luscious auburn hair that I regularly piled into a haphazard knot on top of my head. Living in the land of perfect bodies and routine cosmetic procedures was enough to give anyone a complex and, after a particularly disastrous run-in with bleach and a hair straightener years ago, Lottie and Matthew had both intervened.

"Stop trying to make yourself look like everyone else. It's not going to happen." That had been from Lottie, a woman who had perfected the art of not following the crowd.

"You're ruining a beautiful canvas." Matthew had held up an orange strand of my hair, a disgusted look on his face. "Lottie's right. You're trying to take everything that makes you unique and turn yourself into another copycat Barbie doll. News flash, it's never going to happen. Just embrace who you are...men love confidence more than they do perfection. Perfection is, ultimately, terrifying. Especially for fragile male egos. Stop trying to be Manet when you're decidedly a Rubens."

That had been a turning point for me in how I viewed myself and my body, though it had taken some time to reframe negative self-commentary. Now, I narrowed my eyes back at Matthew.

"I didn't mean that he was too pretty for me in a self-derogatory manner. I meant, like, I'm just a little rough around the edges. I think I need someone who aligns with that a little better, you know? I mean, Chad took longer to get ready than I did," I said, wincing as an oncoming car brushed close to us on the exceedingly small and winding road we were currently barreling to our deaths upon.

"Well, you're certainly in the land for it. If it's burly rough-edged men you're looking for, that is." Matthew shot a pointed glance at our driver, who admittedly met those descriptors.

Harold had thought ahead and, knowing we'd likely be tired from the flight, had arranged for a driver to take us from Edinburgh to Loren Brae, a small village on the banks of Loch Mirren. I'd been given very little information about MacAlpine Castle from Harold, besides instructions to find Hilda. Also provided, a set of keys and well-wishes for a safe trip. When we'd walked out of the airport and were greeted by a surly driver and sheets of pouring rain, I'd been grateful for the assistance. Not only did I doubt my ability to drive a car on the other side of the road, but the thought of attempting to navigate a roundabout made my stomach sour.

Even though the driver had barely spoken four words to us since we'd arrived, I'd always thought Scotland to be a hospitable country and wondered if there was a burr stuck in this man's kilt. Because, yes, much to Matthew's delight, our driver wore a traditional kilt. Matthew's sharp intake of breath at the sight had been confirmation that I was in for a detailed fantasizing session later.

"I'm not looking for a new man, thank you very much," I said, wincing as the little car rocketed around another tight curve. "The only thing I'm looking for is to get out of this car alive."

At that, I could've sworn I saw the driver's lips twitch in the rearview mirror, and I realized I should probably keep my thoughts to myself.

"Not to worry, lass. This is Loren Brae." The driver finally spoke as we drove over a narrow bridge and onto the main street of an enchanting village. Cradled on the banks of Loch Mirren, the village of Loren Brae was picturesque in the way of places that made you want to pack your bags and move there. Which is kind of what I was doing, I realized with a start, and craned my neck to see more of the town. Rows of buildings with colorful doors, arched windows, and hand-painted signs lined the jaw-dropping loch hugged by rolling green mountains. An almost perfect circle of an island was situated smack dab in the middle of Loch Mirren, and I immediately wanted to explore. A dreamy sigh escaped as I felt the charm of the village settle over me like a warm hug from a loved one. For the first time in the tumultuous past few days, I felt a glimmer of hope.

"It's beautiful here," Matthew said. "But a bit quiet, no? Is it off-season? There are so many places with windows boarded up. I wonder if they do that in the low season."

Matthew looked pointedly at the driver who did not offer any more information.

However, now that I looked more closely, I could see what Matthew had noticed immediately. Beneath the surface delight of the village, I realized that it was, indeed, very quiet. Many of the buildings were dark and nobody walked the sidewalks, though that could also be due to the weather. Many of the arched windows that I had thought to be lovely were covered with thick slabs of plywood. The rain intensified, adding to the gloom. What had caused this unpretentious village to fall into such disrepair?

The driver, apparently having exhausted all words in his vocabulary, offered no other information. He turned off the main road and drove through a gorgeous wooden gate flanked by tall hedges. I didn't envy the person who had to trim those, and kept my eyes glued to the window as we wound along a paved road that followed a long line of towering trees. Finally, we turned, and our destination revealed itself like an actress popping from behind the curtain on Broadway.

"Oh my." Matthew grabbed my hand. "That's certainly some pile of bricks that you've inherited there, Sophie."

"I... I had no idea," I whispered. My heart picked up speed as we neared the imposing castle. This was no ruin tucked away in the overgrown Scottish Highlands. Calling it a ruin was like calling a Rolls-Royce a beater. The castle all but preened for us as we turned into the gravel parking lot and passed a ticket booth, rolling to a stop in front of a large arched double wooden door. The castle was a classic rectangle shape, easily four stories high, with honest to God turrets. Immediately, I imagined myself running through the hallways in a flowing dress living out my best romance novel dreams. What was the point in owning a castle if I couldn't pretend to be a historical romance heroine? I made a note to order a fanciful dress for just such a moment. Honestly, though? I was floored. A building of such stature required somebody with knowledge far more than I held to return it to order. Just what had my uncle Arthur been thinking? I was no more equipped to restore this castle to order than the taxi driver was to hold a coherent conversation. Feeling faint, I forced myself to breathe slowly to push away the panic that threatened.

"Right then. That's you." The driver got out and had already deposited our luggage at the top of the stairs before I'd even worked up the courage to open the car door.

Matthew tapped a finger on my arm. Turning, I looked at my best friend, my eyes wide.

"What have I gotten myself into?" I asked.

"It's an adventure, darling. Just look at the architecture! I'm telling you, this is going to be a load of fun to restore. I'm already getting the most fantastic ideas. Give it a chance." Matthew's face lit with excitement for the first time since I'd picked him up after he discovered his boyfriend's infidelity. I reminded myself that he probably needed this as much as I did. If anything, it made me feel better to think that I was doing this for Matthew instead of for myself. If I was doing it for myself, I had to examine why my old life wasn't working out. Such self-analysis required far more dedication than I currently could muster, so I would just leave that for Future Sophie to handle. The taxi driver waited at the door, clearly not wanting to jump back into the driver's seat until he made sure that we had left his car.

"Are you ready?" Matthew asked, and I took a deep breath and stepped into the rain. A giggle bubbled up as I raced up the steps, the cold drops of rain a shock against my skin, jolting me awake far better than a cup of coffee would. Once we'd reached the door, the taxi driver gave us a terse nod, and before I could offer to pay him or even tip him, the taillights winked out of sight as he whipped the car around the corner of the castle.

"*Delightful* fellow," Matthew purred.

"I have the keys right here, so one of these should work." I dug in my serviceable leather crossbody travel bag and found the set of keys that had made me laugh when I first saw them. They didn't look like the keys we had in the United States. Instead, they were several inches long, slender, and had a notched head. I'd had a miniature version of just such a key for an antique jewelry box that I'd had as a child. I finally found one that fit into the lock and turning it, I pushed the massive door open. My skin tingled, foreboding washing over me, as the door creaked on its hinges.

A shriek split the night.

Matthew and I both squealed. We grabbed each other and looked wildly around as the security alarm screeched.

"Do you have the code?" Matthew demanded.

"No, I wasn't given a code. I wasn't expecting a pile of ruins to have a security alarm." I half laughed, half gasped as the siren increased in volume.

I stilled as the alarm ground to an abrupt halt and silence filled the hall.

"Sure, and that's a bonnie lass who's trying to break

into my home now, isn't it? Can't decide if I'm to be flattered or angry." The rasp of a strong masculine voice, the lilt of the Highlands dancing on his words, shivered across my skin. I trailed my eyes up from roughened work boots, over thick muscular legs clad in worn denim, and across a broad chest, until I reached a face that would give an opponent nightmares and women wicked dreams. Piercing blue eyes, rough-cut cheekbones, and thick dark hair completed the picture. Once again, I heard Matthew's sharp inhale, knowing full well he was having the same response that I was.

"What do they serve in the water here?" Matthew whispered to me as I worked to form a coherent sentence.

"I, um, I'm sorry about that." I gestured lamely with the keys. "I wasn't sure where to enter." Matthew snickered softly beside me at my words, and I flushed, immediately thinking about being entered. Knowing that my fair skin would show my embarrassment, I tore my eyes away from the walking fantasy in front of me and scanned the expansive foyer. High ceilings arched above me with intricate plaster moldings, and what looked to be a hand-painted mural with clouds and a floral design rose far above my head.

"Sorry to inform you, but we only offer tours on the weekends." The imposing man crossed his arms over his chest, and I tried to ignore the bulge of his muscles under the flannel shirt. This was *so* unlike me. I was all but drooling over this man.

"Oh! We're not here for a tour. My name is Sophie MacKnight. I, um, well, I guess I own the place." At that, the relaxed expression on the man's face disappeared and was replaced by ice. I involuntarily took a step back, and Matthew's hand came to my lower back to keep me in place.

"I'm sorry. What was that you said, lass? Did you say you're a MacKnight?" His eyes narrowed.

"I...yes, I am. Arthur MacKnight was my uncle. He's bequeathed the castle to me with direction to restore order here. Though, honestly, I'd say it's already in pretty good shape, wouldn't you? I mean, the gardens alone look to be spectacular. And this foyer...well, just look at these floors. Are they travertine?" I stepped forward while looking at the ground, babbling because I was nervous, and promptly slammed into a wall of unmovable man.

"You're the MacKnight?" The man's lips curled as he gripped my arms to steady me. In the meantime, I had to take a few moments to recover my breath after touching this man's chest. These were no designer muscles like Chad had developed in his Pilates class. Oh no, this man, was, well, *all* man. And I'm sure I'd come up with a better way to describe him after I figured out why he looked hell-bent on escorting me off the premises.

"Aye," I said, testing out my Scottish. Matthew snorted, and the man's nostrils flared like an angry bull ready to charge. "And you are?"

"Lachlan Campbell. I live here. And you don't. You'll need to be seeing yourself out." Lachlan gripped my shoulder and made to turn me around, but I dug in my heels.

"That's going to be a hard no from me, buddy. Take your hands off me before you learn why Jason from summer camp couldn't walk straight for an entire week," I bit out, keeping a sunshiney smile plastered on my face. I'm sure the combination made me look unhinged, but hopefully that only added to my threat.

"Och, you're a tetchy one, are you? I can't believe my life," Lachlan grumbled, and a flurry of barking bounced through the foyer before a twelve-inch ball of terror ricocheted its way across the floor at us.

"Stop," I said, pointing a finger at the dog, who skidded to a halt so fast that he ended up tumbling over his head. Immediately feeling horrible, I bent over and scooped the little guy up. "Sorry about that, buddy. I didn't want you racing out into the rain and getting wet."

The dog trembled in my arms, his dark-brown eyes wide and assessing before he lifted his snout and gave me a single lick on the chin. I guess I'd been approved.

"You've got to be kidding me." Lachlan shook his head. "You're meant to be a man."

"Am I? Funny, I'm pretty sure you were the one calling me a bonnie lass just a minute ago. What's with all the lass stuff, by the way? Is that just an act you Scots put on, or do you really use the term? Either way, I'm fairly certain we both know I'm not a man." I glared at him, continuing to pet the trembling dog.

"If you do prefer men, however..." Matthew raised his hand next to me, earning a deathly glare from Lachlan. "No? Not the way of it?"

"While you're handsome enough, it's the ladies I prefer," Lachlan said, surprising me. Some men didn't take well to being propositioned by another man. "I'll let you know if that changes."

Matthew almost fainted.

"Did I hear the security alarm?" a woman's voice called,

and the dog squirmed in my arms. I bent to place him on the floor, and he raced down the hall with another flurry of barks. High-speed and loud must be his autopilot, I mused as a woman rounded the corner, wiping her hands on a tea towel. With kind eyes, a smile on her face, and an apron tied around her neck, she immediately reminded me of the mother that I wish I'd had growing up. "Oh, who's this, then?"

"This is your knight, Hilda," Lachlan said and grabbed a rain jacket from a coat stand by the door. Without another word, he disappeared into the downpour while we gaped after him.

"Really, the men here..." Matthew mused, tapping a finger on his lips. "Short with their words, but fascinating nonetheless."

"Hilda?" I asked, smiling hopefully at the beaming woman, the dog dancing at her feet. "I hope you are *the* Hilda that I'm supposed to find. Otherwise, I've just broken into the wrong place. And apparently, was also born the wrong sex."

"Och, ignore that one. He's been a beast lately. We'll leave him to his mood. Come on then, tea's on." With that, Hilda disappeared down the hallway.

"My, my, my. I do believe your adventure has begun, Sophie. And if you're lucky, it will start with you relieving that *beast* of a man from his bad mood." Matthew hissed into my ear.

"Oh, would you stop? He clearly doesn't want me here." I swatted Matthew's arm as we picked up our suitcases. "I'll be lucky if he ever speaks to me again. Actually, scratch that. He'll be lucky if I ever speak to him again. I'm not interested in dealing with that kind of negativity right now. Nope, he can just stay far away from me."

"I hear your words, but your eyes are still looking out that door for him." Matthew laughed when I jolted and then swung the door closed on the rain. It slammed, the noise echoing through the hallway, the sound a staunch reminder that my old life was now behind me.

I guess the new Sophie did slam doors after all.

CHAPTER FIVE

Lachlan

They'd sent a *woman*. To be a "knight."

I tried to ignore the tug of interest I'd had for the American woman who'd stood on my doorstep, dripping, disheveled, and nibbling on her lower lip as she'd taken in her surroundings with wide blue eyes. The color of the loch after a winter storm, leaning more to gray and moody, her pupils dilated when she looked at me. I knew that look, it was the same many women had thrown me through the years, and in any other time I would have been asking Sophie on a date. Already, images of her pale skin flushed with pink after a hearty session in bed danced in my head, and I cursed.

"Another," I said, holding up my glass.

"Another...*please*," Graham, my best friend, and owner of the Tipsy Thistle, glowered at me.

"Away and shite, Graham," I said, raising my eyebrow at him.

"Och, this one's got himself a mood on, does he now?" Graham stopped in front of me, wiping a pint glass with a towel. "Could it be because of the two guests I dropped off on your doorstep not all that long ago?"

"It's a long drive from Edinburgh. You couldn't have warned me?" I asked. Some best mate he was.

"And ruin the surprise? God, no." Graham laughed and pulled another pint for me. I stewed in my annoyance, glancing across the pub when the front door opened.

The Tipsy Thistle was a proper Scottish pub. With uneven stone floors, rugged stone walls, and a deep fireplace where a fire danced merrily, it was a cozy meeting place for everyone in the village. Several rooms broke off from the main, having been added through the years, to create a hodgepodge space to relax with a pint and a meal. The main room showcased the bar, an ornately carved wooden circle, that flaunted a startling collection of some of the finest whiskies in Scotland. It was a place to watch a match with your mates, to bring your family to celebrate an occasion, or like tonight, to sink into a dark mood.

If your best mate would let you, that is.

"There's Agnes. It's pissing down out there, isn't it?" Graham called to the newest arrival, who promptly crossed the bar and took the stool next to me.

"Heard you have some visitors," Agnes said, running her hand through her short mop of curls that glinted with rain.

"Gossipy old coo, aren't you?" I directed this at

Graham, as he was the only one who'd known of the arrival of the Americans.

"When I want to be." Graham smiled and put a full pint of Brewdog IPA in front of me. "And for you, my lovely lady? Might I say that color looks brilliant on you?"

"You may," Agnes said, smiling evenly at Graham. She'd been one of the few in the village to resist his charms. At this point, I wondered if he was even attracted to her, or if it was just the challenge of it. Either way, their flirty banter had gone on for years, with no headway gained. "I'll take a cider, please."

"Coming right up. Food for either of you tonight?" Graham asked. The pub was empty on this rainy evening, and while I would normally say it was due to the weather, it was empty more often than not of late. I worried for Graham, and that he would have to close his business, a landmark in Loren Brae.

"Just whatever soup is left," Agnes said, and I nodded in agreement. Graham would send his cook home to his family if we didn't want anything else. He disappeared to the kitchen and Agnes turned to me.

"So your guests? Shouldn't you be entertaining them?" Agnes asked. A petite woman, perpetually with paint under her nails, and a laser-sharp intelligence, she owned both a pottery shop and a bookstore in town. Both of which had suffered a similar fate as Graham's business. Tourism was drying up, and I hated that I couldn't find a way to help the people I cared about.

"Not my job," I bit out, taking a sip of my beer.

"Isn't it, though? You're the one out there in your kilt, making tourists squeal with your 'bonnie lass' compliments, and leading tours. I believe it quite literally *is* your job to welcome new people to town," Agnes said. She tucked a wayward curl behind her ear and studied my face. I didn't like what I saw in her eyes, and I already knew the direction this conversation was headed.

"Only on the weekends. Hilda can handle them," I said. I knew I was being stubborn, but I didn't care. There was too much bad history surrounding the arrival of one Sophie MacKnight for me to sit around and make nice with her over a meal. The woman had no idea who she was dealing with. If she thought she could come in and change everything just because she was the new owner...

"Easy, boyo," Graham said, pulling my empty glass from where I gripped it tightly. "I'll not be having you break another glass on my watch."

"Sorry," I said, clenching my fists.

"Be a good lad and tell us what you learned on the ride up," Agnes said, pivoting her inquiry to Graham.

"I'd like to be a good lad for you anytime...or very bad, depending how you like it..." Graham wiggled his eyebrows suggestively at Agnes.

"I like it with a man who's cracked open a proper book at least once in the past decade," Agnes purred.

"Even better." Graham made a great show of pulling out a tattered copy of a bartender's drink guide and thumbing through it before shooting Agnes a devilish grin.

"That hardly counts. There are pictures in it," Agnes pointed out.

"I'm going to need a ruling on this one," Graham said, tossing the book in front of me. "What say you? Is this a proper book or not?"

I pursed my lips and flipped the cover open, giving careful time and attention to the publisher's information before closing it and sliding it back to Graham.

"It pains me to say this, Agnes, but it seems it's a proper book. At least one publisher deemed it so." I shrugged. Fair was fair.

"Och, you lads always side together," Agnes complained.

"I side with the truth, Agnes," I said, and Graham bumped his fist against mine.

"If that's the case, then why are you refusing to accept what's happening in this town?" Agnes asked. Her words hit like perfectly aimed arrows, and I winced. Even Graham, usually up for any and all banter, turned away to wipe down the bar. Notably, he was wiping a bar where no patrons sat, and I hated knowing how difficult business had become for my friends.

"Because if the Kelpies, and the Order, are real, then where does that leave me?" I asked, the words bitter on my tongue. Graham straightened and turned, surprised that I spoke of this. I never, and I mean *never*, spoke about the mysterious myth that clung to our village like a sticky spiderweb.

"In what way are you meaning?" Agnes's voice was soft, and she leaned over to bump her shoulder softly against mine. We'd gone to school together, growing up playing on the banks of the same loch that had claimed my mother's life, and I knew she loved me like her own brother.

"I don't know how to fight this," I admitted, a long breath escaping me as my stomach knotted. It was the first time I'd ever admitted that I couldn't handle something when it came to helping the village. I'd made it a point of honor through the years to be the go-to man to help however I could. But this? This was bigger than my skills. It would also mean unlocking all the emotions that I'd neatly boxed away and shoved deep into a shadowy corner of my soul when it came to my mum.

"But—"

"If, by chance, this is all real, don't you see? Where this leaves me? I don't know how to change it. I hate...and I mean this one thousand percent...*hate* what is happening in our town. Do you think I enjoy looking around the pub and seeing it empty like this? Or not seeing tourists stopping to buy gifts at the local shops? I love this place. I love our people, and I *hate* that I can't fix this. And what's worse? Is that...*if* I admit this is true, then I'm going to have to question everything I've thought to be true about how my mum died. And I *can't*. I feel like I just can't go there. Because where does that leave me? At least if she drowned, I can make sense of it. Drowning happens. It's a normal thing that happens. If..." My voice broke, and Agnes leaned closer but didn't say anything. Graham slid a dram of whisky across the bar. "If...a Kelpie is *actually* responsible for my mother's death...how do I even process that? How do I avenge her death? The Kelpies aren't real. What? I turn into a doddering old man rocking on the corner screaming about water horses killing people? It's mad. I can't go there." I took down the dram of whisky in one gulp, not caring that it wasn't proper. I needed to feel the burn down my throat to stop the tears that threatened.

"Lachlan." Graham leaned over the bar forcing me to meet his eyes. "I say this to you with nothing but love for you in my heart. You're like a brother to me. And I loved your mum as well. You're stuck on the point of *how* she died, and it's stopping you from accepting or grieving the fact that she *did* die. And in doing so, you are hurting our town as well as potentially putting someone else in harm's way."

The whisky roiled in my stomach, and I clenched my fists. I wanted to punch him, someone, *anything*. I hated this feeling of being out of control and was uncertain how to proceed.

"The thing is, Lachlan? We *do* know how to fix it," Agnes added. I turned to her, a comforting blanket of anger settling over my shoulders, but before I could open my mouth, she put her finger to my lips. "Wheesht. Let me speak."

"Och, I like this dominatrix side of you, Agnes," Graham said, lightening the mood.

Agnes shot Graham a withering look before continuing. "As you know, I run a bookshop and have come across many interesting things in my research. Including some historical documents about the Order of Caledonia, which I believe once belonged in MacAlpine Castle. I haven't given them to you out of fear of you tearing them up due to your complete stubbornness. However, if you would step back and ask for help for once, I'm available."

"Have you been talking to Hilda? This sounds like something that she would set up," I asked.

"Of course, Hilda and I talk about this. As does everyone else in the village. It's only you that nobody talks to about it, Lachlan. Don't you see? Look around." Agnes gestured to the empty pub. "It's right in front of your eyes.

Everybody is talking about this. We all believe in the Kelpies. And now everyone in Scotland believes that this town is cursed. Whether it is true or not, does it matter? The belief itself is enough to hurt people. And that's what's happening right now. And nobody can talk to you about it because you throw a fit like a child throwing all his toys out of his pram."

"Surely that's not the way to get me on your side." I glared at Agnes.

"Well? Being your friend and allowing you to be stubborn and turn your back on help hasn't done anything, so now it's time that you listen," Agnes said, and then drained her cider.

"Tell me about the Americans," I said, the request almost getting stuck in my throat. Agnes released a small sigh of relief, and I couldn't bring myself to look at her or Graham. Their words hurt, not because they were *trying* to hurt me, but because they were true. I was stubborn, and the evidence was around me. For years the curse of the Kelpies, the rumor of a truth stone, and the Order of Caledonia had clung to Loren Brae. No matter how much I invested in the tourism campaigns for the village or held events like the Highland Games. Like the weeds that Archie pulled from the gardens each spring, the myth was pervasive. For a while, it had added to the town's appeal, until recently when things had changed. Now the otherworldly shrieks in the night, which I tried to convince people was the wind over the hills, were turning tourists and villagers away. No longer was the myth a draw. It was now a drawback.

"I liked them," Graham surprised me by saying.

"Sophie is not only good-looking but I suspect she'll be up for a bit o' banter. She seems smart."

"And the friend?" I asked.

"He seems smart too. Dry humor. Sounds like he's a professor of history, which might be handy."

"Is that right?" Agnes perked up. "Is he handsome as well? Not that it matters of course, I am much more cerebral than to only be focused on looks," Agnes sniffed at Graham.

"I suspect he's far more interested in Graham than you," I said, and at her crestfallen look, I found that I could smile. Graham preened.

"And another one felled by the mighty Graham," Agnes growled.

"I can't help that my charm is far reaching," Graham protested. "Jealous are you, darling?"

"No, I'm just in awe that you can hold your head up under the weight of that ego of yours." Agnes gave a saccharine smile. A bell went off from the kitchen, signaling our food, and Graham disappeared into the back.

"If... if I'm correct," Agnes said, her tone gentle. "The arrival of Sophie, our knight in shining armor so to speak, would be the beginning of restoring the Order. If that's the case and you choose to accept the hand that you have been dealt? Then the time has come. We *can* take action. And we can protect the truth stone, protect our people, and rebuild our village. But it starts with you, Lachlan. Nobody else. Everyone is too scared to say something to you and instead they're leaving or closing their business. You don't want to rule like that, do you?"

"I'm not even a ruler," I pointed out to Agnes as

Graham came out carrying steaming bowls of soup. "I don't even have a title. I haven't even been voted into power. I don't know why I have to be the one to lead this charge."

"Because you saddled up a long time ago," Graham said as he slid the bowls onto the bar in front of us. "And we all followed you and trusted you because we knew you loved this town. But that doesn't mean you get to turn your back now when things get a little too uncomfortable for you."

"I have to say I admire your delivery," Agnes said, stabbing her spoon into the soup with annoyance. "You do have your moments, Graham, I'll give you that."

"Just like I've been telling you for years, darling, I'll wear you down eventually."

"I think we've got a few years yet before that happens. Perhaps when I'm sixty and have given up all hope on men," Agnes said. Graham let out a whoop of joy.

"Did you hear that, Lachlan? I think that's the first time she's ever agreed to have a date with me."

"When I'm sixty. And not married," Agnes said, annoyance in her voice.

"Nevertheless, there's hope for me yet. If that's the case, I think times are changing, don't you, Lachlan?"

The silence drew out as both of my best friends waited for my direction. Looking down at my soup, I nodded.

"You can bring your papers by."

that Arthur used to tell me, and I feel like I'm not welcome here."

"I don't know about that. Hilda seemed absolutely delighted to see you," Matthew said, taking a sip of his wine. "It's that grumpy Scotsman that's gotten in your head, hasn't it?"

"Well, you can't say he was particularly enthused about my arrival." I tried to ignore my reaction to Lachlan, knowing full well that my current emotions couldn't be trusted. It was obvious that I was fatigued, on edge, and stressed out. Which was why when my eyes had locked on his, and my heart seemed to sit up and take notice, along with other parts of my body, I refused to think too deeply about it. Lachlan had shown us what kind of person he was, and I certainly didn't need that energy in my life.

"On the contrary, I think he was *very* interested in your arrival," Matthew said, a smirk hovering on his lips. "I think he doesn't like *what* your arrival signals. But I don't think that has anything to do with you as a person. For some reason, it seems like you being here means change, and he kind of reminded me of a territorial dog protecting his turf. And you certainly didn't help matters by coming in and announcing that you were the new owner of his home."

"No." I sighed. "I suppose that probably wasn't the best approach, was it? However, I was feeling so awkward because I'd just set off the alarm and stumbled into somebody else's house. I wasn't expecting anyone to be there. And then he was all this grumpy, massive muscular man up in my face, so I just wanted to prove that I had the rights to be doing what I was doing."

"And unintentionally threatened his ego and his home and his livelihood."

"Do we even know if he lives here? For all we know, he's just a worker or maybe he's Hilda's son," I pointed out. *Please don't be Hilda's son.* I already liked the woman and didn't want to dock her points for having an abrasive son.

"I guess we will learn more on our adventure tomorrow," Matthew sing-songed.

"*Mooooooo.*"

"I'm sorry, what?" I had been looking at the electric fireplace, which I had to admit was still very soothing even if it wasn't the same as a real fire.

"That wasn't me," Matthew said, holding a hand to his chest, an affronted look on his face. The sound came again, and we both stared at the door.

"Is that..." Matthew tilted his head.

"Come on," I said, shocked to find a giggle working its way up my throat. We scrambled from the couch and raced to the door, easing it open quietly. Holding our breath, we both poked our heads out to look down the long dimly lit corridor that led from our apartment. Like the rest of the castle, the walls were stone, the hall narrow, and rugs had been thrown over the uneven floor. I did a double take at what I saw in the murky light at the far end of the hall.

"Um..." I whispered. Matthew grabbed me, pulling me tight against him, and I held on as we stared at the apparition.

A semi-transparent Highland cow raised its head at us at the end of the hallway, stamping its hoof once into the rug.

"A ghost coo," Matthew hissed. He pulled me back

inside, slamming the door and locking it behind him. Something about him locking the door against a ghost allowed my laughter, or more likely my hysteria, to escape, and I doubled over, clutching his arm.

"I can't...I just can't..." Tears streamed down my face, and I fought to breathe. "That...it can't...no way was that real. That has to be, like, a thing they do for tourists."

"What? Like we're at Disney? Like this is some 3D hologram show? No way. That's an honest to God ghost. A ghost coo. In our hallway," Matthew exclaimed, pointing at the door, his expression torn between awe and fear.

"If you say so," I said, wiping my eyes, refusing to accept that a ghost coo wandered the hallways of this castle. Like, sure, I could see maybe a little girl who had died of sickness years ago haunting the hallways—also, on a side note, why are child ghosts always the creepiest ones? There was something about the thought of a toddler ghost clutching her doll that was innately horrifying. Nope, I'd take a ghost coo any day if that was the way of things here. Not that it was, because ghosts weren't real, but I'd still choose that option if someone came to me and asked me which haunting I would prefer that evening.

"I do say so," Matthew said, and I saw the moment where fear gave way to interest. "*Fascinating*. I'm going to have to get my hands on some books about the area as I'm suspecting this room doesn't come with Wi-Fi. This makes sense, though. It's not uncommon for buildings of this age to have records of hauntings, though it's hard to say if those sightings are exaggerated or not. Often, those stories weave their way into local lore, and add to the appeal of historical places such as this one seems to be. I suspect, since your man said he ran tours here, that this castle benefits from the addition of a ghost story."

"He's not my man," I protested, moving past the ghost coo and narrowing in on Matthew's assumption. "I want no man. I just had a man, remember? I got rid of him."

"Darling, that Chad of yours was a child. His mirror was an echo chamber of validation that he enjoyed preening in front of more than spending time with you. He was after your money. Even if it's an ugly thing to say," Matthew said, glancing once more at the locked door, before tugging me back to curl up on the couch.

"It *is* an ugly thing to say," I said, stung by the truth of it. "And I hate that you're right. Not because I really loved him. I know that I didn't. But I liked being in a relationship. I liked the certainty of it. The continuity. The..."

"Routine? The security?" Matthew asked. He hooked an arm around my shoulders, and I curled into him. "You need that, Soph. I get that. Your parents, worthless twats that they are, never gave you any semblance of a normal childhood. You lucked out in Arthur and Lottie, but let's be honest here. They certainly weren't normal either. It makes sense that you would crave the stability of a partner. Just not Chad. Please don't serve me up another Chad. I think my tongue is damn well bloody from biting it all these months."

"Seriously?" I grimaced. Had everyone else been able to see what I had missed? "I didn't think he was *that* bad."

"He got regular facials and asked not only Lottie, but me, how much you were worth," Matthew said, and I reared up at that, turning to him in surprise.

"He asked you how much I was worth, and you didn't tell me?"

"I told him, in no uncertain terms, that if he ever again gave a hint of wanting you for something other than your delightful personality, that I would ruin him. He backtracked quickly. He said it was out of curiosity, but not anything he needed and that he was happy with his job."

"He had seemed happy with his work, I'll admit. And, I don't have any money, well, I didn't, aside from what I'd built of my own savings." I sighed. Chad had only wanted me for my money. There. I said it. If even only to myself. Not a fun thing to admit, no it was not.

"Please tell me, at the very least, he was good in bed?" Matthew pleaded with me.

"Um." I winced, and Matthew threw his head back and laughed. "It was very mechanical."

Matthew laughed harder, his shoulders shaking, and punched his thigh.

"Mechanical, she says..." Matthew wheezed.

"Yeah, like he was following a manual. Insert Part A into Part B. Twist, and complete."

"Oh. My. God." Matthew pounded his leg. "We are getting you laid. That's it. Not only did you have to deal with Chad but bad sex too? Nope, sorry. New mission. Forget restoring order to this place, which by the way looks lovely. I'm requesting a *new* order. Find Sophie a proper man."

"Nope, no way." I stood and put my empty glass on the table. Stretching my arms over my head and yawning, I turned to the first guest room door and saw my suitcase. "Much like you, my dear friend, I'm on sabbatical."

"All sabbaticals come to an end," Matthew yelled after me, and I closed the door, but not before flipping him off, even though I couldn't help but laugh. I let out a happy sigh at the sight of the bed, piled with puffy pillows and thick blankets, and barely made it through my nighttime bathroom routine before I was sound asleep.

Later that night, I was thrust from an easygoing dream of walking the beach with Arthur by what sounded like a shriek. Sitting up, I pawed at my eye mask and ripped it from my face, my head swiveling as I tried to remember where I was.

Right. Scotland. In a castle. What had that sound been? I'd only caught the tail end of it when I'd been jarred from my dream, and I wasn't sure that I wanted to hear the sound again. It was bone-chilling and jarring in a way that made me deeply uncomfortable. Did ghost coos shriek? I slipped from my bed and padded to the window in my tower room.

The rain had abated, and a sliver of light showed on the horizon. Below me, movement caught my eye. Lachlan strode across the gravel parking lot and climbed a set of stairs that led to a wall. There, he began to walk, back and forth, and I realized he was on top of what was likely a battlement.

He was standing watch. A shiver rippled across my skin at the thought of just what he might be standing watch for. When he turned, his gaze coming to my window, I stepped back, not wanting him to see me at the glass, watching him.

Diving back beneath the thick fluffy comforter on the bed, I pulled it up to my chin, waiting for the fear to settle in. Something was up at this castle and, apparently, I was in charge of putting things to rights. The image of Lachlan, a lone figure in the dusky dredges of dawn, standing on the ancient wall came back to me. Oddly, knowing he was out there, watching for whatever secrets the wind held, comforted me, and I slipped back into a dreamless sleep.

CHAPTER SEVEN

SOPHIE

"Och, don't worry yourself about Clyde, hen. He'll do you no harm." This came from a man who sat by the fire, a box of feathers and threads next to him, a folded newspaper at his side.

I jolted, as I hadn't even seen him sitting there, or I wouldn't have been rambling on about supposed ghost coos wandering the halls. I took in the man's attire, roughened work pants, a faded flannel shirt, and shaggy white hair and wondered if he was making fun of me.

"Clyde, is it?" Matthew asked, his eyes lighting, and crossed to the man. "Is that the name of the ghost coo?"

"Aye. Was Hector with him?" the man asked, biting off a piece of string in his mouth, and then twining it around a small feather.

"I can't be sure. Who is Hector? Also, I'm Matthew."

subtle shake of his head. I wasn't sure why I was antagonizing Lachlan except that I couldn't handle rudeness before I'd finished my first cup of coffee for the day. Lachlan's hands tightened and then he dropped his fork to his plate and pushed back from the table.

"The Internet code is on the back of the router by the television in the corner," Archie said. Lachlan glared while I smiled sweetly at Archie.

"There now that wasn't so bad, was it?" I asked Lachlan.

"You seem to think that you have free rein to make any changes you want here. If that's the case of it, I'm not sticking around to watch this place fall into ruin." Lachlan stood and while I enjoyed getting the best of him, for a moment I saw the very real flash of pain in his eyes. This was more than just anger, there was something deeper here that I didn't yet understand. When one wounded soul recognizes another, it was hard to hold on to annoyance. I stopped him from walking away by raising my hand in the air.

"Lachlan. I don't want to be at war with you."

"You don't have to be, then." Lachlan jerked his chin at the door toward the entrance. "There's the door."

"While I don't *want* to be at war with you," I amended, "I think you should know that I truly not only have no idea what I'm doing here, but I also have no intention of coming in and taking over. In all honesty, I didn't even know this was a fully functioning castle or that it held tours or even that people lived here. As demonstrated by me walking into the place and setting the alarm off yesterday. Hilda has been kind enough to give us a little time to rest before we talk about what it is specifically my uncle wanted from me when it came to this castle."

"Your uncle clearly didn't care much about this castle, or he would have been more helpful when we've needed it lately," Lachlan said, bitterness lacing his tone.

"I can't say why my uncle made any decisions that he did. However, I can say that knowing my uncle, I find it highly unlikely that he wouldn't have helped where help was needed. This is truly the first time I knew that he owned this castle and I'm sorry if you haven't gotten the support that you needed from my family."

"Seems to me your uncle probably enjoyed the idea of owning a castle far more than the realities of running one," Lachlan said, still standing by the side of the table. Hilda came into the room in time to hear his words, and she smacked him across the shoulders with her tea towel.

"Lachlan Campbell, you will not speak to a guest in this house this way."

"Och, she's not a guest. She owns the place as she's pointed out several times now," Lachlan said, his arms crossed over his chest.

Matthew stood and walked forward until he faced off with Lachlan. Though Lachlan was several inches taller than him and much more muscular, Matthew simply raised his chin and met his eyes dead on. When he spoke, his voice was low and dangerous.

"Have a care with your words there, *mate*. Arthur was like a father to Sophie, and she's just buried him. It seems that none of us know the real story behind how Arthur came into ownership of this place. You are bleeding on someone who didn't cut you." Matthew's hands were held in loose fists at his side as though he was readying himself for a fight. I'd never been prouder of my best friend in my whole life. While I knew that Matthew had faced a lot of challenges in his life, the sheer size of Lachlan was terrifying.

Lachlan's head dropped, and he studied the floor for a moment before taking a deep breath and then looking at me. "I'm sorry for your loss. It's a hard thing to lose someone you care about. I wasn't thinking about it in that manner. There are a lot of things at play here that perhaps neither of us understands. I don't like change. And I don't like not understanding the bigger picture, and it's making me a touch prickly."

"A touch prickly?" Hilda laughed. "You're worse than the hedgehog that Sir Buster tried to get his teeth into yesterday." We all looked over at where Sir Buster had taken up residence at the end of the table, ever hopeful for a little bit of scrambled eggs or bacon.

I swallowed past the rough lump in my throat, not expecting such a sincere and direct apology from Lachlan. For a moment, it had felt like he commiserated with me over losing someone important, and I wondered briefly if he'd also experienced such a loss in his life.

"There now. That's better. I'm away to put the kettle on as I think Agnes is coming around soon enough." A loud gonging sound reverberated through the room, sending Sir Buster off in a flurry of barks and protective rage. "Right, that must be her then. I'll be right back."

Lachlan sat back down in the chair, and I tried a smile on him. "Just think of me like your annoying kid sister who will have a thousand questions for you."

"Och, lass, it's not a sister I'll be thinking of you like." His meaning was clear, and his heavy-lidded look did little to stop my mind from descending into a very naughty space. I caught Matthew's delighted grin over Lachlan's shoulder.

"*I told you*," Matthew mouthed.

I had to look away, knowing my face was likely burning, and now I was torn between wanting to smack Matthew and Lachlan, but both in *very* different manners. I looked dubiously down at my glass of water. Maybe there was something different in the water here. I'd never had such lusty thoughts about someone I'd just met before, and here I was, ready to crawl over the table and into the lap of one very annoyed Highlander.

A scurry of paws across the tile floor gave me an excuse to turn to the hallway to see a slender woman in a bright red sweater, fitted jeans, and a twisted mop of auburn curls. She carried a backpack with her and was unwrapping a brightly woven scarf from her neck as she spoke with Hilda.

"I'm sorry to come so early, but once Lachlan had given the green light I figured I didn't want to miss my chance."

"Lachlan gave the green light?" Hilda asked excitedly, and we all looked at the man in question. He gave a curt nod and went back to studying the liquid in his coffee cup. I was beginning to realize there were many curt nods in this town, and the quiet and succinct nature of these people was a stark contrast to my town, where everybody eagerly talked about themselves.

"I was just trying to decide if it was best we started with the castle tour or got into the thick of it," Hilda said.

"Hi, I'm Sophie," I said, giving a little wave since nobody seemed inclined to introduce me.

"Och, of course, where are my manners?" Hilda laughed. "I was so distracted by Lachlan's change of heart that I forgot to introduce you two. This is Agnes. She owns a bookshop as well as a pottery studio in town and went to school with Lachlan."

Immediately, I wondered if they'd ever dated and then wanted to kick myself for wondering. What business of mine was it who Lachlan had dated or not dated? I was here because of Arthur and, as I had told Matthew last night, I was on sabbatical from men. "It's nice to meet you," I said, "and this is Matthew who is going to become your new best friend because you own a bookstore."

"Aye, you must be the history professor then. You're welcome at my shop anytime." Agnes beamed.

"Word travels fast," Matthew hummed.

"Welcome to life in a small town," Hilda said. "I think since you're here and before we go any further, we might as well get started. Clyde's already shown himself to her so I'm sure she has questions."

"Did he now?" Agnes exclaimed. "That's unusual for him. He must have taken a shine to you. I'm going to take that as a good sign that we are on our way to restoring the Order." And for the first time after all the times I had repeated the words of the will to myself, did my brain finally click over to what they were *actually* saying. These people did not want me to restore order to the castle. They wanted me to restore *the* order. My eyes met Matthew's across the table, and I realized we'd both reached the same conclusion. The phrasing of it immediately made me think of one of those scary religious cults from documentaries on Netflix, and I pressed my lips together. Worry slipped through me. Maybe there was a good reason that I'd never heard about this place from Arthur.

I couldn't do this. While I wasn't a particularly vain person, I was so not down with awkward cult hairstyles and bland matching dresses. Nope, cult life was not for me. Unless they worshipped cheese, of course. Then I could perhaps be persuaded.

"Shall we?" Hilda asked.

Oh, we shall, Hilda, we shall. I narrowed my eyes at her, seeing if I could get any cult vibes from her attire, but nothing popped. I'd have to pull Matthew aside and get his read, but for now? It was time to find out what ride Uncle Arthur had bought me a ticket for.

CHAPTER EIGHT

Lachlan

There was no way around it. I wanted Sophie MacKnight. Under me. Over me. In any way she'd give me, really. Never had I had such a visceral reaction to a woman before and, while Graham may hold the title for charming the most ladies, I'd certainly been no slouch in that department either.

And still.

This woman, with fair skin that flushed easily, messy hair that I wanted to run my hands through, and short bursts of confidence, all but undid me. She reminded me of a colt, first learning to walk, the way she alternated between bouts of uncertainty and haughty declarations. I wondered which way she'd be in bed and had to push such thoughts aside as we all followed Hilda to the library. I trailed at the back of the group, knowing that I was being difficult, but not really caring at the moment. Much like the hedgehog, I needed some sort of armor against my intense instant attraction for the woman who now, quite literally, held the key to my future. I suppose, both metaphorically and literally, as I recalled her waving the keys in my face yesterday.

That way lies ruin, I thought, as I watched Sophie's thick thighs, ensconced in tight black fabric, cross over each other as she took a seat at the wide table that dominated the middle of the library room. Turning away from the table—because I needed something to do with my hands before I did something stupid like throw Sophie over my shoulder and steal her away from here so I could learn the softness of her skin at those aforementioned thighs—I crouched at the large stone fireplace that dominated one wall of the room. Though it wasn't horribly cold by Scottish standards, I noticed Sophie rubbing her hands up and down her arms in the thin jumper she wore and was reminded that she came from a much warmer climate.

The library was one of my favorite rooms in the castle, not only for the large collection of books that the floor-to-ceiling shelves housed, but because I had some of my best memories of my mum in this room. We'd sit in the oversized chairs pulled close to the fire on cold winter nights, reading stories, or acting out make-believe plays. It was those simple memories, rich with love, that still hung on the wall of my mind like the most treasured of paintings.

"I could live in here," Matthew said from behind me, and I couldn't blame him. Even if he didn't really understand the extreme amount of work that went into upkeeping a castle of this size, the library was one of those rooms that worked its magic on everyone. "This hunter green color is gorgeous for the walls, and with that massive fireplace and high ceilings? If you can't find me for, well, however long we're here for, just come to the library. I'll just bring my pillow and comforter down here."

"Ah, a man after my own heart." Agnes laughed. "It's marvelous, isn't it? I've always envied Lachlan for being able to come here every day. It's a room for dreamers, isn't it?"

"It is," Sophie agreed, her voice like a caress, and I sucked in a breath. Surely I must be going mad if the mere hint of a woman's voice gave me shivers. Cursing softly, I struck a match and set it to the tinder, the erupting flames mirroring those in my soul.

"That's a nice fire, Lachlan. I forget our guests must be chilled," Hilda said, and I returned to the table. I took the seat she offered, putting me directly across from Sophie, and I wanted to remind Hilda that Sophie wasn't a guest. We were now *her* guests. I waited to see if Sophie would say anything to the like, but the moment passed without her asserting her power in this situation. Maybe she'd been truthful at breakfast, and she was willing to be here with an open mind. God knows, I needed one.

"Let's start at the beginning?" Hilda looked around the table. Archie entered the room, tacklebox in hand, and took a seat by the fire where he resumed working on his flies. "Just how much do you know about MacAlpine Castle and our history?"

"Erm," Sophie said, biting her lower lip. "Until two days ago, I didn't know this castle existed."

"At all? But I thought the sale went through six months or so ago?" Agnes turned to me.

"Sophie's uncle, Arthur, purchased the castle. Sophie inherited it this week after her uncle passed away," I said.

"Such a shame," Agnes said, sympathy crossing her face. "I'm sure that's a lot for you to be processing then, isn't it? You came very quickly as well."

"It was a directive in the will. I'd been given leave of my job and needed to be on a flight as soon as possible. He'd even arranged for use of his private plane, which I can only guess at the costs for that. It seemed imperative that I be here, and quickly, though I'm still not certain how I can be of use to you. But I can try. I like a challenge and I'm great at brand management." Sophie gave a half-hearted smile.

Brand management? What was she on about? Distracted from the way her round body shifted under her jumper, I cocked an eyebrow at Hilda, my meaning clear.

"That's a fine attitude to have, Sophie." Hilda smiled, while Agnes put several leather books on the table in front of us. More documents, tucked in protective slips, followed.

"Shall we begin?" Agnes asked, her tone serious.

"Should I be taking notes?" Matthew asked. He reached into his pocket and pulled out a small notebook and pencil. Sophie rolled her eyes.

"Ever the professor..." Sophie smiled.

"You can take the nerd out of academia..." Matthew winked.

"You can, if you'd like. But best to just jump into it, right?" Agnes looked at Hilda.

"You'll need to suspend your disbelief for a bit." Hilda leaned forward, prompting Sophie to meet her eyes. "This may all sound a bit fantastical, particularly to an American who might not be used to living with myths. I'll just ask that you hear us out before drawing judgment."

"If this is a religious cult, I'm out," Sophie said, raising her hand. "I don't do blind obedience."

The thought of her being obedient, only for me, sent a bolt of heat straight through my body, and I shifted in my chair, turning to look across the room.

"No, I'll concur with Sophie on that one. Plus, the outfits are horrible, no?" Matthew agreed.

"No religion. Promise," Agnes said.

"So a non-religious cult then?" Sophie asked, and despite my misgivings at all of this, my mouth twisted in a smile.

"No cults. Well, I guess...och, I never really thought about it that way. Would the Order be a cult then?" Agnes scrunched her nose at Hilda.

"No, it's the person's choice to step into their power or not." Hilda shook her head.

Sophie's eyes widened at that. "Excuse me, did you say... step into our power? Care to explain?"

"Start at the beginning. The Clach na Fìrinn. The Stone of Truth," Archie's voice boomed, cutting off the chatters, and Agnes took a deep breath.

"The Stone of Truth. It's a rumor whispered at night, a legend told over a pint, and the truth is only ours to hold," Agnes began.

"One of the holy grail," Matthew interrupted, his eyes wide. "Say it isn't here?"

"Aye, it's here," Agnes said, and Matthew's face went white.

"Wait, didn't you *just* say this wasn't about religion?" Sophie interrupted, concern crossing her face.

"I guess I'm using the holy grail loosely." Matthew turned to Sophie, stroking her arm to soothe her. "From what I remember, The Stone of Truth is one of those famous items through history that people go on great quests, even crusades, to try to locate."

"Like Indiana Jones?" Sophie asked.

"Yes, except this wouldn't pertain to eternal life, would it? It's a knowledge stone, if I remember correctly." Matthew leaned back and steepled his fingers together as he thought about it. "Any person who had possession of the stone could gain all the knowledge of the universe. It's as though the stone is one big microchip, and you can download any knowledge you wanted. In the wrong, or well, even the right hands, it could be catastrophic. No one person should be privy to that much knowledge."

"Like...what? Like the mystery of the pyramids or if there are aliens?" Sophie leaned forward, biting her lower lip as she looked over the documents on the table.

"Exactly like that," Agnes said. "The Clach na Fìrinn not only holds the knowledge to all of the universe, but it also knows the truths that everyone hides. While it can be used for good, the possession of the stone and the sheer insurmountable knowledge it holds can quickly descend the holder into madness. Few who have possessed it have lived long to make use of it, the sheer force of its power quickly becoming overwhelming. A few have managed to briefly harness its power, as in managing to use it for *incredibly* short moments—minutes even—and coming away the better for it. For a brief time, quite recently, it had slipped from its protection due to one greedy man. He allowed access, for a price, to a select few. It might even be why Scotland is known as a place of great inventors."

"No way," Matthew breathed. "Fascinating. And the stone didn't drive this man mad?"

"Oh, it certainly did, and the Order was sent to recover it and return the stone to its proper and protected resting place," Hilda said, her eyes trailing to the tall windows that bracketed the fireplace. Sophie's eyes followed.

"The lake?" Sophie asked.

"Loch," I automatically corrected.

"Loch." Sophie rolled her eyes, and I bit back a smile.

"The stone is protected in a small fortress on the island in the middle of the loch," Hilda continued for Agnes. "MacAlpine Castle was built to house the Order of Caledonia, those tasked with the protection of the stone."

"The Order of Caledonia," Matthew mused, pursing his lips together. "I can't say I know it."

"You wouldn't. It's not a recognized order in Scottish national records," Agnes said. My stomach twisted at the discussion of the order and my skin felt itchy, and I stood, needing to pace for this discussion. Sir Buster stood as well, walking across the room, cocking his little head to peer at me. I bent to pick him up, ignoring his growl of disapproval, and tucked him into my chest as I began to pace.

"The Order of Caledonia was formed by a group of individuals who saw the need to protect the stone from falling into the wrong hands. Because of the nature of the stone, and its ability to recognize truth, the Order was given its own power. Well, powers I should say. Each individual in the Order of Caledonia is imbued with power when they step into their role." Hilda said the last bit evenly, and I paced, awaiting Sophie's response.

"Um...power? Like magick?" Sophie asked, her voice soft and breathy. I counted my steps as I paced, Sir Buster trembling at my chest, and waited.

"Correct. I understand that seems ridiculous but remember, Scotland is a country with a wealth of myths and legends. And there's always a kernel of truth rooted deep in these stories. This is our truth, Sophie, and we need you to accept it," Hilda said.

"We'll withhold our comments until we hear more," Matthew interjected, stopping Sophie from speaking. I suspected Sophie had been about to tear apart the story about magick and, I had to admit, I'd likely have done the same. In fact, I'd been doing just that for years now. It was easier not to believe than it was *to* believe.

"Through the years, the stone has come to rely upon the Order of Caledonia for protection, however it has a last line of defense if the Order dissolves and it is left without protection," Agnes said, and I waited, wondering just how much the Americans would take before throwing up their hands and hightailing it back to the airport.

"You speak as if it is a sentient being," Matthew observed.

"To a point, it is. With that much power, it has learned through the years to make decisions for self-protection."

"And this last line of protection?" Matthew asked, toying with his pen.

"The Kelpies," Archie boomed from his chair. "You'll have heard them this morning, likely. They'll scare every last

CHAPTER NINE

SOPHIE

"Soooo, you're saying there's a magickal stone that knows the secrets of the universe that has given this Order of people magickal powers to protect it, and when all else fails, it unleashes hell through the form of mythological water horses that terrorize anyone who gets too close to the stone. Is that correct?" I asked, my eyebrows at my hairline.

"Aye, that's the way of it," Archie answered. If it had been anyone else, I might have made a joke, but there was something about the steadfastness of Archie's nature that gave me pause.

"And, as next in line to this Order, I, too, will somehow gain magickal powers?" I continued, enunciating carefully as though I was speaking to someone who was still learning English.

"Yes, from what I can gather," Agnes said, peering

down at the protected documents through reading glasses she'd perched on the end of her nose. "It's an unusual situation, as there's more or less been at least a partial Order for years now. This is the first time that no current members of the Order have stepped into their position."

"There's more then." Matthew steepled his fingers in front of his face, his gaze thoughtful. "So why Sophie? Why does she come first?"

"You believe this?" I turned to Matthew, my voice rising, not caring that I was being rude.

"Soph"—Matthew turned to me, an earnest look on his face—"at heart, I'm a student of nature. If I've learned anything in all my years of studying history, it is that *anything* is possible. Leaders make unexpected decisions. Brilliant minds discover new mathematics, artists create unimaginable works of staggering beauty, writers weave stories that stand the test of time. All with fewer tools than we have at our disposal now. I've learned that if the matter is important enough, whatever that may be, the solution finds a way. In this instance, I'd say that the Stone of Truth is pretty damn important. It's found a way to protect itself and, while it may not make sense to us in the regular way of things, that doesn't mean it isn't true."

"Let's say this is true," I said, leaning into a debate with Matthew. It was a comfort zone for me, bickering with him over various points on whatever we were currently reading, and the routine of it helped to soothe the tangle of nerves in my chest. "Say the rock is true, the Kelpies are true...how then, does one suddenly just have magick? I can unequivocally tell you that thus far in my life, I have shown no gift for magick. Nada. No matter how many times I twirled three times on my bed and wished for my parents to come home." Oops, I thought, wincing as I revealed too much about my past for my comfort. Matthew, immediately understanding, jumped in.

"I think that's what we're here to learn about. The transfer of magick, I presume? It likely comes down to energy. Magick is a universal energy, therefore it can be passed to anyone else. Energy doesn't just disappear."

I blinked at Matthew, my head spinning, as I tried to push all the various parts of this story around in my head like a forklift stacking boxes in a warehouse. I needed to frame this in a way that would make sense to me or I'd never be able to move forward.

Magick is the great equalizer, Sophie. It isn't reserved for the rich or the powerful. The most humble of beings can hold the mightiest of power in but a spoken word. Never underestimate its power.

Uncle Arthur's words floated up from the recesses of my brain, and I leaned back, crossing my arms over my chest and closing my eyes as I thought about all the times that Arthur, even more so of recent, had wanted to talk about the myths and legends of Scotland. Particularly, magick. Lottie and I had thought it was his newest thing, as he had a habit of hyper fixating on one area of interest for six months to a year before abandoning it to the next hobby. I suppose, it was more than likely that Uncle Arthur had been undiagnosed for ADHD, but at this point, that made little difference. Arthur had been trying to tell me, in his own convoluted way, that magick existed.

"If...if I am to believe all of this...what happens next?

And why me? Why did Arthur take on this castle instead of another member of this Order?"

"We don't know where the others are. It took us ages to find Arthur." Agnes and Hilda exchanged a look, and Lachlan stopped his pacing behind me.

"*You* found Arthur?" Lachlan's voice held a note of danger that pricked the fine hairs at the back of my neck. Should I find this sexy? *I really shouldn't*. I liked even-keeled men, not ones that ran to fits of intensity or grumpiness like Lachlan did. "You're the reason the castle sold?"

"In fairness, I didn't know he'd buy the castle. But we did need the help..." Hilda trailed off as Lachlan marched to the fireplace and gently deposited Sir Buster on his bed before turning and storming from the room. I noted that he had been gentle with the dog, and he hadn't slammed the door on the way out of the library, so the man had some restraint it seemed.

"What's his deal?" I asked, no longer caring about being polite. These people were asking me to accept magickal powers and fight water beasts, so I think we'd turned the corner on proper etiquette a while ago.

"His bark is worse than his bite," Archie said, snipping a piece of wire with tiny scissors.

"His mother, like Lachlan, didn't much believe in what she considered to be nonsense. A lovely woman, but fiercely pragmatic, she swam too close to the island one day. She'd never done so before, and perhaps curiosity finally got the best of her, but she drowned that day. The locals believe it to be the Kelpies. Lachlan will only accept that she drowned. Because of this, the entire discussion about the Order of Caledonia is an uphill battle with that one."

"I saw him. This morning. He was standing on the wall when the...the shrieks..." I turned to Matthew and grabbed his arm. "Did you hear them as well? Early this morning?"

"No, I had my earplugs in." Matthew's forehead creased in confusion. "Was there screaming and you didn't come wake me?"

"Aye, the Kelpies," Hilda said softly. "He'll still protect us, you see? Even when he's stubborn to the point of infuriation, he'll still take watch."

Unbidden, the image of Lachlan, alone on the wall, facing down an unknown beast that might have been responsible for his mother's death, rose to my head. My heart twisted, and I found myself with the inexplicable urge to go find Lachlan and comfort him. I almost snorted. I had a feeling that trying to console Lachlan would be like trying to hug a bull.

"He believes," Archie said, quietly. "Just give him time to work around to it."

"It's been years." Hilda rounded on her husband. "We're running out of time. Loren Brae is losing people. They're leaving. Tourism is drying up. Businesses are closing. Next, people will start getting hurt. It's a responsibility we have, Archie, to see this through. We owe it to our people and to our place in history to protect the Clach na Fìrinn. It's us who can restore the Order, the guardians, and I'll not shy away from such a task. Even if it hurts Lachlan. I love him, och, you know that I do with all my heart, but some things are bigger than one person's feelings."

It was her impassioned speech to her husband, the firelight glinting off a sheen in her eyes, that convinced me that I needed to honor their story. It was wild, oh goodness, was it wild, but also...a part of me wanted it to be true. More than anything, that last bit surprised me. For someone who thrived on the predictability of a routine and the comfort of the mundane, this entire story should have sent me running for the next flight out of Scotland. Instead, something inside me warmed to it, my blood beginning to hum and, for once, I listened to my gut instead of making a neat pros and cons list to lead my decision.

"This is wild," I said, drawing everyone's attention back to me. "Like, well and truly wild. But I'm open. I want to know more. Particularly...why me?"

Matthew almost fell out of his chair.

"You're into this?" Matthew asked, the look on his face like he'd just discovered I visited bondage sex clubs in my downtime.

"I don't know that I'd say it quite like that." My lips quirked. "But, yes, I'm in the information-gathering stage, Matthew. I want to know more. I'm...I'm listening."

"That's a good lass," Archie said. His praise warmed me, as he didn't seem like one to dole it out unnecessarily, and I turned to the two women across from me who now wore matching hopeful expressions.

"Why me? Tell me," I reiterated.

"I'll take this," Agnes said, shifting through the papers in front of her before pulling one to the top. Peering at it, her lips moved slightly as she read through the words before lifting her head to look at me in the weird way that people do when they try to talk to you while looking over their reading glasses. "The Order of Caledonia was originally comprised of individuals that played a role in the maintenance and upkeep of the village."

"So not a traditional Order, then?" Matthew leaned forward, his pen flying across his notebook as he took notes. "It's not like the Knights of the Round Table or something of that nature?"

"No, it's not," Agnes said. "Each member of the Order has different and valuable roles. But there is a knight."

The room went quiet, and I felt a touch of...something...dance across my skin. My eyes widened.

"Me?" I whispered.

"Aye, Sophie. You're the knight. The first of the Order of Caledonia. It always starts with the knight. Your duties, should you choose to accept them, will be to step into your power and to restore the Order to its fullest. In doing so, you'll bring peace and prosperity back to our community and protect one of the greatest gifts and threats to humankind that has ever existed—the Clach na Fìrinn," Agnes said. Her words fell like a curse or a benediction. It was hard to say, really. The weight of them settled on my shoulders, a mantle of responsibility and, for a moment, I almost bowed under the pressure. Looking down at the table, I forced myself to breathe and tried to sort through my emotions.

This is your birthright.

"So no pressure, right?" I smiled weakly, and Matthew chuckled next to me.

"It's immense pressure." Hilda regarded me stoically. "And a great honor. The knight is chosen because they are capable of handling both."

"Wait...why not Sophie's father, then?" Matthew interjected, his hand in the air.

"He must not have been worthy." Agnes shrugged, flipping through the pages as though the answer to my father's inability to care for anyone outside himself would be found there.

"You hear that, Soph?" Matthew asked. "*Robert* wasn't worthy. But *you* are. This stone—one of the most sought after in the world, mind you, that knows all the truths of the universe—decided that your father wasn't worthy. And you have been chosen. I think that's a pretty important point, don't you?"

"Duly noted, Professor," I said, my heart thundering in my chest. I rose from my chair. "Do you mind...I think that I just need some time to digest all of this?"

"Why don't we take a break and meet back here before lunch for a quick castle tour? I think you'll enjoy the history." Hilda stood, twinkling up at me as though I was her savior. The crux of it was...I already didn't want to let these people down. Aside from Lachlan, they'd all been incredibly nice. How could I tell them that fairy tales were for kids and leave them behind? Either way, I owned this castle, which meant I was in charge of its future, even if it came with a whole bag of ghosts.

Not waiting for Matthew to accompany me, I left, my own ghosts haunting me as I tried to decide if I could handle what came next.

CHAPTER TEN

LACHLAN

I needed to blow off some bloody steam.

A half hour later, after sledgehammering a section of the old wall that Archie had been moaning about needing replaced, I finally straightened. Sweat dripped down my body beneath my shirt, and I headed for the burn to cool off.

As spring days in Scotland went, it was a fairly mild one. The rain had been chased away by the first soft rays of the sun that filtered through the clouds to where my secret swimming hole was. Most people wouldn't dare dip their toes in such frigid waters, but I loved it. I dove beneath the surface, the icy water making my skin burn, and relished the spike of adrenaline that rushed through my body. While these cold plunges weren't for everyone, I always felt invigorated after, and the shock always managed to help me clear my mind in times of trouble. I had been coming to this swimming spot since I was a wee lad, and the familiarity of it soothed me.

Surfacing, I brushed my sodden hair out of my eyes and took several deep breaths. The music of the river, the water racing gently over the rocks, and the wind shifting through branches of the trees, brought peace in a way that nothing else could. I floated on my back and looked up at the sky, letting my thoughts drift for a moment.

A voice at the riverbank jolted me upward, and I turned, treading water as I looked toward shore. There, one Sophie MacKnight stood, her arms crossed over her thin jumper. I could see her shivering from here.

"Can I help you?" Immediately, I thought of one way I wanted to help her which was to peel those threadbare leggings off and bury myself between her thighs. Despite the frigid water, my cock twitched, and I was grateful that my body was hidden from sight beneath the surface.

"Have you lost your mind? How can you possibly be swimming in this water?" Sophie asked. "You won't catch me in a pool unless it's above eighty degrees."

"Eighty degrees and we'd all be dead," I poked at her, knowing full well that she meant Fahrenheit even though we tracked temperature in Celsius here.

It took her a moment, and then her eyes narrowed on me. I couldn't help it. My lips twitched as I realized that I quite enjoyed poking fun at Miss Sophie MacKnight. Perhaps she wasn't aware how her emotions played across her face, but she was wildly interesting to watch and, despite myself, I drew closer to the river bank. There was only so long I could stay in this frigid water anyway before I would start to shiver myself.

"Is this how you bathe?" Sophie stared dubiously at my pile of clothes on the rock. "I'm fairly certain the castle has indoor plumbing. At least in my apartment it does."

"Och, the showers are only for the fancy folk. Us *help* must bathe in the rivers like the livestock." I affected a deep Scottish accent, and it took Sophie a moment to work out what I was saying. When she did, indignation flooded her face along with a bonnie pink flush. I bit back my smile.

"Well, that's positively barbaric. I'll see to it this morning that you have use of the showers. This is no way to live and allow me to apologize on behalf of my uncle if this is how you've been treated," Sophie said, tightening her arms across her chest.

I realized quickly that she had taken me at my word. Even though the thought of me washing regularly in this river during the height of a Scottish winter made me laugh, I kept it to myself.

"*Sophie*. I have a shower. I just do this on occasion when I need to clear my head."

"I'm certain there has to be a less painful way to clear your head," Sophie said. I could think of one such way, but I suspected the thought would send her running. Sophie's coltish nature made me want to both poke at and protect her, and I truly wasn't sure how I wanted to proceed around her. I hated that she had the power to now direct the future of this castle and this town, and at the same time, apparently, she also held the power over my arousal. I stayed in the deep water even though the cold was starting to get to me, in order to hide my *very* visible reaction to Sophie.

"There is nothing wrong with a bit of cold water. It's a good shock to my system, and I find it invigorates me in a way that coffee just doesn't," I said, my eyes on hers. She continued to huddle into her jumper, her eyes darting everywhere and, for a moment, she looked so lost and alone that I wanted to go to her and cradle her into my arms and tell her that everything was going to be just fine. Following that urge, I met her eyes.

"I'm sorry about your Uncle Arthur. I know it's not easy to grieve." *At least it wasn't for me.*

"And I'm sorry about your mom," Sophie said, and my stomach twisted.

"I guess you were bound to hear about her death," I said, shrugging one shoulder awkwardly. "It was a long time ago." There wasn't much else I could say.

"I don't know that time is relevant when it comes to love," Sophie mused. "It's just there, isn't it? It doesn't go away. It just becomes woven into the fabric of your soul."

I paused, stuck on her words, realizing that she phrased grief for me in such an eloquent way while at the same time not making me feel embarrassed for missing my mother.

"Tell me one of your favorite things about her." Sophie surprised me with her question.

"She talked to birds." I had no idea where the memory had come from or why that popped out of my mouth but, nevertheless, that was the first thing that rose to my mind. "She would have full conversations with them. Particularly the crows. They used to bring her little gifts. Shiny bits and bobs. For a long time, I thought she was a magickal queen of the forest or something of the like. Talking to her crows, feeding all the other birds. They'd follow her around, as well. I still have a coin that one of the crows brought for her." My hand went to where I had threaded the coin onto a leather cord around my neck. It was a whimsical part of my mother that I'd always carried with me, and now I had to question when I had stopped letting whimsy and wonderous moments into my life. After her death, I had shouldered the burden of trying to take care of everyone else, barely allowing Hilda to step into the role of mothering me. There'd been no time for childhood games as I learned the role of taking care of the castle.

"I love it," Sophie declared. "I've watched videos on that. On the crows, that is. They're meant to be really smart, and I've always wanted to see if they would really bring you gifts if you fed them."

"Well, we have plenty here. No one is stopping you," I pointed out, and Sophie's mouth dropped open.

"Are you saying that I could train a crow army?"

This time, I did laugh.

"I don't know why the thought of you leading a crow army terrifies me but, yes, I suppose you could attempt to train the crows to fight your battles for you." I smiled openly at Sophie. "Tell me a favorite thing about your Uncle Arthur."

"His love of the ridiculous," Sophie said immediately. "When he finally found his last wife, Lottie, I think he really felt comfortable enough to embrace his eccentricities. She's such a creative spirit that she leaned into it as well, and you'd never know from one day to the next what oddball thing Arthur would bring home or news story that we'd be discussing over dinner. Like the one time he took up a campaign to knit sweaters for some penguins that needed them. I can't even remember where or why now, but there we were, all learning to knit these tiny little penguin vests for a good six months until the organization finally wrote to Arthur and said that they had more than enough." The memory brought a wide smile to Sophie's face, transforming her from coltish and uncertain to beautiful. Her smile was like the sun coming out from behind a cloud, and my breath caught. I wanted her to look at me like that.

"He doesn't sound quite like the evil overlord that I was making him out to be in my head," I said, a shiver working through me as the cold water started to numb my body. "I apologize for thinking dark thoughts about your uncle. I thought he was just maybe another rich man coming in and snapping up a piece of our heritage with no care for the history held within."

"I imagine that probably happens a lot here, doesn't it?" Sophie looked at the forest where the castle jutted proudly over the tree line. "It's hard not to visit somewhere like this and wonder if you couldn't have the fairy tale for yourself too."

"Unfortunately, this fairy tale comes with its challenges, and potentially some very real danger," I said. There, I had brought it up. I acknowledged the truth of what I'd spent years avoiding.

"No kidding," Sophie exclaimed. "At least you've had some years to get used to it. All of a sudden, I'm supposed to be a knight capable of attacking water beasts. Did I mention that I don't like going into cold water? How am I supposed to kill a water horse if I can barely swim when it's too cold?" Sophie demanded.

"Is that the thing you're going to fixate on? Of all the

intricacies and history that lies with the myths around this, you're worried about getting in the cold water?" I raised an eyebrow in disbelief.

Sophie brought her hands to her hips, and I could almost see her stamping her foot like a child having a tantrum. "Did I not mention that I hated cold water? This isn't exactly a walk in the park for me."

"Speaking of cold water," I said. "It's time for me to get out. I'm going numb."

"Nobody is stopping you from getting out of the water," Sophie said, her brow furrowed in thought. "So how am I supposed to just be a knight? Isn't that, like, reserved for men? Or does it matter? We are in the days of gender fluid and non-binary. Well, at least acknowledging it more, as it's been around forever but, nevertheless, I suppose that means it doesn't matter what gender the knight is. Right?" Sophie scrunched up her face as she rambled and paced the banks of the river. I drew closer, wondering if she would even notice that I was naked, and a part of me wanted to test her response to me. I'm not saying it's a great part of me, and yet, here I was. Even when I knew that she was the last person I should be getting involved with.

"I don't think it's about the gender of the knight, though I'll admit that I had expected a man to take this position. However, it is the code of conduct and the characteristics of the person who makes the knight, not the gender." The water was now at my waist, droplets running down my chest, and I paused a moment, wondering if Sophie would realize what was happening. I wasn't a shy man, but I wanted to give her a moment to react.

"Okay, that's fine. I like that. Right, so it's not about whether I have the biggest dick or the strongest muscles. It's really about how I carry myself. I mean, are any of the qualities of good knights about being organized or focused on details? Because I'm good at that. I can make a killer spreadsheet. Is that a knightly duty?" Sophie finally stopped talking, and her mouth dropped open as I walked out of the river completely naked.

"Aye, I can't say that I know whether efficient spreadsheet skills fall under the duties of the knightly code, as I'm sure that's more Agnes's department, but we can be asking her later," I said, leaning over to grab my T-shirt and dry the water from my chest. Sophie gaped at me, frozen, and my smile widened.

"You're naked," Sophie declared, all but stammering, her cheeks turning a delicious shade of pink.

"Aye, lassie," I said, infusing my voice with a thicker accent. "Did you think I was swimming in my clothes then? You saw the pile right here."

"I didn't know. Most people wear swimming suits where I come from," Sophie said. I noted that she didn't turn away. Instead, her eyes dropped below my waist. Grateful that my arousal no longer showed, I winked at her.

"The water's cold if you ken my meaning."

Sophie's hands flew to her face.

"You are an impossible one, aren't you? You know exactly what you're doing." Sophie's hands descended back to her hips. "You're just trying to ruffle my feathers. I'm onto you. And I'm going to tell you that you can't get rid of me this easily."

"Who said that I'm trying to get rid of you?" I bent and

pulled my jeans on, zipping them before walking closer to Sophie. Her eyes followed my legs all the way up my shirt- less torso before finding my face. She bit that lower lip in her unconscious habit, and I desperately wanted to lean down and nibble it myself. Her eyes widened as though she understood where my thoughts had gone.

"You've been nothing but rude to me since my arrival. Not saying I don't blame you"—Sophie held up her hand —"but nevertheless, it's rude you've been, and I know you don't want me here."

"Don't stay if you can't cut it, Sophie." I issued the challenge. "I lost my mother because of this. And my father, while alive, vacated shortly after. The Order of Caledonia isn't for the faint of heart. And I'd rather soldier on without you than have someone who thinks this is just a whim or something fun to take a stab at, who will then up and leave us when we need her most. If that's the way of it, and who you are as a person, don't get our hopes up. I'd rather you leave now instead of making things worse."

The moment drew out, suspended between us. Sophie grappled with the meaning of my words while, for the first time ever, I placed my future in someone else's hands. I didn't like this control she had over me, and it was a feeling that reminded me of being a child with no voice in my future.

I wanted Sophie to stay, but not if she couldn't hack it. Even at the basest level, the responsibility of the upkeep and maintenance of a castle of this size as well as the holdings in town was enormous. It wasn't meant to be managed care- lessly from afar by someone unfamiliar with Loren Brae's needs. I needed Sophie to stay for many reasons, one of which I wasn't ready to admit.

"Is that a threat?" Sophie asked, raising her chin at me. I liked the spark of fire that came into her moody eyes and hoped that spoke of her spirit.

"I don't have to threaten anything, but I can promise you this. If you hurt the people I love or play with their livelihoods, you will regret it."

"And here I thought we'd made some headway just now," Sophie said. Something about the way she crossed her arms and tilted her head made me think I was about to get scolded by my teacher. "I haven't decided what I'm doing yet, Lachlan. I'm not prone to impulsive decisions, so I'm taking a little time to gather information. I'll be sure to inform you of my decision when I've made one." Sophie turned on her heels and stormed up to the top of the brae, turning back just as the clouds opened and icy droplets of rain began to fall. "And the next time you flash me, I won't be as kind as I was today. You'll need to protect your little man there—if I can even find him."

My mouth dropped open as she disappeared over the banks.

"The water was bloody cold!" I shouted after her, glancing down at my jeans. Was I really that small? I hadn't had any complaints in the past. Annoyance rippled through me along with a healthy appreciation for her banter. Despite everything, I laughed as the skies unleashed their fury, drenching me.

I guess that was the Scottish version of a cold shower.

CHAPTER ELEVEN

SOPHIE

"I'm going to need details," Matthew said later that evening as we walked into town. "Very exacting and in-depth details. Leave nothing out."

"I mean you've got eyes in your head, don't you? I'm sure you can imagine what he looks like without clothes on," I said.

I snuggled more deeply into the sweater that Hilda had handed me before I left the house. A man's sweater, it was a heather-green wool and smelled faintly of soap and smoke from the fireplace. I resisted asking if this was Lachlan's sweater and had gratefully accepted the added layer of warmth. While everyone else had been walking around talking about what a mild day it had been, I continued adding layers from my meager supply of clothes. If I planned to stay here any longer, I would need a shopping trip soon before I caught my death from pneumonia.

"Oh trust me, I have tried. So why don't you add to the picture just to make sure that my mental imagery is correct. Is he clean-shaven?"

I rounded on him and grabbed his arm. "Down there?"

"Well, I was talking about his chest, but now that I know you've seen him completely nude, I'm going to need even *more* details," Matthew all but panted, and I poked him in the chest.

"Let's just say I could easily see him gracing the cover of one of those men's calendars. You know the ones where the firemen raise money for charity by posing half naked while cuddling puppies or kittens?" I asked.

"Go on..." Matthew exaggerated his breathing. "I really had no idea how...virile the men here would be. Now if I could just find one that is just a little bit nerdy and not too overwhelming, I'd be all set."

"You and me both." I laughed. "Except I'm not here for that, remember?"

"Well, honey, you may be getting it whether you like it or not," Matthew said. "If I'm reading this situation correctly."

"Lachlan is not interested in me. He's trying to scare me away more than anything." Of that, I was certain, after he'd laid out his threat earlier that day.

"Oh sure, I also like to expose my dripping wet gorgeous naked body to someone to get them to leave. Yes, that's the first tactic I would use to chase people away." Matthew rolled his eyes as we crunched down the gravel path that led from the castle to the village.

"I mean it would scare *me* away," I teased, and Matthew's mouth dropped open.

"Wow, Scottish Sophie is bitchy," Matthew said. "I like it."

I laughed and hooked my arm through Matthew's as we left the gates of the castle and crossed the road to the sidewalk that lined the banks of the loch. Loch Mirren was gorgeous in her vastness, far larger than any lake I had seen back home, cupped gently by rolling green mountains in the background. Gorgeous skyscraper clouds lined the horizon, and the setting sun tinged their curves pink. My eyes caught on the small island a far distance from shore, where I could just make out a pile of stones between the trees. I paused, looking across the still waters that reflected the mountains, and wondered if the myths were actually true.

"It sure grabs your heart," Matthew observed, leaning against the stone wall that lined the walkway. "It's a stark contrast to the strip malls and hills cluttered with houses back home."

"It's like an uncut gem," I said, my breath catching. "I think the roughness of its edges adds to its beauty. It's not a polished landscape, is it? But something in that wildness appeals to me."

"When was the last time you took a vacation?" Matthew turned to me. "Or left the office for any discernible amount of time?"

The wind picked up, bringing the icy scent of rain with it, so we continued our walk toward town. Clustered on the banks of Loch Mirren, Loren Brae reminded me of an old friend waving you over to sit a while on her porch. I realized with a jolt that I wanted to stay, to listen to her whisper her secrets into my ear, and to wander the banks dreaming about what-ifs and what-may-comes.

It was out of character for me, but a lot of things had been since I had arrived in Scotland and maybe I just needed to embrace this side of myself. "It's probably been a year or two since I've taken a proper vacation," I admitted, stopping to smile at a charming statue of a unicorn tucked next to a weathered wooden bench.

"See? That's your problem as well. You only ever see the inside of your office and your shabby little apartment. Maybe coming here is exactly the change you needed."

"I wasn't aware that I needed a change," I protested. "Why does everyone else always think they know what's best for me? When am I not allowed to be the one who can be trusted with decisions for her own life?" I wasn't really mad at Matthew, but I did feel a little annoyed at his line of questioning.

"When you can show me a proper work-life balance, a level of self-care that isn't leading you toward a stroke at the age of thirty-five, and a touch better decision-making when it comes to the men in your life, then maybe I won't interfere so much," Matthew said as we came upon a building with light spilling from its arched windows. A sign over the door pronounced it to be the Tipsy Thistle, and I decided that I was going to go in for a pint. If I was going to be a temporary local, then I should have the proper Scottish experience.

"Just like you're so great at picking the men in your life?" I arched a brow at Matthew.

"She *is* bitchy. For your information, I'd already taken my sabbatical for *me* prior to agreeing to go on that dig with

to be the way of how they grew them here, stood and raised his pint glass to me. "To our Knight! Sláinte!"

I raised my glass, unsure of how to respond to their adoring looks, but a part of me warmed to the challenge. I didn't know the first thing about being a knight, let alone any rules of magick, but I did know one thing—I liked to help people. I was a fixer at heart, forever taking care of extra duties both in my uncle's company, at his house, and in all of my friends' lives. I was always the first person people called when they had a problem, and I loved nothing more than feeling like I was needed. Perhaps it stemmed from my parents ditching me at such a young age, and therefore I sought validation through being of service to others, or at least that was what my therapist told me before I stopped going to her. Nevertheless, there was no way I was going to let the sweet grandmother down. Or at least, not without giving this whole knight thing an honest try. It felt funny to think of myself as a knight even though our family business was built on protecting people. At that thought, I almost dropped my pint.

"Matthew, a thought just occurred to me," I said.

"Oh, just one? That's a record for you." Graham snickered from where he'd overheard, and Matthew preened.

"I guess I'm not the only one who's bitchy in Scotland, am I?" I arched an eyebrow at Matthew.

"It's not just Scotland, darling, as you well know." Matthew smoothed a wrinkle in his pant leg.

"As I was saying...do you think that there is some corre-lation of our family business being a security company and this whole magickal knight thing?" I took a proper sip of the beer and was surprised to find that I enjoyed it. I was more of a wine girl, but the beer had some light citrus notes and a dry aftertaste that was different from some of the lagers I had forced down in the past.

"I definitely had the thought when it came to your last name," Matthew agreed. "However, I hadn't thought too deeply about your uncle when it came to his protective services. That's certainly interesting, isn't it?"

"What's interesting?" A gravelly voice at my side had a shiver of awareness dancing over my skin. Turning, I looked to see Lachlan taking the seat next to me, fully clothed this time and looking like he just stepped out of a catalog for rugged Scotsmen. What was it with the people in this town? Particularly the men? Not to say that the ladies weren't likely appealing as well, I was just paying more attention to the broad-shouldered hulking overabundance of masculinity that dominated.

"I see you found your clothes," I said, raising my glass at Lachlan.

"I'm not sure being naked around the lass is any way to woo her," Graham said, leaning onto the bar. "If anything, it's enough to send her screaming for the hills."

"That's not what your sister said," Lachlan said, and my eyes rounded. Before I could intervene, Graham grinned.

"Having her stitch up your bum because you tripped on a rake doesn't exactly qualify for a romantic rendezvous. Not to mention she was seeing you naked in a professional capacity." Graham rolled his eyes.

"You tripped on a rake?" I asked. The very thought of being impaled on a rake and the fact that he needed stitches made my stomach turn.

"More like I was shoved." Lachlan glared at Graham.

"All's fair in love and war. I couldn't let that pretty Lisa Murphy think you were the stronger one, now could I?" Graham asked.

"Did you have to maim me in the process?" Lachlan asked.

"Och, it was nothing but a scratch," Graham said, sliding a pint in front of Lachlan. "You'd think you'd had open-heart surgery the way you still moan about it."

"I only moan about it to remind you that your plan backfired, and the pretty Lisa took pity on me and nursed me back to health." Lachlan smiled sweetly at Graham.

"So why were you seeing our lad here naked?" Graham asked, returning his attention to me. "And might I offer my deepest apologies. We do try to be a welcoming town, but it seems someone needs to work on his definition of welcoming."

"Yes, Sophie? Why did you see him naked?" Matthew asked, his eyes dancing with laughter. "Also, I think you need to describe what you saw in great detail."

"He's a fine specimen at that," Agnes said, joining Lachlan. "I'm sure it wasn't a hardship on your eyes."

"Specimen, is it?" Lachlan looked aggrieved. "Is that all I am to you ladies? Just something to be ogled at?"

"Don't flatter yourself. There are not many eligible bachelors left in this town. So we need something to look at...anything at all," Agnes said.

"Yes, Sophie," Graham said, deepening his voice and leaning closer with a sultry look on his face. Even though I got the sense that he was putting this on for show, I flushed. "Anytime you'd like me to put myself on display for you, I'd be more than happy to."

Agnes snorted and picked up Lachlan's beer to take a sip.

"Well," I said, fighting through the natural shyness that wanted to take over, "I suppose it would be only fair that I saw you naked as well. In that case, I could make a ruling on who is the finest specimen. For research purposes of course."

Lachlan muttered something under his breath next to me.

"This is a full-service pub, hen," Graham said with another one of his delicious winks. "You just say the word, and I'm more than happy to serve."

"Surely, that doesn't work on you, Sophie," Agnes interjected, rolling her eyes.

Matthew fanned himself with a napkin from the bar. "It's working on me."

"And I don't see why you're giving him a hard time for being less than welcoming," I interjected, wanting to take my mind away from the constant loop of Lachlan's naked body currently playing in my head. "You barely said two words to us the whole ride from the airport."

"That's called good service," Graham argued. "You want a driver with his eyes on the road, particularly in the rain."

"You weren't driving when you dumped our luggage on the front door of the castle and disappeared with barely a word," I continued, my eyes narrowing as a man appeared from the kitchen with two plates in his hand. "Is that the haggis? I think it's the haggis. Oh, tell me what it is again, Matthew."

"Best not, I think," Matthew said, rubbing his hands

together in anticipation as our steaming plates were deposited in front of us.

"Ah, a proper pub meal for you." Lachlan leaned over, nodding his approval. I caught the same whiff of soap that the sweater I was wearing had, and suddenly the pub felt much too warm. Leaning back, I raised my arms and stripped the sweater from my shoulders.

"Trying to return the favor?" Lachlan asked, his eyes heated when I'd gotten the sweater over my head. Confused, I glanced down to see that I'd pulled my undershirt almost to my neck and my neon-pink lace bra was on shining display for everyone in the pub to see.

"At least it's not your old sports bra," Matthew said, tugging my shirt down while I sat there frozen. "I've seen those, and they aren't pretty."

"I...I..." My brain had just about short-circuited. I wasn't sure if it was the embarrassment of showing my breasts to the pub or the way that Lachlan looked like he'd happily bury his face between my cleavage, but either way... thoughts were not coming forward.

"Don't fuss too much, Sophie. We're an easygoing lot," Agnes said. "Nothing to be embarrassed about. Not like this one over here and how he all but rolls over for any skirt that walks through the door." Agnes nodded to Graham.

"I sit up, shake, and bite on command as well, darling," Graham said to Agnes, his voice silky again, and I instantly wondered what the undercurrents there meant.

"Do you fetch as well? If so, fetch me a cider then, *darling*," Agnes said, rolling her eyes, and Graham blew her a kiss before bending over to grab a glass from the shelf.

"What is what?" I asked, my voice low, leaning toward

Matthew as I picked up my fork. The plate held crumbled dark meat, which looked a bit like ground beef, and then a pile of steaming white mashed potatoes and orange sweet potatoes. Deciding to start with the easiest, I took a bite of the sweet potatoes and grimaced.

"What...is that not sweet potatoes?" I asked.

"Neeps," Lachlan said. I glanced over to find him watching me closely, his arms crossed over his chest. It appeared I was going to be the show this evening. I flushed, thinking once more about how I'd flashed him, and blew out a breath. At least I'd put on a good bra today. Matthew hadn't been wrong—my typical sports bras were not the most flattering.

"And...a neep is what exactly?" I asked, washing the mouthful down with a sip of beer.

"Turnips," Matthew supplied, and I paused, looking at my plate differently.

"Sure, okay, that makes sense. I guess you wouldn't serve sweet potatoes and potatoes on the same plate, right? That would be silly," I said.

"My mother serves both at Thanksgiving," Matthew said, dipping into his plate and nodding when Graham tapped his empty pint glass. "Another for you, Sophie?"

"Um, while I said I wanted the proper Scottish experience, I'm not sure I'm up for whisky tonight. What else would you suggest if I don't want a whisky?" I asked Graham.

"Gin," Graham said, pointing at a line of pretty bottles. "Gin's grown quite popular here over the past few years. It doesn't take as long to make as whisky does."

"Oh, I like the pink one," I said, pointing at a pretty bottle with soft pink liquor inside.

"Matches your bra," Lachlan said as Graham retrieved the bottle. "Good choice."

"At this point, I'm just glad I was wearing underwear. Unlike yourself," I pointed out.

"If that's a bother for you, I suggest not asking to look under a man's kilt, then," Lachlan said, and I stilled.

"Is it true?" I turned to him, curiosity getting the better of me.

"Hard to say, really. You'll need to find that out for yourself." Lachlan grinned, and I narrowed my eyes at him before turning back to study my plate. So the brown stuff had to be the haggis. Deciding it was best to just get it over with, I scooped up a bite with my fork.

Everyone stopped and looked at me, waiting. I paused mid-chew. Had I done something wrong? Was there a proper order in which to eat this? Was I supposed to recite a traditional poem first or do a native dance? Swallowing, I smiled at Graham.

"It's tasty," I said. "Why is everyone looking at me?"

"No reason," Graham said, putting a large goblet with my pink gin drink in front of me. "Have a sip of this and see if it's to your taste."

I complied, making a mental note to look up haggis when I had Wi-Fi back at the castle, and smiled up at Graham.

"It's perfect, thank you."

"Nae bother, hen. I'll be here to serve you all night," Graham said with exaggerated charm, and Agnes coughed into her palm.

"You gonnae no do that..." Agnes muttered.

"How no?" Lachlan replied, and the two cackled like old crones. Knowing I was missing some inside joke, I turned to Matthew.

"Do you ever feel like the square peg trying to fit in the round hole?" I asked. Which pretty much summed up my whole life, I realized. I'd been off-kilter since I'd arrived in Scotland, well, really since I'd lost Arthur, and I vacillated between wanting to crawl into bed for days and wanting to explore this gift he'd given to me. This week had felt like the one time I'd tried bodyboarding at a beach in Mexico and misjudged the waves. I'd gotten stuck in an endless loop as wave after towering wave crashed into me, sending me tumbling across the sand and depositing me very ungraciously in front of an old man reading his book. He'd taken one look at me, covered in sand and spitting sea water, and had moved to another chair.

"You will. For a bit. Soon, you'll be sitting here, laughing along with everyone else about a joke that you're included in. These things take time, Sophie. Look at how excited that woman was that the Knight had finally arrived. I know the magick and myths of this place seem flat-out ridiculous, but there's something to it. Historically speaking, many myths are rooted in truths. You may not be able to see the truth *yet*, but your heart can still listen, can't it?" Matthew used his lecturing voice, which I responded well to. I'd always liked learning and, as a rule follower, being given explicit directions was right up my alley. Things like listening to my heart fell more into a gray area for me because I liked exact and precise answers. However, perhaps that was part of what Uncle Arthur had been trying to teach me for years with his obsession with the mystical. He'd given me the love of fencing—an exacting and precise sport—and then tried to fill my head with magick stories at other times. I'd always loved his story time but, to me, it always had been just that—stories. Now, it seemed like I'd stepped into my own real-life fairy tale.

Complete with a few handsome princes, I supposed, my gaze darting between Graham and Lachlan.

"Another?" Graham all but purred, leaning over the bar and tapping my hand gently with his finger. Lachlan bristled next to me.

"Lay off, would ya? The lass just got here," Lachlan grumbled.

"Even better." Graham grinned at me and, I'll admit, there was a little flutter of interest that danced through me. "You fools haven't had a chance to turn her against me yet."

"Because your charming disposition on the car ride over was meant to win me over?" I asked. Graham threw his head back and laughed.

"Treat 'em mean, keep 'em keen." He took my empty glass and began mixing me another drink.

"Oh please, would you listen to this one? And that is why I'll never be dating the likes of you." Agnes blew out a breath and, leaning over Lachlan, she grabbed my arm. "Don't be taking up with that man, Sophie. I'm warning you, it's a heartbreaker he is."

"You have to have a heart first for me to be breaking it," Graham said easily, placing a fresh pink gin drink in front of me. His tone was easy, but I noticed a glint of something else in his eyes when he looked at Agnes.

"Lachlan, what time for the games tomorrow?" the tall

man who had raised his glass to me earlier called from across the pub, interrupting the conversation.

"Games? What games?" I asked, turning to Lachlan. I *loved* games. They spoke to my rule-follower heart.

"It's the Highland Games," Lachlan said and raised his voice. "Half ten for tomorrow."

The man threw his fist in the air and whooped, and everyone else in the pub clapped.

"That sounds like something we must go to." Matthew leaned forward. "Will there be kilts?"

"Aye," Lachlan said, his lips twitching.

"It's settled, then. We're going to have us a proper Scottish weekend, aren't we, Sophie?" Matthew clinked his glass against mine.

Too many pink gin drinks to count later, Matthew and I stumbled our way home to the castle. Lachlan had left much earlier to prep for the games that weekend, which left the two of us to traipse precariously up the gravel road that led to the castle. Once we'd passed through the gates, the streetlights no longer lit our way, and we were at the mercy of the wan light from the half-moon that hung low in the sky. Still, it was enough to see the road and the trees that lined it. A flash of white caught my eye.

"Matthew." I hiccuped as I grabbed his arm, catching my toe on a rock and stumbling a bit. "Look!"

"Is that...?" Matthew squinted, hooking my arm and pulling me closer to him.

"It's Clyde," I hissed, though I'm sure they could probably hear me in the next village.

Sure enough, Clyde, the mysterious ghost coo from the night before, poked his head from among the trees.

"*Moo*," Clyde bellowed, causing me to jump. A snort escaped me.

"I think..." There was no way I was going to keep my laughter down. "I think...that's his version of..."

"Don't say it," Matthew warned. His shoulders shook with laughter.

"He's...I think he's..." Tears ran down my face. "He's yelling *boo*. But it's..."

"Moo!" Matthew and I screamed together. Clyde danced forward, clearly delighted that we understood his cow joke, and followed us the whole way back to the castle.

CHAPTER TWELVE

LACHLAN

I t wasn't the turnout that I had been hoping for.

Twice a year, I helped to host a Highland Games on a grassy field behind the local school in Loren Brae. Typically, the event was a huge draw for the community, with people coming from all over to partake in the games or to enjoy a day spectating. But now, as I looked at the smattering of people who milled around the field, my heart fell. I could no longer ignore the fact that the Scots held tightly to their superstitions. The word was out—the Kelpies had returned—and people weren't going to risk visiting here. Archie had been right. It didn't matter that it was more comfortable for me to try to ignore the legend. What had Matthew said last night? A blind man can still listen? Something of that nature. Either way, it was time for me to be a leader.

Which meant I needed to train a knight.

As though my thoughts had conjured her, Sophie wandered onto the field wearing her leggings and threadbare jumper again. She'd plaited her hair into pigtails and wore no makeup, and something about the way she looked around the field with wide searching eyes made me want to cross to her and put my arm around her shoulders. There was something earnest and appealing about the way she handled herself, and I couldn't help but admire how she'd held her own with a bit of banter the night before. As Scots, there was no faster way to our hearts than being able to have a proper banter with our mates.

I was warming to Sophie as much as I wanted to push her away.

Liar.

Okay, fine, so I wanted to pull her closer. But I couldn't because I had to step into the role of preparing her as a Knight of the Order of Caledonia. Which, to be honest, I had no freaking clue what that involved. Agnes would, though.

Snagging Agnes's sleeve as she passed by on her way to the food tent, I bent to her ear.

"I'm in. We need to train Sophie in whatever is necessary to get her started on restoring the Order. Look at this turnout. Worst I've ever seen. I won't stand in your way anymore, I promise you that."

"Well then, ice must have formed on the lakes of hell." Agnes gave me an approving smile. "Tonight, then. We'll get started."

"Tonight?" Usually, we'd all gather and celebrate after the games concluded.

"Tomorrow, then," Agnes conceded. "You'll need to be patrolling the loch. With an unusual amount of activity, the Kelpies may feel threatened."

"Och..." I started to protest but caught the look she gave me. "Right then, I'll be on patrol."

"That's a good lad." Agnes patted my shoulder. "I'm off to grab a sausage roll before I start." Agnes often announced the games when she wasn't overseeing the crafts tables. Today, seeing the paltry turnout, she was likely comfortable with letting her assistant handle any purchases while she called the matches.

"Did you move the caber toss to later?" I asked. The ever-popular caber toss usually drew larger crowds, so I was hoping that by moving the event, more people would show up.

"I did. It's the lesser events to start, and then we'll go into broadswords before we end with the caber toss, hammer throw, and weight for height." Agnes pulled her phone from her pocket, checking the time, and disappeared with a little wave.

As days went, it was another mild one—weather-wise— and though clouds still hugged the sky, I was grateful that rain hadn't yet fallen. Hopefully, the promise of a relatively dry day would add to the appeal, and more people would show up by day's end. I rubbed a hand over my chest, scanning the field for any problems I could solve, my eyes drawn back to Sophie like a heat-seeking missile.

Graham had found her, and my lip curled in distaste as she threw back her head and laughed at something he said. Why did he always have to zero in on every available woman who came to town? Didn't he know that Sophie was off-

bone to chew on, he wasn't going to let it go. "I'm just having a wee chat with the lass."

"You can drop the lass and lad, mate," I said, accentuating my accent. "None of the tourists are around to hear."

"It's become a bit of a habit, I'll admit. And, when you've got a bonnie lass such as Miss Sophie there, well, it's hard not to be appreciating her..." Graham trailed off as I drove my fist into his stomach, pulling much of the power of the punch but using enough force to have him expelling a long breath of air. "Her mind, Lachlan. Her mind. The lass has good banter, that's all."

"Keep it at that," I warned.

"You're claiming her then?" Graham asked, rubbing the spot in his stomach where I punched him. A part of me wished he'd thrown a punch back, as adrenaline hummed just below my skin, seeking a release.

"Surely it's not the olden days, is it then? Claiming her?" I arched my brow at Graham.

"You ken what I'm saying..." Graham said, crossing his arms over his chest. We both nodded in approval as one of the men on the field flipped the other onto his back and pinned him. Matthew clapped exuberantly, and I had to imagine he was deeply enjoying this particular competition.

"I just think if she is the actual Knight that you all have been waiting for, perhaps it is best not to distract her. Right?" I asked, turning back to where Graham studied me with that stupid gleam in his eyes again. "You're the one all up in arms about protecting the village. Well, according to you all—it starts with her. And then you want to move in on her and pull her attention away from what she is here to do?"

"So you're *not* claiming her then?" Graham clarified, and I almost punched him again.

"No, neither of us. It has nothing to do with..." I trailed off, knowing he was smarter than this. "Don't be deliberately obtuse. Just back off, all right?"

"No," Graham said, shooting me a cheeky grin, and my mouth dropped open. I was so used to people listening to me that it took me a moment to respond. By then, he'd joined Sophie at the fence and fury raced through my blood. I strode forward, ready to give him a piece of my mind, and stopped short when Sophie turned and beamed at me.

That smile.

Since I'd met Sophie, most of the time her face had been furrowed in deep concentration, suspicion, or annoyance. The rare times I had seen her smile had all but taken my breath away. But this? This was the first time her smile was just for me.

It was as though someone had tossed a caber right into my gut, and I almost bowled over from the force of it, as I discovered a new desire. Now, instead of just poking at Sophie to get a rise out of her, I now wanted to make her smile. While she still made me nervous, knowing that she could up and leave us hanging at any point and thus putting the castle and our village in a precarious position, I reminded myself that she could also decide to stay here. I'd fallen into an overly cautious way of thinking about the situation, always assuming the worst, a habit I'd learned after my mum had died. If I could anticipate the worst possible outcome, then I could prepare for it. But now, seeing Sophie smile at me like I'd just given her a gift, I allowed myself to think optimistically. *What if*? What if Sophie stayed? What if she made an actual difference to our lives? Maybe, instead of being the harbinger of doom, she might be the angel of hope.

"Look at you," Sophie exclaimed, and I glanced down at myself and realized she was excited about my kilt. Matthew turned and waggled his eyebrows at me.

"My, my. The man does clean up well," Matthew purred.

"I have my moments," I said with a smile. "How are you feeling today? You were out late last night."

"You heard us?" Sophie asked, a guilty look flashing over her face.

"Honey, the whole village heard us," Matthew said. "Don't you remember us howling with laughter the whole way up the drive? Clyde?"

"Oh! Clyde! I'd forgotten he'd walked us home." Sophie slapped a palm to her thigh. "He...he mooed at us."

"Yes, well, that is what coos are known for," I supplied, amused at her.

"Yes, but a ghost coo...like, first of all, can we just stop and appreciate how quickly I've grown to accept the fact that a ghost coo wanders about the castle? And that I can see him? Like...that fact alone is something that two weeks ago I would not have readily accepted. But, you know. *Boo. Moo.*" Sophie looked at me expectantly while Matthew started to laugh behind her.

"It's still funny, Soph. Even if Grumpy McKiltsman doesn't get it," Matthew said, bumping his shoulder to hers.

"I'm not grumpy," I protested, and the whole group

laughed at my words. Was I grumpy? Maybe I was too serious at times, but everyone looked to me to solve problems. I had to be serious, didn't I? "I'm practical. Assertive. That's not grumpy."

"Methinks you doth protest too much," Matthew said out of the side of his mouth as he turned back to the field where two new wrestlers circled each other. "Now this is a sport I can get into."

"I prefer a weapon," Sophie mused, turning back to the field, leaving me feeling like the sun had gone behind a cloud. "Are there swords in any of these games?"

"Aye, broadswords is up next," Graham said.

"Is it? Now that is what I'm into," Sophie said.

"I'm not grumpy," I said from behind them, unable to move past their words.

They all turned to look at me, and Graham got a calculating look on his face.

"Yes, you are." Sophie shook her head and sighed.

"No, I'm not," I said, parroting her head shake.

"As I'm on the receiving end of it, I can tell you that you're grumpy," Sophie insisted.

"Perhaps grumpy means something different in the States." I narrowed my eyes at Sophie.

"Nope, pretty sure it's a universal concept," Sophie insisted.

"Oh, like your fanny?" I asked, hands on my hips.

"My fanny?" Sophie peered over her shoulder and raised a hand to brush her bum. "Is there something on my pants?"

"Fanny isn't..." Matthew leaned in and whispered in her

match between man and woman because, let's be honest, it's the weapon that levels the playing field, right?"

Cheers greeted her words, and then Agnes turned to me.

"The field's yours."

"Thanks," I grumbled, settling on my stick. The smooth weight of it in my palm felt right, and I hefted it lightly in the air.

"That's a good lad," Graham said at my ear. "Prove to her that you're not grumpy by pummeling her with a stick. Well done, you."

"Oh, bugger off," I muttered, striding onto the field, already berating myself for allowing this to happen. The people of the village drew close, shouting their encouragement to Sophie, and I hated that I was going to have to trounce her in front of everyone. Nevertheless, my pride refused to allow me to throw the match, but I would at least make sure not to hurt her.

When I reached the middle of the field, I rolled my shoulders, anticipation buzzing lightly through my body. I turned, my mouth dropping open.

Sophie had stripped off her loose jumper and wore only a fitted black tank top that hugged her body like a second skin. The same bright pink bra from the night before was easily visible, and her cleavage was a siren's song for my gaze. It was the first time I'd fully seen Sophie's body without baggy clothes covering it, and my mouth went dry. As promised from my brief glimpse the night before, her breasts were ample and inviting. A rounded stomach, a high bottom, and thick thighs led down to shapely large calves. Both muscular and soft, all in one, I realized, and I appreciated her confident swagger as she approached me. Sophie came to a stop in front of me, the stick in her hand, and bit at her bottom lip.

"Is this how I hold it?" Sophie asked, her wrist loose as she lifted the sword at an awkward angle.

"Keep your wrist straight," I said, showing her how I held the stick so that the end of it rested against the inside of my wrist. Closing my hand around the stick, I turned it upward. "Then the sword will be an extension of your arm, and you'll have more control."

"Oh, thank you," Sophie said, batting her eyelashes at me, and a warning sounded in my brain. "That's kind of you to help me."

"It's only fair that you know how to properly hold your weapon. I don't want you to get hurt," I said, my tone gruff.

"So how does this work then? If I stab you, then I win?" Sophie asked. Agnes drew close and heard the tail end of her question.

"I'd like to avoid you stabbing me," I said with a smile. Even though it wasn't a sword, those sticks could leave marks.

"This is the way it will work," Agnes said. "I'll call the start, and the first person to get three strikes, wins. By strikes, I mean that your stick will get past your opponent's defenses. You don't have to physically strike the other person to score a point, but it should be clear that you've breached their defenses. Though, you're welcome to give this one a strong poke in the ribs, Sophie." Agnes nodded to me, and Sophie grinned.

"Sure, and that's a fair and impartial judge now, isn't it?" I muttered.

"No hits to the face as neither of you has guards on," Agnes pointed out.

"Why are we using sticks and not swords?" Sophie asked, blinking at the stick in her hand.

"It's a touch safer, as many people are still learning the sport," Agnes said. "Right, then. Three strikes decides the winner. Sophie, make us proud."

"Gee, thanks. Where's the hometown loyalty?" I groused, stepping back and assuming the on-guard position.

"Sorry, mate. Gotta go with the lady on this one." Agnes shrugged and stepped back, holding her hands in the air. Sophie stood, the stick pointed at the ground, her eyes wide in her face. I sighed. This was going to be like stealing candy from a baby. But at least I'd get a kiss out of it. The thought cheered me, and I smiled at Sophie.

"Begin!" Agnes shouted, and cheers erupted around the field. I waited for Sophie to lift her stick, knowing I could have advanced and struck her already if I had wanted to. Giving her time to adjust, I stepped lightly forward, brandishing the stick in front of me.

"You might want to lift your sword," I suggested.

"You might want to try being less grumpy," Sophie said, lifting her stick and advancing so quickly that the point of her stick was already in my side before I could take a breath. What...the...

How had that just happened? I blinked at her as Agnes called for the point, the crowd screaming, and I danced backward out of range, just in case she pulled another move like that. Where had that come from?

"I'm not grumpy," I insisted, stepping back into on-guard position. The wind had picked up slightly, bringing with it the promise of rain, and I waited for Agnes to call the start again. "I have a lot of responsibilities on my shoulders."

"Gee, like nobody else has to deal with responsibilities?" Sophie rolled her eyes and brought her stick up at the last moment to clash with mine as I attempted another parry. Hmm, she was quick, I would give her that. I retreated, my sword up, and met her eyes.

"That's not what I'm saying," I said. I advanced, hoping to get past her again and end this quickly.

Again, Sophie brought her stick up at the last moment, even though she wasn't standing in a protective position, and caught my stick before I could strike her.

"It sure sounds that way. You know...my Uncle Arthur," Sophie said, taking a few steps back, her sword held more carefully in front of her now. "He had a lot of responsibility. I might suggest even more so than yours. His company is responsible for thousands of people's livelihoods around the world." She danced out of the way of my next strike, pivoting so that my stick flew past her body and turning to bring the tip of hers into my side.

I stared at her, aghast, as I realized she'd already claimed two strikes on me. I needed to get my head in the match and not listen to her words. Ignoring the laughter from the side of the field, I brought my stick up and waited for the call. Advancing immediately, I thrust my stick forward only to be met, once again, by Sophie's stick. This time, she parried, and I was forced back a step. Our sticks connected, and we danced, the wood striking as we blocked each other's attempts. Breaking, I retreated, and Sophie grinned.

"As I was saying, my uncle had a lot of responsibility. Not only for those he employed, but also the fact that his company is responsible for protecting our clients' homes and businesses around the world. I would say that is significantly more responsibility than what lies on your plate." Sophie lunged, and I had to retreat three steps to miss her attempt. My eyes narrowed. She'd administered that move in almost perfect form.

"And you know what?" Sophie continued, falling into an exact on-guard position. I raised my sword, matching her, and waited.

"What's that?"

"He was never grumpy." Sophie lunged, and I retreated, my stick clashing with hers.

"In fact, Arthur was one of the most cheerful men that I knew. Maybe that's because he knew how to channel his frustrations in the appropriate manner."

"Like how?" I grimaced as our sticks clashed once more, worry racing through me as Sophie pushed me backward, keeping me on the defense as she compound attacked after I feinted.

"He had his hobbies...like fencing." Sophie's mile-wide smile stopped me long enough that she almost got past my defenses. At the last moment, I dodged her blow. Realization dawned as Sophie cut over, her stick grazing mine, and I stepped back. I'd been had. Sophie was hustling me. My adrenaline kicked up and, no longer caring about playing nice, I attacked.

Our sticks met in a vicious clash, and the crowd gasped as I thrust forward, lunging toward Sophie. Sophie parried, and then feinted, and I twisted, already knowing that she'd gotten me. I hadn't expected the feint, and if she was any good, she'd follow through with a disengage. When she did, her stick coming beneath mine and hitting my rib once more, I dropped my head as the crowd went wild.

"Knight! Knight! Knight!" the crowd chanted, and Sophie stepped back in perfect position before bringing her sword to her side and bowing. I'd been well and truly hustled.

"It seems that I am grumpy then," I bit out, the words stinging, along with my pride, as I bowed to Sophie.

"Oh, so he admits it now? Only took a fair lass beating you at a tough man sport to get you to agree, didn't it?" Sophie pursed her lips and gave me a knowing look. It rankled, I'll admit, but there was nothing I could say. She'd won, and I accepted my loss.

Sophie sighed, and then shook her head. "I've always had a soft spot for the losers. Come here, grumpy."

I came closer, curious, as she beckoned me with two fingers and a mischievous look in her eyes. I swear, if she bopped me on the head with her stick, I would tackle her right there. Instead, Sophie surprised me by placing a hand on my chest and leaning up on her tiptoes to softly brush her lips against mine. The roaring of the crowd matched the roaring of my blood when her mouth touched mine. Acting on instinct alone, as all conscious thought had fled my mind, I dropped my stick and wrapped my arms around Sophie, hitching her up so her legs straddled my waist.

Just like I'd expected, her soft body pressing against

mine drove me wild, and I angled my head to deepen the kiss, swallowing her exclamation of surprise when our tongues touched. Fire raced through my veins, and I held her tight to my body, my hands cupping her generous bottom, and lost myself in the kiss.

"Ahem," Agnes shouted into my ear, and I pulled back, blinking rapidly as my surroundings returned. Sophie looked up at me, her moody blue eyes dazed, her lips already swelling from my kisses. More, my mind demanded, and I bent my head.

"Go away, Agnes."

"There are children here," Agnes hissed, putting her hand over the top of the microphone. "Don't make me whack you over the head with the sword."

"Bloody hell..." I blinked down at Sophie, who visibly gulped for air, each breath causing her chest to hitch. My eyes were drawn to her cleavage, where her breasts trembled with her breaths, and I had to forcibly pull my lust back from taking over.

"Grumpy fires run hot..." Sophie muttered as I let her go, her body slipping down mine, and she took a shaky step back. Without another word, I turned and stormed off the field, embarrassment clinging to me as the crowd jeered at me for my loss.

"The best man won," I agreed, accepting some good-natured insults, and kept going until I was in the car park, far away from other people. There, I bent at the waist and gulped for air.

I wasn't embarrassed that I had lost. Oh no. In fact, I admired Sophie for her skill and allowing me to assume she wouldn't know what she was doing. It was smart of her, and she was clearly a skilled opponent. No, it was the fact that I'd been seconds away from dropping to my knees on the field and burying my face between her legs. My grasp on my control had been so thin that it shook me to my core.

"I've got a cold pint waiting for you at the pub," Graham offered at my side. I didn't even look at him as I nodded, needing to get away from this place, from Sophie, as fast as I possibly could.

CHAPTER THIRTEEN

SOPHIE

"You gave it laldy, lass!"

The villager's approval still warmed me the next day, though I'd had to request translation of that term. Apparently, it meant that I'd enthusiastically gone after Lachlan even though he looked as though he'd crush me.

Crushed me with his kiss instead. I tried for the thousandth time to push his kiss from my thoughts. Let's just say, I'd had an eventful evening after my win—where I'd been heralded as the new Knight, fed numerous pints at the Tipsy Thistle, and even been carried on one enthusiastic man's shoulders. Lachlan had been nowhere to be seen, and I was actually just fine with him not being at the pub. It was a welcome respite from the confused emotions that tangled in my gut and had kept me up most of the night.

Reliving the kiss.

He'd just...he'd just picked me up like I'd weighed nothing at all. It was something so simple, I supposed, and yet I'd never experienced it. Perhaps it didn't help that aside from Chad, my previous boyfriends had run on the weak side, but still. It was the kind of move that I'd read about in romance novels, and nobody had ever tried with me before.

Because I'm...before the thought could go down the wrong track, I redirected it. Because I picked the wrong men, I told myself. None of my past boyfriends had the sheer muscular brawn of Lachlan, whose muscles were clearly more than strong enough to lift me as though I was nothing more than a bag of groceries. I'd relived that moment several times through the night, my hand dancing over my stomach and reaching between my legs, seeking the relief I hadn't known I needed until Lachlan had hauled me into his arms. It had been like wrapping my body around a massive tree, his body hard and unmoving, as he'd banished the history of all kisses I'd ever had from my mind. Nothing mattered before or since that singular kiss, forever seared into my head, and now I felt like a drug addict craving her next hit.

I hadn't known it could be like that.

As I descended the stairs to the lounge area, I realized it was the type of kiss that had made the world fall away, and all I could do was feel. When he'd finally let me go, his eyes stormy with need, the crowd's cheers and my location had rushed back into sharp focus. At that moment, when Lachlan had turned on his heel and left the field while the crowd had screamed for me, I'd decided to stay. I know I'd said before that I would give this a little time, but I'd been fairly noncommittal up until that point. But hearing the crowd cheer for me while the hottest man I'd ever seen in real life, let alone kissed, had stormed away from me because he'd barely been able to control his need—well that, my friend, is an experience that every woman needs at least once in their life. Whenever I was feeling insecure or unconfident in the future, I promised myself that I would bring that memory to mind and step forward like the badass that I was.

I'd turned to Agnes after we'd watched Lachlan leave the field and told her as much. Which was why, now, when I entered the lounge, Agnes was already at the table enjoying a scone and a cup of tea. Today was *the* day.

It was time for me to start my training as a Knight in the Order of Caledonia.

"There she is." Agnes toasted me with her mug of tea. "Our fearless Knight."

"And her ever faithful companion," Matthew said from behind me, making me smile. Turning, I raised an eyebrow at him.

"Isn't a knight's companion their horse? Should I ride you then?"

Matthew opened his mouth to retort, but Lachlan stepped into the room just as I'd finished speaking, and the last words I said hung in the air. My eyes caught on Lachlan's, and my face instantly heated.

"Should I make the obvious joke here?" Matthew wondered.

"It's too easy." Agnes shook her head.

"Sit down, get started on your brekkie. We've got a big day ahead of us," Archie surprised me by saying as he put his tackle box aside and stood. His words held an air of

147

authority that everyone instantly acknowledged, and soon I was nibbling on a buttered piece of crusty toast while Archie took the chair at the head of the table.

"I've brought along everything that I could find about the Order." Agnes nodded to a stack of books and notebooks on a small table by the fireplace. "Between all of us, I think we can make some real headway this morning."

"No need," Archie said, his voice gruff, though I noticed he dropped a bit of scrambled eggs on the floor for Sir Buster. The dog gobbled it up and then raced around the table three times, a blur of excitement, and Archie shook his head. "Settle yourself." The dog skidded to a stop back at Archie's chair, his eyes hopeful.

"Why's that?" Hilda asked, pausing at the kitchen door with her hand on her hip and teapot in her hand. "You've got us sorted then?"

"Aye, I do," Archie said, continuing to steadfastly make his way through his breakfast. "Have a seat then and we'll get to it."

I worked up the courage to look at Lachlan and found him staring at me, well, my mouth, and heat flashed through me again. My skin felt charged up, like I'd touched a live wire or something, and I found myself barely able to sit still in my seat. I tried to tell myself it was nerves about learning to be a knight, but even I knew that was partially a lie.

Lachlan's kiss had shaken me, rattling my bones, so to speak, and woken me up. His kiss had been like what it was like to learn to read for the first time. An entire new world had awoken inside me, something I hadn't known I'd been missing, and now I craved more of it. Not just his kisses, but him. I was hyperaware of his presence, and now I tried to subtly study him to see what else I could learn. He'd drawn his gaze from my mouth back to his mug of coffee, and his shoulders were hunched, his face drawn, as he waited for Archie to speak.

While this may be a bit of a lark for me, it was Lachlan's whole life. There was some very real and very serious history here, particularly when it came to the death of his mother, and I needed to tread carefully as we proceeded so as not to hurt Lachlan's feelings.

Not that he'd let me know, the prickly man that he was. Despite myself, my lips quirked, and I buried my face in my mug of tea as I remembered Hilda calling Lachlan a crabbit hedgehog the first night we'd arrived. She wasn't far wrong.

Luckily, I thought hedgehogs were cute.

Hilda returned from the kitchen and sat, patting Lachlan's arm, before fixing her attention on Archie.

"Well then? Go on."

"Right, here's the way I see it," Archie said, his terse voice jolting me from my thoughts about Lachlan, and I turned to give him my full attention. He wore his usual uniform of faded denim and a worn flannel shirt and, for the first time, I noticed a glint of gold at his wrist. Leaning a bit closer, I realized it was an ID bracelet of sorts with something inscribed. "What?"

I jumped as I realized Archie had stopped and was staring at me. Gosh, I was on edge this morning.

"I was just looking at your bracelet. I hadn't noticed it before," I said.

"It's passed down to the Keeper of the Order. That would be me." Archie angled his wrist so I could better see the inscription. Two swords met in an inverted V, under which a Celtic-style horse, or dragon, was etched. Words that I couldn't decipher were beneath the emblem.

"Is this the crest?" I asked, looking up to meet Archie's eyes.

"Aye, lass. That's the Kelpie in the middle there. The phrase means pure of heart. Only those with the purest of intentions are deemed worthy of protecting the Clach na Fìrinn."

"It's beautiful," I murmured. The gold had a rich buttery sheen to it, and the etchings were blackened, showing their age, and I imagined this piece had been passed through the years.

"I think, given the state of things, it's best if we crack on with the teaching and the initiation," Archie said, turning to look at Hilda. "We could spend hours going through those books, or I can just be telling you what's needed done. Do you have a preference?" The last bit he directed at me, and I realized that everyone at the table was waiting for me to make the call.

For some reason, the way they all waited on me to make a decision, shook me. A tumble of emotions backlogged in my throat, and I swallowed, overcome.

"I need a moment," I said, shoving back from the table and racing down the hall. Sir Buster skidded after me, abandoning his campaign for more scrambled eggs, and followed me out the large arched door we'd first arrived through. Once I was outside, I sat on the steps, gulping for air as I tried to sort through my convoluted thoughts.

Sir Buster, normally so crochety, seemed to sense my mood. Two little paws landed on my thigh, and then he licked my arm with his tiny tongue, his body vibrating as he waited on me. With a sigh, I scooped his trembling body onto my lap, and he curled up, propping his chin on my arm, and I was instantly soothed.

"Therapy doggo," I muttered, stroking his fur, lightly though, in case he'd growl at me like he usually did. It was like cradling a landmine and brought equal parts anxiety and enjoyment. Much like life, I realized, finding the metaphor of a loveable rageball of a chihuahua somewhat apt to describe myself as well.

"Are you all right then?" Lachlan's voice sent a delicious shiver over my skin, and Sir Buster raised his head in annoyance.

"I apologize for my dramatics. I just needed a moment I guess." I looked out across the gravel parking lot and over the battlement to where Loch Mirren lay resplendent in the morning light. From here, I could just see the island, and I wondered if the Stone of Truth could possibly know that I was here.

That *I* was the one sent to protect it.

A hysterical giggle escaped me, and Lachlan dropped to sit next to me, not touching, but my skin warmed at his nearness.

"Tell me," Lachlan, man of many words, said.

"I'm an afterthought," I spit out, the words surprising even me, and I waited for Lachlan's response. When none came, I took a deep breath and continued. "I've always been an afterthought in everyone's life. My parents barely noticed me until I became a hindrance to them, and then they sent me on my way. My work? While I'm great at my job if I do say so myself, I'm still viewed like I've just been handed the position by my family. Even when my suggestions or ideas are the best in the meetings? They're dismissed until one of the other team members can rephrase it in a way that he gets credit for it. My boyfriends? Well, let's not even go there."

Silence met my words and, again, I admired what an effective tool it was to get someone to talk.

"I'm a doormat, Lachlan." I turned and met his eyes. Those moody, stormy, stunning eyes. "I'm no knight. And, I haven't known all of you all that long, but I don't want to fail you. It's...yesterday was the first time in my life that I'd ever felt the way that I did." I left out the part where he'd kissed me senseless. "To have a whole crowd of people cheering me on? To accept me? To be excited that I am here to help them? And not because of my money or who I know, but because I, *me*, Sophie MacKnight, can possibly save them from an ancient curse? It's...I'm scared. I don't want to let people down."

"So don't," Lachlan said, and I huffed out a small laugh when nothing more came from him. The man, if nothing else, was succinct.

"You make it sound so easy."

"I didn't say it was easy. But it doesn't sound to me like being a doormat is any easier either." Lachlan shifted, drumming his fingers against his thigh. "Seems to me like you were trying to make yourself fit in somewhere you didn't really belong, Sophie. Yet in a few days here, you've won over an entire village, made friends, bested me at broadswords, and even convinced this crabbit beastie to love you."

My heart skipped a beat before I realized he was talking

about Sir Buster and not himself.

"I feel like the last part is a tenuous agreement," I said, running a hand over Sir Buster's fur. A low growl emanated from his body, and I grinned. "See?"

"Aye, he's a moody one at that. But most of the Scots are. The other thing about us Scots? We're a bloody strong lot." Lachlan rose, and I looked up at him, the sun haloing his head. "While it seems you can play an important role in helping us, this doesn't all rest on you, Sophie. If you weren't here, we'd figure something else out. Our people are survivors with pure hearts, and we persevere. No matter what."

Lachlan left me on the doorstep, and I took a moment longer, turning his words over in my mind like one of those crystal prisms, holding them up until they caught the light.

Pure of heart, I repeated to myself. It had never been heart I'd been lacking. Oh no, if anything, mine was too open and desperate for love. I'd lucked out when Lottie and Arthur had stepped in, helping me to fill the void, but now I understood what they'd been trying to teach me all along. Only I could give myself the love that I'd sought so desperately from others through the years.

Oh, yes. My heart was huge and I had *so* much to give. Instead of looking at all the ways I could fail the lovely people I'd met here, maybe it was time for me to show them all the ways I could help.

Me. Sophie MacKnight.

The Knight of the Order of Caledonia.

To think I'd always been looking for a knight in shining armor when the person I needed to rescue me had been staring back in the mirror all along.

CHAPTER FOURTEEN

LACHLAN

"The Knight is the first position in the Order of Caledonia," Archie said, and I listened carefully. Once I'd agreed to take this seriously, I stuck to my word. It wouldn't help anyone for me to vacillate on my decision, and if we were going to work together to save Loren Brae, then I had to be a helpful part of the team. As much as my pep talk for Sophie had been meant to help her, my words were also a stark reminder for me.

"And you said that not all positions are knights, correct?" Matthew asked, scanning his notebook. We hadn't even bothered to move to the library. Instead, we dived right into the matter at hand after breakfast had been cleared.

"Correct. In an unusual diversion from a typical Order of olden days, the Order of Caledonia is filled with various roles that combine to create a happy and healthy village. Through the years, we've seen members that are healers, astrologers, blacksmiths, and so on. And roles not only held by men, either. However, it always starts with the knight. In this case, Sophie," Archie said, steepling his hands before him. "For Sophie to step into her role and claim her power, she'll need to pass three challenges. Three is a sacred number of the pagan ancestors, and the order is built on multiples of three. You'll see this repeated as we go along."

"Do we know what the challenges are? And how are they deemed passed?" I asked.

"The Clach na Fìrinn will deem it so," Archie said, and I couldn't stop myself from scoffing.

"You're saying an inanimate object will tell Sophie if she's passed these challenges?" I raised my eyebrows at Archie. "Sure, and you ken why I may have a hard time with all this."

"It's magick," Agnes said, turning to me with a wondrous look on her face that stopped any further words from pouring forth from my very skeptical brain. "That's the beauty and frustration of it. Magick doesn't explain or ask to be understood, it just *is*. It doesn't care if you accept it or not. Magick doesn't try to fall neatly into little boxes in your mind. Magick exists because everyone needs to hold on to the possibilities of what-ifs. In a world where we are told no more often than not, magick is the hope that whispers sweetly in our dreams."

Maybe I was someone who needed to see it to believe it, but what I *could* see just now was that the people I loved needed me to believe, if only to be the glue that held everything together. While I might reserve judgment on whether magick existed, I wouldn't be the one to block their progress either.

"That's fair enough, I suppose," I said and reached over to squeeze Agnes's arm so she knew that I was being serious and not just humoring her.

"Challenges sound scary. Particularly if I have to battle a Kelpie or something." Sophie worried her bottom lip and my thoughts went to a different type of magick—the miracle of her kiss that had almost dropped me to my knees.

"A knight's responsibilities include courage, generosity, mercy, sacrifice, hope, honor, perseverance, and chivalry. There are more, but those are some of the main ones. To pass your three challenges, you'll need to demonstrate, unequivocally, your ability to shine in one or more of these skill sets."

"Fascinating," Matthew mused, tapping his pen against his lips. "And will she need to declare before each challenge that she is going for a particular trait? What will be the measure of a challenge being met? Because Sophie has more courage than most on any given day. How would we know?"

Sophie reached over and squeezed Matthew's hand, and I saw a sheen of tears in her eyes. I was grateful, given what sounded like a turbulent past, that she had someone like Matthew in her life.

"We'll start by touring the four corners of the property. At each corner, we'll burn a bunch of dried thistle and declare our intentions to restore the Order. After we've begun the rite, we'll return to the weapons room, and Sophie will choose her sword. It's there that we'll learn how her magick will manifest."

"Wait...I'll get magick? Before I even complete the challenges?" Sophie raised a hand in question.

"Correct." Archie nodded. "Once you begin the rite, the magick will find you. How that manifests for you is yet to be seen. However, there will be physical indicators when you pass a challenge. For example, in the past, one knight had gold bands appear on his armor. Every time he passed a challenge, a new gold band would appear. We won't know what that looks like for you until we start."

Silence settled on the table as we all looked at each other. Honestly? It felt like I was at one of those murder-mystery evenings where people go to a castle for dinner, and one of the servers dies, and then everyone attending the dinner has to discover the killer. Suspending my disbelief was going to be a heavier chore than I had originally anticipated.

It would be far more difficult if I hadn't heard the screams echoing across the loch in the wee hours of dawn. They were occurring more frequently now, and each time I went to the battlement, I stood, unsure what I would do if a Kelpie did emerge from the waters and attack the castle. The one time that I had seen the Kelpies? I'd frozen, still a young boy and disbelieving in what I was seeing. To this day, I explained that encounter away by blaming the stolen Guinness I'd imbibed and having zero tolerance for alcohol. Now, I climbed the battlements at night, understanding that I needed to make my presence known. I'd fight, no matter what, even when I didn't completely understand what I was fighting against.

But at least I knew what I was fighting *for*.

I'd fight for Hilda, my second mum, with the purest

157

heart I'd ever know. I'd fight for Archie, a steadfast cornerstone in my life, and for Agnes, a woman who brought knowledge and creativity to our village. I'd even fight for Sir Buster, the little rageball that he was, because even the smallest of knights needed backup once in a while.

And Sophie.

Her eyes were huge in her face, and a fine tremble showed just at her collarbone, her pulse revealing her nerves. I wanted to kiss the skin just there and ease her worries, and though I'd only known the bonnie lass just a few days now, I was already gone. Too far gone, I realized uncomfortably, for someone who had made a living of not forming attachments in case the person I loved was taken away from me.

I understood that it wasn't the healthiest outlook on dating, but it had served me just fine until recently. But now? Now I wanted Sophie to stay, and I wanted to unpeel the layers of her and learn where her fierceness came from. She was a fighter, even if she didn't see it yet, and I couldn't wait to watch her bloom.

"I suppose no time like the present, right?" Sophie looked around at everyone, breaking the silence. "Shall we get on with it?"

"Meet by the stables in fifteen minutes. Bring a rain jacket." With that, Archie stood and disappeared down the hallway, Sir Buster trailing him.

"I've got an extra jacket for you," Hilda supplied before Sophie could open her mouth to ask. The lass still hadn't had a chance to go clothes shopping, and I made a note to offer her a ride to the next town over to pick up some warmer clothes.

Fifteen minutes later, we were gathered at the tack room of the stables, where Archie was sizing up Matthew for a pair of wellies. I crossed to where Sophie leaned against a stall door, stroking the nose of a pretty chestnut mare.

"Lady Loren likes you," I said, watching as the horse blew into Sophie's palm, searching for a treat.

"Of course you're a lady, aren't you, pretty girl?" Sophie crooned, and the mare's ears perked up at the attention. I wanted Sophie to fawn over me the same way, and uncomfortable with the need that rose inside me, I turned when Archie called us over.

"Sophie, you'll need to put some wellies on. What's your shoe size?" Archie asked.

"Ten in our size. I'm not sure what that translates to for UK shoe sizes," Sophie said, and Archie disappeared back into the tack room. Shortly he returned with a pair of dusty hunter-green boots and offered them to Sophie, who immediately slid off her trainers. I reached out an arm so she could lean on me while she shoved her right foot into a boot. For a second, something flashed behind her eyes before she offered the group a cheerful smile.

"They don't fit," Sophie said.

"That should be the right size." Archie scratched his head.

"Shoe size. Not calf size." Sophie shrugged, the smile still on her face. "Big girl problems. Our calves don't fit in normal boots."

I wanted to reassure her that I loved her thick legs, outlined so beautifully in the fitted leggings she favored, and where she saw large, I saw strong and womanly. But, before I could offer any placations, I stopped myself. Sophie hadn't asked for them, and she wasn't apologizing for who or what she was. She was a smart woman. I'd only insult her if I rushed to reassure her that she wasn't big. At the end of the day, there was nothing wrong with being larger, and I, for one, couldn't wait until Sophie let me get my hands on her again.

"Och, of course. You'll be needing a knight's boots then," Archie said smoothly and disappeared into the tack room before returning with a men's pair of boots. This time, the boots slid on easily, and Sophie stomped around the yard a few times, making sure they fit, a smile lighting her face.

"That's better. I can walk properly in these instead of the boots squishing uncomfortably at my ankles," Sophie said.

"We'll start with the east," Archie directed, pointing toward Loch Mirren, and we dutifully fell in line as he led us to a narrow footpath that wound around the stables and over gently sloping hills. The group was silent, each of us caught in our own thoughts and, aside from the wayward birdsong and the rustling of the wind in the trees, our walk was peaceful.

"It's here." Archie crouched and brushed wild grasses away from a spot on the ground, and we formed a circle around him. Peering down, I saw an old stone plaque with a Celtic insignia on it.

"Is that a Kelpie?" I asked, leaning closer.

"It is," Archie said, glancing up at me. "You've never seen these before?"

"I didn't know they were here," I admitted, surprised.

I'd spent hours running all over this land since I was little, yet I'd never come across this stone before.

"It's really lovely." Matthew pursed his lips as he crouched next to Archie. "The carving is quite detailed, and I imagine quite old. For it to withstand the elements and remain in such good condition is remarkable."

"Magick," Agnes offered, and despite myself, I grinned. Magick, indeed.

"Here you go, lass." Hilda held out a bundle of dried thistle wrapped in twine, and Sophie took it with a worried look on her face.

"I'm not sure what to say?" Sophie asked.

"You'll be repeating after me," Archie ordered, and Sophie nodded quickly.

"Aye aye, Captain."

Archie's lips quirked, but he said nothing else as he stood, his gaze across to the loch.

"Go on, light it." Hilda offered Sophie a lighter. Soon, a thin curl of smoke emanated from the bundle of dried flowers, and Sophie held it in front of her over the stone. Her stance was tense, her lips tight and, without thinking, I reached out and kneaded her shoulders. She didn't look at me, but I caught the gradual loosening of tension in her back and hoped that I had helped a little bit.

"I, Sophie MacKnight," Archie said, "the First Knight in the Order of Caledonia, announce my arrival."

Sophie repeated his words, waving the bundle of smoking flowers over the stone.

"I accept the responsibility of protecting the Clach na Fìrinn and promise to restore the Order to its fullness. In doing so, I show myself worthy of the magick of Clach na Fìrinn."

Sophie repeated the words, stumbling a bit over the Celtic language, but powering through, nonetheless.

"It is with these words I establish the Order of Caledonia as the first line of protection for the Clach na Fìrinn and alert the Kelpies to my arrival. I accept the power bestowed upon me."

Once more, Sophie dutifully repeated Archie's words, and then we all waited. When nothing happened, I glanced at Archie.

"All is well. On to the south." Archie nodded once, a pleased look on his face as he stared across the still waters of Loch Mirren, and I realized then that something could have not gone well. Had we potentially been putting Sophie in danger? Annoyed with Archie and his lack of clear information, I moved to his side as we began the trek to the southern point of the property.

"What would have happened if the Stone hadn't accepted Sophie?" I asked, keeping my voice low.

"Why ask questions that you don't want to know the answer to?" Archie parried, and I narrowed my eyes, frustration twisting in my stomach. I didn't like feeling defenseless against an unknown entity.

"I do want to know the answer."

Archie stopped, turning to me, his eyes serious.

"No, lad. You don't." With that, he resumed walking, and I knew Archie well enough to know that was all I'd be getting from him.

We came upon a small stone hut situated at the far end of the property that had seen better days. Sophie paused, her face lighting, and ran a hand across the stone wall.

"This is so cool. I just love all the old stone walls and cottages that you have here. There's just this sense of history to how things are built to last across time that you don't often see in the States. I imagine this was for a small family. The father coming home from working the fields, the mother tending to the children," Sophie mused, her eyes dreamy.

"It's a loo," Archie said, and Matthew snorted.

"A loo?" Sophie glanced at me, and I crossed to her, a smile on her face. I hated to ruin her charming little fantasy of what this cottage was used for.

"It was once an outhouse. A toilet," I supplied, and disappointment flashed across her face.

"Oh, right. A loo. Ahhh." Sophie beamed up at me, and I could have lingered there for hours so long as she kept smiling at me that way. "It's where you go for a gobby."

Archie choked and coughed into his palm while Hilda swatted him on the back. A soft chuckle came from Agnes while Matthew bent to Sophie with a pained look on his face.

"It's not where I'd typically prefer to go for a gobby, darling," I said, infusing heat in my voice and arching an eyebrow at Sophie. "But I'm willing if you are."

"Um..." Sophie's eyes darted to Matthew as he whispered in her ear.

That delicious pink flush that I was determined to be the cause of one day crept up her neck and over her cheeks as mortification filled her face.

"Oh. Oh, no." Sophie wheezed, fanning her hands in

front of her face. "Tell me I didn't just proposition you for a blow job in an ancient toilet."

"I believe *jobby* is the word you're looking for?" I asked, keeping my voice serious, though every ounce of my being wanted to laugh at her discomfort.

"Jobby! Yes!" Sophie all but screamed. She turned away from the toilet and stomped up the path to where Archie stood with his back to us, his shoulders shaking with laughter.

"Erm, just so you know, Sophie, it's not really polite to say you're away for a jobby, either. It's akin to saying you're taking a shite," Agnes supplied.

"Thanks, Agnes, just keep heaping salt into my wound, why don't you?" Sophie seethed, and then I lost it. Bending over, I laughed until I gasped for breath, Matthew clapping me on the back as I did.

"Well, she gave it a good try," Matthew said, wiping his eyes as I straightened.

"I can't remember the last time I've laughed so hard," I admitted, following a furious Sophie up the hill. "Och, but I needed that."

"Here? Does this translate?" Sophie turned and held up her middle finger at us, and I laughed once more.

"We use two fingers here, darling," I called, just to infuriate her further. When her growl of frustration echoed across the hills, I shook my head.

I was well and truly gone for this woman, and that was the truth of it.

CHAPTER FIFTEEN

SOPHIE

By the time we'd finished the rite and returned to the castle, I'd mostly recovered from my embarrassment. And, if I'm being honest, part of my reaction had to do with the way my entire body heated when Lachlan had leaned into my misunderstanding, his eyes heavy with meaning. He was all broad-shouldered and muscular and masculine and his nearness was starting to bring me to distraction in general, let alone when blow jobs were on the table.

Which they weren't, to be clear.

Or on a toilet, for that matter.

To also be clear.

Now, we found ourselves in the weapons room, with Matthew exclaiming over the display of swords and knives and other sharp instruments that I couldn't possibly know the names of but understood would be rather painful if taken to the face.

"See anything you fancy?" Lachlan asked, his voice warm at my ear, and I shivered. This man's presence was becoming a liability, I decided, and surely I couldn't take on challenges when all I could think about was having another taste of his mouth.

It appeared Scottish Sophie was a wanton woman.

And, since I'm being honest, I kind of liked this side of myself. Back home, I was always convinced that men wouldn't really take a second look at me or, as I'd told Lachlan earlier that day, that I was just an afterthought. Sex, and the pursual of it, had sort of taken a back seat in my life, yet now it was like someone had flipped a switch, and lusty thoughts flooded my brain. Which, I'll admit, came at a slightly inopportune moment as I was supposed to be picking my weapon of choice and not bringing to mind the image of Lachlan in his kilt yesterday.

What was it about a kilt that just about made my mouth go dry? I suspected it was the easy confidence of the men wearing them that made them appealing.

Or the easy access, Slutty Scottish Sophie whispered in my brain, and I felt heat rush to my cheeks.

"They're all very pretty...and terrifying," I said, refusing to look up at Lachlan lest he guessed where my thoughts had wandered to. "These are nothing like a fencing foil. I mean, these are pretty heavy-duty swords..."

"What's a knight without his...er...*her* sword?" Agnes asked.

"Sharp-witted, I suppose," I said, and warmth bloomed

in me when Lachlan laughed. He'd only laughed a few times since I'd arrived, typically defaulting to his surlier nature, and I had to admit that it made me feel good to bring a smile to his face. Not to mention, it transformed his visage from almost overwhelming intensity to much more approachable. Not that I planned to approach him, or touch him, or...

Down, girl.

The weapons room was a large room with stone walls, low ceilings, and lights that mirrored the old-time torch look, like the ones that lined the hallway to our apartment. It had a cozy and intimate feel, as though we were there to share our secrets, and I supposed in some ways the room was doing the same with us. Indescribable amounts of history were woven into the craftsmanship of these blades, with each sword having different etchings and emblems carved into the hilts.

"How do I choose?" I asked, looking up at Archie. "Are there any that are off-limits?"

"None are off-limits, lass." Archie rocked back on his heels and crossed his arms over his chest. "Pick the one you want."

"But..." I nibbled my lower lip as I surveyed the vast array of weaponry before me. I hated being put on the spot to decide, particularly in an area that I wasn't well-versed in. When it came to my job, I trusted my instincts and made strong choices. Asking me to pick which two scoops of ice cream I wanted on my cone was a whole different challenge and often resulted in me having odd flavor combinations like mango with pistachio. I didn't like feeling pressured when I knew I could let down an entire village of people, and now my gut twisted as I tried to figure out which sword most "spoke" to me.

"Hear what he said, Soph." Matthew came to my side, sensing my distress. "Pick the one you want. Period."

"Just...*any* one I want?" The sword that had caught my eye a few times wasn't as grandiose as the others on display.

"Yes, any of the swords. No explanation required." Matthew tapped his chest where his heart was. "And no pressure. Take your time."

I took them at their word and wandered the room, making sure I saw each of the swords displayed there, from slender and sharp to large and terrifying. And still, my eyes danced back to one tucked in the corner, almost as an afterthought. Finally, after a full circle, I returned to the sword I kept looking at and stood in front of it.

"Are you mine?" I asked, and then flushed, feeling foolish for talking to a sword.

The blade was significantly shorter than the others, and the metal was dulled as though it needed a good polishing. The hilt was a simple hammered gold and ebony, although upon closer inspection, I realized it might also be brass. I couldn't imagine it was all that smart to make swords with a gold handle, not when they could be so easily stolen from a knight. With no embellishment, it was a simple, unassuming sword. I liked it, however, because while it wasn't as long as my fencing foil, it seemed like a sword I'd be able to maneuver comfortably should I need to. "Can I touch it?"

"Of course. You can pick up any of them and test their weight and see if they are a good fit. Once you've chosen, we'll close the rite," Archie said.

Reaching out, I hovered my hand over the hilt of the

sword for a moment and waited, reminding myself that I could turn around and leave. I didn't owe anyone anything, and even though Uncle Arthur had wanted me to come here, I didn't have to fulfill his wishes. If I moved forward with this, well, it had to be for myself and no one else. I took just a moment, taking a few careful breaths as I checked in with myself.

Who was I kidding? I was *so* in.

Reaching down, I picked up the blade, and immediately, a zip of energy raced up my arm as though I'd stuck my finger in an electrical socket, and a nervous giggle escaped my lips.

"Is that the one?" Matthew came to my side and studied the blade.

"This is a dirk, actually," Lachlan said, coming to my other shoulder. "While not technically a sword, no proper Highlander would have been caught without one. It's perfect for hand-to-hand combat and was also used for food preparation and hunting."

"Oh, should I not..." I looked up at Lachlan, worry in my eyes. "I'm supposed to choose a sword."

"You're supposed to choose the blade for you," Lachlan said, his expression patient as he looked down at me. His words soothed, and I looked back at my blade.

Yes, *my* blade. It fit me, simple and unassuming yet strong and capable. A blade that could be underestimated by your opponent, I thought, hefting it in my hand carefully. Much like I was, at times.

Not anymore.

Turning, the sword at my side, I smiled at Archie.

"I choose this one."

"An honorable choice for a Knight of the people." Archie bowed his head and then motioned for me to come to him. "We'll now complete the rite."

We'd already burned the bundles of thistle and recited our chants, so I wondered what came next. I seriously hoped it didn't involve slicing my hand open and coating the blade in blood or something of that nature.

"Cardamom oil," Hilda said, coming forward with a small pot in her hands. "For love and clarity of thought."

"Why love?" I asked, suspicion coating my voice.

"Love is the universal thread that binds all things," Hilda said, offering the jar. "There is more than just romantic love, my dear."

"Of course," I said, feeling foolish. I dipped a finger in the oil and then brushed it where the blade met the hilt, careful not to cut my finger on the sharp edge.

"I, Sophie MacKnight, have chosen my blade. With pure heart, I accept the honor and duties of the First Knight of Caledonia," Archie intoned.

I repeated his words, staring down at my blade as I did so, gasping when the room went dark when I finished speaking.

Except for my blade. It glowed. And not in a lightsaber neon red kind of glow. But in an ethereal, starlight captured in a jar kind of way. I gasped, hypnotized by the beauty of the pearlescent glow that clung to the edges of the steel, as a cool balm rushed through me.

"The lights will go back on." I heard myself saying and caught Matthew's raised eyebrows when the lights blinked back on in the room.

"Interesting," Archie mused, tapping a finger on his lips.

"Interesting?" I parroted, my eyebrows at my hairline. "I just made the lights go on by command, and my dirk glows in the dark. And *interesting* is all you have to say about it?"

"Yes," Archie said and left the room.

"Wait...now what?" I looked at Hilda, who I deemed next in command, and she looked at Agnes, who just shrugged.

"That's it. You're the Knight now. I guess you'll need to figure out how to start your challenges," Hilda said.

"Oh sure, right, okay. That's easy enough, isn't it?" I rolled my eyes. Needing to get out of the weapons room, which now felt like the ceiling was closing in, I followed Archie up the stairs and back into the main part of the castle. There, I detoured to the library, a room that had given me solace before, and dropped into the chair next to the fireplace. Closing my eyes, I leaned back with my sword in my lap and tried to take stock of the emotions that tumbled in my stomach. Elation mixed with fear, I realized. Elation because something about this blade made me feel stronger than I had in years, and fear because I didn't know my path forward. I was the person who, when booking a vacation, had my spreadsheet already started with ideas and itineraries. Since the moment I'd stepped foot on the private plane to come here, with haphazard packing and no idea what was waiting for me on the other side, I'd been out of my comfort zone. Now, I was supposed to just willy-nilly conquer a few ancient challenges and fend off a few dangerous mythological water beasts hell-bent on terror-izing a small village.

It was Archie who found me, staring up at the ceiling and contemplating how to proceed, and put a mug of tea by my chair.

"You need to tell me how to fight these challenges. Or the Kelpies. Something. I need *some* direction, Archie," I said, still staring at the mural on the ceiling. I realized little elves or cherubs were hiding among the painted vines. "I can't just banish the Kelpies with no information."

"You won't banish them no matter what," Archie said, dropping into the other seat by the fireplace and reaching for his tackle box on the floor.

"Wait, what? I thought that was what this was all about?" I asked.

"It is. But you can't do it all on your own. You're the first step. Once the full Order is restored, the Kelpies will return to rest. Ideally, you'll lessen their presence and be able to control them. As the Knight, you'll have the most power over your horses so to speak."

"Wait, the Kelpies are mine?" Had I just inherited some crazy water horses as my pets?

"The Kelpies belong to themselves. But, in theory, when your powers manifest, you'll be the one best suited to keeping them in check."

"Right, of course, and how am I to do that again?" I narrowed my eyes at Archie as he took a feather from his box and studied it.

"Magick." Archie snipped off a bit of the feather and, deeming that one appropriate, he put it aside.

"So what do I do now?" I asked, tapping the hilt of my dirk with one finger.

"I suggest you have a rest. None of this is going to happen overnight. Today was a big step forward. Soon enough, the challenges and how they manifest for you will reveal themselves."

"A rest?" I asked in the same tone as if he was offering me cocaine.

"Yes? You've heard of it, surely? Close your eyes. Kick your feet up. Read a book. Things of that nature..." Archie shrugged as I stood. Rest? This man was crazy. I was way too keyed up to relax. What I needed was action. Or a job. Something to keep me busy.

"Did you see where Matthew went?"

"He's off with Agnes to visit her bookstore," Archie said. "And Hilda's gone to get the messages."

I still wasn't certain what that term meant but narrowed my eyes as a clap of thunder rattled the window. The sound of paws skittering down the hallway reached me, and Sir Buster tore into the library, his eyes wild, and darted for the cushion on the floor in front of the fireplace.

"That's a good lad, then. I'll just get a fire going here, and we'll cozy on up against the storm, won't we?" Archie said, putting his flies away to crouch at the fireplace. Leaving them to it, I wandered into the hallway and down to the lounge, peeking my head in to see if Lachlan lingered there. Finding it empty, I turned and decided to head back to my apartment. Maybe I could take a nap? Another clap of thunder sounded, and I nudged that idea aside. Though cozying up under that thick comforter on my bed did sound lovely.

Uncertain, and unused to time off, I wandered down another corridor, stopping to study several of the portraits that hung between the tapestries strung up to cover the stone walls. I wondered if the tapestries were hanging to display their beautiful artistry or if it was another way to provide insulation against the damp cold that seemed common to Scotland. A grunt of frustration tore my attention away from a portrait of a woman in a blue ball gown with a small dog on her lap. If I squinted my eyes, the dog could have been an ancestor of Sir Buster's. Turning, I saw an arched doorway with the door only partially closed and light spilling into the corridor. Curious, I stopped at the door, nudging it with the hilt of my dirk until it swung a touch wider.

Lachlan sat at a desk, paperwork strewn about in a mess that immediately made me itchy, and ran a hand through his hair. My mouth went dry. It was the wire-rimmed glasses perched on his nose that did it. Never had I wanted to jump a man more than I did at this moment as he cursed long and low at the computer screen.

"I don't think Siri responds to curses," I said, and Lachlan jumped in his chair. Turning, he narrowed his eyes at me.

"Who is Siri?"

"Um, she's the...voice-activated assistant. In your Macbook there?" I pointed at his computer, and he just looked blankly at me. Taking pity on him, I leaned against the doorframe and glanced around the room. It was clearly his office and was a really cool room. The stone walls were painted white, and a shallow arch showcased a matching curved window, and the ceiling rounded above it. An oriental-style carpet was tossed on the floor, and a cluttered bookshelf hugged one wall. Two lamps cast a warm glow across the room, and I felt some of the tension ease from my shoulders. Here was a man with a problem, and I could help. At least it would give me something to do.

"I don't know what you're on about," Lachlan said, glancing back at the computer.

"Spreadsheets giving you trouble?" My fingers literally vibrated with the need to nudge him out of the way and tidy up his desk.

"They are the bane of my existence. It's what makes me so tetchy, I swear it." Lachlan glowered at the pile of papers in front of him.

"Is it to do with the business of MacAlpine Castle?" Oh please, let it be something to do with the business. At least then, I'd have a viable reason for butting in to help.

"Aye, it's the accounts. They're not matching up, but I can't find the error." Lachlan poked at a pile of papers in front of him.

"You know, I quite like spreadsheets. In fact, more than *like*...I'm very good with them," I said, wandering a bit closer.

"Is that right?" Lachlan peered at me.

"In fact, I double-majored in university. Accountancy is one of my great loves."

Lachlan stared at me like I'd sprouted a second head.

"And here I thought I was beginning to like you," Lachlan said with a small shake of his head.

"And since I'm technically the new owner of the castle, it's probably best that I get a handle on the accounts, anyway, right?" Pleasure bloomed in me at the thought of him liking me, but I pushed past that, zeroing in on the paperwork. I needed a distraction that made sense to me, and when everything else failed, the logic of numbers always lined up for me.

"I suppose..." Lachlan said, leaning back in his chair to study me. "Are you saying you're keen to take a stab at these?"

"Lachlan, I'm *begging* you to let me organize this. The mere state of your desk is close to giving me hives. Please, I'm on my knees here. Let me have at it," I pleaded.

The air grew heavy between us, and I realized that my choice of words was perhaps more suggestive than necessary as his eyes heated. The moment held before he shook his head and took off his glasses, tossing them onto the desk. Pushing back from the chair, he gestured with his hand.

"You really are a knight in shining armor if you can make sense of this."

"Oh, phew. I thought I was going to have to threaten you." I held up my dirk, and a grin flashed across his handsome face.

"Why don't you put that aside?" Lachlan gestured to a small table set next to the desk, and I put the dirk safely down. Once I no longer held it, I realized that I felt momentarily bereft as though missing a limb or something. Odd, I thought, glancing at the dirk, an invisible link connecting me to it.

"What's the problem?" I asked, leaning over his desk.

"It's the tours. Based on the persons entering the castle, the money should be higher. I'm not sure if the credit card payments aren't going through or where we're losing it, but there's a significant difference. And the feed for the horses has gone up, so I'm trying to negotiate a new price with a different vendor. Oh, and energy costs are projected to go up, so we'll need to figure out ways to insulate or use less heat. Or increase the tourists who visit..." Lachlan stopped when I held up my hand.

"Is there anything here you don't want me to see?" I gestured to the pile of papers on his desk. "And on the computer?"

"No, this is all business. I have a personal laptop in my study in my apartment."

"Smart," I said. "Do you care if I just dive in? Like, go through your ledger books? Sort the papers? Update the spreadsheets?" I stopped at Lachlan's look.

"You want to just...do this? Like well and truly handle this?" Lachlan's voice rose on a hopeful note.

"Yes, please. But I need to just..." I spread my hands wide over the desk. "Handle it."

"Are you saying..." Lachlan looked like a kid on Christmas morning.

"Please leave," I ordered, and Lachlan was already at the door.

"I'll check in later," Lachlan called, closing the door behind him, but I was already lost to a new challenge to tackle. At the very least, this would give me something to do. Plus, it would familiarize me with the finances of the castle, and I might prove to be useful to the business. All in all, this was shaping up to be a win-win for us both. Delighted that I'd wandered this way, I settled into sorting the papers on the desk and making notes while the storm raged outside. Happily content, I barely noticed the passage of time, instead hyper-fixating on the task at hand.

At some point, food and a glass of wine appeared at the desk. I lingered over both, appreciating the gift but, still, the numbers drew me in, and I sighed, happy to finally feel like I was back in my comfort zone. At the very least, this was an area I could truly help in, and being useful always cheered me up.

It was close to ten in the evening when Lachlan startled me from typing my final bullet points.

"Oh, Lachlan." I held a hand to my heart. "You startled me. I'm just finishing up. I've gotten through most of what you asked about, and I'm typing up the last of my recommendations."

"You..." Lachlan's eyes darted between the screen and my face. "You've finished? As in...found the issues?"

"I believe so unless you have more hidden away?" I raised my arms over my head, stretching the kink from my neck.

"I could kiss you," Lachlan breathed, and this time when the heat flashed through me, I let it, looking up at him from under heavy lids.

"Why don't you?" I invited.

CHAPTER SIXTEEN

LACHLAN

Kicking the door closed behind me, I moved across the room before Sophie could change her mind, having obsessively stolen glances at her mouth all day and needing no further invitation now. Sophie let out a small squeak, her eyes lighting with excitement, as I pulled her wheeled chair out from the desk and turned her to me. Dropping to my knees, I cradled her face in my palms, need consuming me like a spark to dry tinder. Tilting her face, I angled my lips over hers, pausing as her eyelashes fluttered against her cheeks. Her breath came out in soft pants, and I realized she was as turned on as I was. Had Miss Sophie been thinking about yesterday's kiss as much as I had? When her eyes opened, the shock of blue piercing me, I held her look for a moment before pressing my lips to hers.

She tasted sweet, like the glass of wine I'd brought for

her, and I lapped at her tongue, enjoying the dance as she made a soft mewling sound low in her throat. Her hands came up, threading through my hair, and I smiled against her mouth. No, Sophie wasn't immune to my touch.

But I needed her to more than just accept my kiss. I wanted her to crave me like I had craved her the night before, pleasuring myself not once but twice as I imagined being wrapped around the softness of her body. Now, while my lips trailed hot kisses down her neck, I slid my hands to her sides, running them up and down her waist, brushing gently against the sides of her heavy breasts. Would she let me touch? She still wore that threadbare jumper, and I brought my hands to her waist, sliding a finger beneath the hem until I touched the skin of her stomach, and waited while I nibbled at the sensitive skin at her throat.

"Lachlan," Sophie gasped, and I licked her neck, and then blew on her skin, smiling when she trembled.

"Yes, my sweet?"

"Um, what are your plans?"

I chuckled into her neck, understanding now that Sophie was indeed someone who needed order and rules in her life if her obsession with spreadsheets was any indication. She likely wasn't comfortable playing things by chance, so I trailed my lips back to her ear and bit. Sophie squeaked, then moaned when I licked gently at the lobe, her body trembling where my hands stroked the skin just above the waistband of her pants.

"Would you like a game plan, Sophie? A play-by-play?" I asked, my breath hot at her ear.

"Um, yes, please. If it wouldn't be too much trouble."

Sophie's voice rose on a higher note as I kissed just below her ear.

"What the lady wants...the lady gets. First...I'm going to slide my hands across your soft skin and up to your breasts," I said and waited for Sophie to tell me to stop. When she didn't, I let my hands follow my words, and her body trembled beneath my touch. Her skin was smooth, her stomach rounded and soft and, when I found her breasts, I groaned against her neck. But still, I resisted from cupping their weight in my hands, instead returning to kiss Sophie's lush mouth while lightly stroking the silky cups of her bra. I wondered if it was the same pink bra I'd seen the other night or if it was a different color. "Next, I'm going to caress your breasts, teasing your nipples until they ache for my touch, and I'm going to watch you as I do so."

I pulled back, my eyes caught on her face, as I slipped my hands inside of her bra, feeling the weight of her heavy breasts in my hands, watching as her eyes shuttered closed again.

"Look at me, Sophie," I ordered, and her eyes flew open just as I brushed the pads of my thumbs over her already taut nipples. She gasped, her eyes caught on mine, as I stroked her nipples, learning the feel of them, tweaking them gently to see what garnered a response from her. When I had a good idea of the pressure she enjoyed, I leaned back in, needing my mouth on hers once more. There, I feasted on her lips, her mouth driving me mad, certain that I'd die a happy man if I could stay here forever.

"And now, since you've asked so nicely for a kiss, I'm going to give you one," I said, my hands dropping to the waistband of her leggings. "Lift your hips, Sophie."

I smiled when she complied, her eyes hazy with lust, and dragged the black fabric along with her thong underwear down her legs.

"Lachlan," Sophie said, snapping out of her daze, and I lifted my head from her lap.

"Yes? Do you want me to stop?" I asked, stroking the soft skin of her inner thighs. Much like I suspected, her legs were a thing of beauty. Thick, soft, and muscular, they were thighs I looked forward to having wrapped around my waist one day as I drove deep inside her.

But not today.

Today was for Sophie, a woman who'd looked both lost and ferocious upon her arrival. A woman who grieved yet took the astronomical in stride, rising to greet each challenge on her path with a gusto that not many could likely muster. A sweet woman who whispered soft words of reassurances to Sir Buster and stood her ground when I tried to intimidate her. A study in contradictions, I couldn't wait to unwrap her more.

"No," Sophie finally muttered, and I grinned against her thigh. Scraping my teeth against the soft skin I found there, I bit, sinking my teeth into the skin and sucking gently. Hard enough to leave a mark but not enough to truly cause her pain.

"Oh!" Sophie exclaimed, rearing up, and I pressed her back with my hand on her stomach.

"I wanted to leave a mark. Just to remind you that I was here." I smiled up at her shocked expression and winked before burying my mouth between her legs. Her moan echoed off the rounded ceiling, and my office grew warm as

I lavished in the sweetness of Sophie. Here was decadence. Here was a gift.

Here was an answer to my soul's longing.

Taking my time with her, I lingered, discovering her most sensitive areas as I savored her like a delicacy. She arched against my face, no longer seeming to care for my next direction, her moans increasing as she began to thrust her hips against my mouth. Sensing she was close to completion, I slipped a finger inside her, teasing her, as I sucked her clit. When she reared up, exploding around me, I smiled, continuing to pleasure her even as she flopped back in the chair and threw an arm over her face.

I ached to feel her clench around me. Painfully so, and still I stayed on my knees, my hands drawing circles on the soft inner skin of her thighs, wanting nothing more than to see the aftereffects of my ministrations in her eyes. When she finally brought her head up, removing her arm, the look on her face stole my breath.

Her cheeks were pinkened, much like when she grew embarrassed, and her lips were swollen from my kisses. A fine sheen of sweat made her face glow in the warm light from the lamps, and her eyes were heavy with sated desire. It was the first time I'd seen her truly relaxed and vulnerable since she'd arrived.

I never wanted her to look at anyone else like that. The thought almost knocked me backward, so unusual for me it was, but it echoed what I'd thought when I first tasted her. Loving Sophie was like being gifted the most precious and fragile piece of art, and I refused to be the one to damage it. My need grew and, with a grin, I bent back between her legs.

"Wait, wait, wait..." Sophie rolled the chair back, leaving me kneeling on the floor, my hands in the air where they'd once been wrapped around her lovely thighs. "What about you?"

"What about me?" I asked, tilting my head at her. If she had any idea how wanton and depraved she looked right now, with her college jumper still on and her legs splayed open, she'd probably hide in her room for a week.

"Should I...service you?" Sophie asked, biting her lower lip, her eyes dropping to where I bulged against my pants.

I threw back my head and laughed, her words easing some of the tension in my body, and I stood.

"Darling. What a way to put it." I crossed to Sophie and heaved her out of the chair, surprising another squeak out of her, and pulled her against my body. Looking down, I placed a finger under her chin and tilted her head up. Ever so gently, I lingered at her lips, kissing her softly. "Tonight was about you. And satisfying the need I've had to taste you since the moment you broke into our castle."

"I didn't break in," Sophie said automatically, fire lighting her eyes. "I had keys, you know."

"You've already done me a great service tonight." I nibbled Sophie's bottom lip, much like I'd seen her do many times. "The accounts have been a huge time suck and a burden for me. Having you take care of them is...a gift."

"Is this how you pay all your accountants?" Sophie pulled back and narrowed her eyes at me. I couldn't help myself, laughing once more before kissing her indignant nose.

"Of course," I said lightly and stepped back while she pummeled my chest with her fists. "Ow!"

"Oh, shut up. You're much too strong for that to hurt." Sophie pouted.

"Truly, Sophie. You've made my day in more ways than one." I traced a finger over her lips before tilting her head up for a kiss once more. "Let tonight be about just you. A gift."

"I...okay, well, then. Thank you." Sophie stepped back and tripped on her leggings, and we both bent, smacking our heads against each other and staggering as I tried to help her. Laughter consumed me for the second time that day, and I shook with it as she swore and untangled her pants before pulling them up her legs. "Just once, I'd like to do something with a modicum of grace."

"Och, grace is overrated. Plus, can we stop to admire the beauty of this desk? I mean...I'm not sure I even knew what was under here," I said, admiring the gleam of wood that I could now clearly see under the neat stacks of paper.

"I did good, didn't I? While you're here...can I just give you my recommendations?"

"Only you would enjoy an orgasm and immediately return to your spreadsheets." I shook my head in awe.

"It's a toss-up which is more orgasmic for me," Sophie said, a wicked light in her eyes, and then she convulsed in laughter when I bent and whispered a very naughty suggestion in her ear. "Fine, fine, you win. Your orgasms are a smidge better than working with spreadsheets."

Bending over the computer, I pointed at the piles of paper. "I'll take the win, lass. Now, go on, then. I'll try not to pass out from boredom."

CHAPTER SEVENTEEN

SOPHIE

The shrieks awoke me in the muted gray light of dawn, and I pulled myself from the warm cocoon of blankets to scramble to the window. There, I found Lachlan standing on the battlement in dark jeans and a thick coat, his arms crossed over his chest as he stared out to Loch Mirren.

Was I supposed to join him? Was this a job for me now? Unsure of how to proceed, I crossed my bedroom and flipped on the lamp. Reaching for my dirk that I'd placed on the bedside table, I paused.

A glimmer at the base of the sword, near where it met the hilt, caught my eye. Picking the sword up, I bent closer to examine it in the soft glow from the lamp.

Sure enough, a singular sapphire had appeared in the blade, no larger than a carat, and appeared to be strongly welded into the metal. I brushed my thumb over the stone, wondering if it would fall loose, but the gem was firmly rooted in the metal. At my touch, the blade lit, and a cool balm washed through me. The feeling reminded me of the time Lottie had treated me to a fancy spa where, when you left the sauna, you walked through a room with a cold eucalyptus-scented water misting down from the ceiling. The stark contrast from the heat to the refreshing mist had felt much like this power did when it ran through my body.

If this was magick, I could get on board with this feeling.

Returning to the window, I saw that Lachlan no longer stood on the battlement, as the sun now peeked out from foreboding gray clouds that hugged the tops of the mountains behind Loch Mirren. I made a mental note to ask if the Kelpies only arrived in the night, for I'd yet to hear any of the otherworldly shrieks during the daytime.

Not that I would have heard anything last night while Lachlan had done wicked things to me with his mouth. The reminder of his touch sent a flash of heat through me that no cooling eucalyptus mist could tame. My need for him threatened to overwhelm me, and I wasn't sure if this heady rush of longing was exhilarating or terrifying. I'd never considered myself one to have fits of high emotions. Instead, I tended to remain steadfast as I waited to react to what the world threw at me.

And maybe that was what Uncle Arthur had sent me here to change about myself. Something to consider as I traced my finger over the sapphire in the blade once more. Thoughts of his laughter, his shrewd mind, and his thirst for knowledge filled me—both with sadness and comfort—

as I looked out to Loch Mirren. He'd loved Scotland, in all her unruly glory and, knowing Arthur, he'd sent me here with more than one reason in mind. I couldn't help but think that becoming a knight was secondary to a greater goal that Arthur had wanted me to achieve. Even now, when he was gone, his presence lingered closely.

Arthur had loved greatly. He'd not only loved the *idea* of love, evidenced by the numerous times he'd married, but he'd also loved without reservation. Being loved by Arthur was like being consumed by wildfire, Lottie had once told me after a few too many glasses of wine. At first, I'd been grossed out before I realized she hadn't meant in the bedroom. Arthur loved wholeheartedly, embracing the highs and lows of love like a sailor holding fast as the sea tossed his sailboat around in a storm. To be loved like that, Lottie had said, was life-changing and truly a gift.

Now, I wondered if I held the same capacity to love as Arthur had. The thought scared me, sending my heart skittering back behind its protective walls, and I defaulted to putting Lachlan just where I needed him. He was nothing more than a fun vacation fling, someone I could enjoy while in Scotland, but not for the long term. No, Lachlan was a friend, and it appeared he came with some benefits, and that would be all I'd take from him. Making the decision soothed me, tamping the fire that built inside me when I thought of his mouth on mine, and I was happy to have some rules to govern how I treated him.

Friends with benefits. A flirtation. A holiday romance. It all sounded so chic and worldly. I was having a proper European affair, I decided. The kind my friends would talk about when they studied abroad for the summer. That was all this was. It would be silly to attach any sort of expectation to it.

Plus, I had bigger issues to worry about, I reminded myself, as I looked once more at the gemstone in the blade. If I was correct, the appearance of the stone meant that I'd passed a challenge of sorts. The problem was—I couldn't possibly know what that challenge was.

"So the sapphire just appeared?" Matthew asked at the breakfast table later that morning. I hadn't been able to go back to sleep, so instead had spent time in the library going over the books that Agnes had left for me. Hilda and Archie were nowhere to be seen, but a note on the table had informed me to help myself to any food for breakfast. Keeping it easy, I toasted some bread and slathered some jam across the top, and now Matthew and I studied my dirk as we sipped coffee.

"Yup. It wasn't there last night, and now it is here today."

"And nothing happened in the night? You didn't sneak out and battle a Kelpie without me, did you?" Matthew narrowed his eyes at me.

Not a Kelpie, I thought, my cheeks pinkening, but I'd had a different battle of sorts.

"What's that look about?" Matthew asked, leaning closer, his eyes glinting. "You've got gossip, don't you?"

"I do not," I hissed, glancing over my shoulder to make sure that Lachlan wasn't nearby.

"You do, or you wouldn't look so guilty. Spill," Matthew demanded.

"I can't spill. There's nothing to spill."

"Sophie, you are a horrible liar on a good day. Don't

even bother to try." Matthew shook his head at me. He crossed his arms over his chest, one hand holding his mug, and gestured with it. "Details, now."

"I can't. Not here. Plus, we need to figure out what happened with the blade," I insisted. There was no way I was giving Matthew details of what had happened the night before when anyone could walk in at any moment.

"We're going to the bookshop, then. Agnes was going to pull some books for me to pick up today, and I'm sure she'll be able to help with this new development. Or developments, should I say?" Matthew arched a brow. Blowing out a breath, I crammed the toast in my mouth, stopping myself from answering, and shrugged one shoulder. There was no way I'd get out of telling Matthew about what had happened between Lachlan and me, but at least I could prolong it for now.

On the walk to the bookstore, I managed to steer the conversation in the direction of Matthew's views on what had happened yesterday with magick, the town of Loren Brae, and his overall impressions of everyone we'd met thus far. Even if he knew I was dodging his interrogation, he was kind enough not to press me for more information about what had transpired the day before. Instead, we'd enjoyed a stroll in the misty weather, with myself once again snuggled into the man's sweater that Hilda had given me. One of these days I was going to buy proper clothes for the Scottish weather.

"Is this her shop?" I asked as we turned from the street that wound along the loch and onto a side street with stone buildings tucked next to each other in a neat row. *Bonnie Books* was carved on a cute wooden sign that hung over a bright blue door. Two large arched windows showcased a display of books and art, and I was immediately charmed. I had to admit, I hadn't realized how much I loved an arched window or door until I'd seen so many around the village. It was those little details that added to the appeal of the village.

"It is. I'm just going to pop into the market to see if they have hibiscus tea. I'll be right along." Matthew gestured to a small supermarket across the street, and I nodded.

Pushing the door open, I heard Agnes's voice raised in anger. It was so unlike the Agnes I had met that I paused just inside the door, unsure of how to proceed.

"Och, and you're a clarty bastard, aren't you? I've told you again and again that I don't have the money. Nobody in the town does. Tourism has all but dried up. I bloody well don't have an extra pound to be paying you. You can't be closing my shop!" Her voice rose in anger, and worry twisted my stomach. "David Goodwin, you're not a proper gentleman if you're forcing this through. All of Loren Brae is suffering. You don't need the money. You're just being greedy."

Silence filled the air as Agnes listened. She paced the shop, still not having seen me, and dread gripped me. David Goodwin was a name I was well familiar with. If I was correct, he was the New York business manager who oversaw many of Uncle Arthur's properties around the world. A part of me hoped that I was wrong, but with a sinking feeling in my stomach, I knew that it had to be one and the same.

"Your mother would be ashamed of you, David. I hope

you lose sleep at night knowing you're stealing from the mouths of needy families." Agnes swore and punched the button on her phone before tossing it on the counter. Not wanting to intrude but also feeling uncomfortable, I cleared my throat. Agnes whirled, two bright pink spots on her cheeks.

"Oh, Sophie. You startled me."

"I'm sorry, I came in just as you were speaking...I couldn't help but overhear. I'm sorry, it was rude of me to listen. I shouldn't have..." I crossed to her and took her arms in my hands, searching her face. "Are you okay?"

"No, I'm *not* okay. And don't worry about listening. It's not exactly a secret. Though I'll admit my pride often prevents me from moaning about it." Agnes sighed and pulled me in for a quick hug before retreating behind the counter. "It's this New York landlord. Some investor bought up a lot of the properties a while back and has no empathy for the hard times we've fallen upon. While I understand it is business, it would be nice if he could at least be a touch understanding during this hard time. It's not like he'll find other tenants to take this spot, not with the way people are steering clear of Loren Brae. Better a partially paying tenant than none at all, right?" Agnes asked.

"I agree. One of the reasons my Uncle Arthur had such a strong business is that he understood that the people who worked for him were human. He didn't care if mothers had to leave early to pick up kids or go to a doctor's appointment. He trusted his employees to get their work done around their schedules and insisted on balance in all things. In turn, he built a loyal employee base and had little turnover. He'd always told me that while the common advice was to treat everything like a business and not personally—that advice quite simply wasn't true. People *do* take business personally. It's their livelihood. It's how they introduce themselves at parties. It's where they spend a huge chunk of their time. It's never just business, and anybody who doesn't understand that is operating without a heart." I made a mental note to double-check that David Goodwin was indeed the man I was thinking of.

"I think I would have liked your Uncle Arthur," Agnes said, her eyes going to the door as Matthew barreled in, brushing his coat off.

"It's coming down out there now," Matthew said, shaking his coat and hanging it on a hook on the wall.

Turning, I took a slow scan of the room, my heart giving a happy sigh as I took in the space that Agnes had created here. Clearly, it was a place for book lovers and dreamers alike. A low-slung leather couch was tucked beneath the tall front windows, and two comfortable-looking armchairs bookended the sofa with small tables on either side. A variety of intricately woven rugs were splashed across the wooden floors, and bookcases in varying heights and sizes created nooks around the room. A fireplace on one wall was framed by a pretty carpet, floor cushions, and more low-slung cushy chairs. I realized that must be a space for children to curl up and listen during story time. Long wooden beams crisscrossed the ceiling, and white floral garlands were hung among strands of twinkle lights. Along the walls, bold paintings in bright colors added interest to the space, and I already wanted to wander the room and lose myself in the offerings found there. She'd done an incredible job of creating ambience, and I was itching to explore the bookshelves.

"Cup of tea for you?" Agnes called from where she crouched by the fire.

"Yes, please. We have very important things to discuss this dreary morning," Matthew said, crossing to the fire and plopping into one of the chairs. Stretching his legs out, he drummed his fingers on his thigh. "But I can't decide which is more important—the reason behind why Sophie's cheeks go pink whenever I ask where she disappeared to for hours yesterday—or figuring out why she's already met the first of her challenges."

"Och, bloody hell. It's quite a morning then, isn't it?" Agnes whirled on me. "And here I'm moaning on about my own problems when you've got much bigger news."

"Yes, see? There's a gemstone in my dirk," I said, pulling the sword from the tote bag I'd brought with me.

"Hold that thought. I'd just put a pot on to boil before you walked in. Let me get it." Agnes hurried through a door in the back of the store, and I took the opportunity to cross to a shelf full of pottery decorated with a delicate purple glaze. Charmed by a small vase, I took it to the counter and continued my perusal. By the time Agnes returned with a tray in hand, I'd added a small painting, four books, another piece of pottery, and a soft scarf in muted storm cloud colors. I'd also avoided any questions from Matthew, though I knew that time had come to an end when I returned to the fire and both Agnes and Matthew had similar expressions of interest on their faces.

"Fine," I muttered, plopping down into a leather

armchair and staring into the fire. "I hooked up with Lachlan."

"There it is..." Matthew snapped his fingers.

"Did ye now? I'm liking that for you," Agnes said, her short crop of curls bouncing as she nodded her head in approval.

"You haven't..." I met her eyes, gritting my teeth as I waited.

"Och, *no*. Not with him or Graham. Those two have been charming the ladies for ages. Far easier for me to stay on the outside of all that," Agnes said and then grimaced. "I should say Graham charms far more ladies than Lachlan does. Lach tends to be more standoffish. And choosy, I suppose."

"That's somewhat comforting to hear." I shrugged one shoulder, unsure of how I felt about knowing Lachlan's past but also grateful that at least I wasn't stepping on any toes where Agnes was concerned.

"You were gone all of the afternoon and evening." Matthew blew on his tea before taking a sip. "It sounds like it was quite the rendezvous."

"It wasn't..." I sighed, tilting my head back to look at where the wood beams crossed the ceiling. "We weren't doing *that* all day."

"More's the pity," Matthew mused.

"So you're thinking that sex with Lachlan caused a gem to show up in your sword?" Agnes nodded to where I'd placed the sword on my lap. "May I see?"

"We didn't sleep together," I said as I handed her my blade. Immediately, I felt bereft at the loss of it, and a tad uncomfortable as she handled the blade. It was like giving someone else your baby to hold, or at least I imagined what that must feel like, and was relieved when she returned it to me.

"It's well and truly embedded, isn't it? Fascinating." Agnes stood and crossed to the counter, bending to pull a folder from a shelf. She returned and began leafing through the folder, nibbling her lower lip as she read. Outside, the rain pattered against the windows, and I glanced up as the sound of bagpipes filled the store.

"My music comes on at ten when the shop opens," Agnes said, catching my look.

"'Amazing Grace,'" I murmured, transported back to Arthur's funeral and the man playing the bagpipes. It all seemed so long ago now, though it had been just over a week since we'd arrived in Scotland.

Just over a week and here I was letting a man I barely knew pleasure me. The thought brought heat to my face once more, and I turned to stare down at where the light of the fire glinted off the dull steel of my sword and picked up the deep blue of the gemstone.

"I'm going to need details, Sophie. Or I swear I'm getting on the next plane out of here." Matthew mocked stamping his foot on the floor as though he was about to have a tantrum. I couldn't blame him. I'd done the same anytime I knew he'd hooked up with a new man.

"Well, I wasn't lying. I didn't spend all day hooking up with Lachlan. Just a small portion at the end of the day," I clarified, giving Matthew a pointed look.

"Hmm, love maybe? I wonder if that's a challenge to be passed," Agnes mused as she flipped through the pages, missing my horrified look.

"No, not love. That was *not* one of the knightly duties," I exclaimed.

"But love was part of the rite, wasn't it? With the cardamom oil?" Matthew asked, and I had to wonder if he was purposely baiting me or just trying to be helpful.

"It's not love," I practically shouted, and both of their gazes snapped to mine.

"I was just...why don't you tell us what else you did with your day?" Agnes hurried on.

"After the rite, I was too keyed up to just sit there. I needed something to do. Some direction. Anything. I don't like all these ambiguities and what-ifs. I'm much more comfortable dealing with structure and rules." I realized that made me sound boring, but I soldiered on. "Anyway, I was walking around the castle and found Lachlan in his office surrounded by an atrocious mess of paperwork."

"Aye, he's bollocks when it comes to paperwork." Agnes laughed.

"I bet that drove you nuts." Matthew's eyes lit.

"You know me." At this, I did smile. "Not only do I work with brand management, Agnes, but I also have an accountancy background. Spreadsheets are like foreplay to me."

"Och, that explains the hookup with Lachlan, then. All those numbers got you all hot and bothered." Agnes laughed.

"You're probably not wrong." I sighed. "Painful though it is to admit it. Either way, I could see he was struggling. And it, legit, agitated me to see the state of his desk. I realized that since I'm technically now owner of the castle, I should understand the business operations. I basically strongarmed him into giving up his mess of paperwork so I could sort it all out for him. By the end of the day, I'd cleared his desk, had the books in order, and had created a list of a few suggestions for him to review in areas he could cut costs in."

"How very..." Matthew's eyes widened. "Chivalrous of you."

"Ohhhhh." Agnes slammed her hand on the arm of her chair a few times in excitement. "Yes! Matthew, *yes*!"

"I haven't heard a woman say *that* to me in years," Matthew quipped to me, and I rolled my eyes while Agnes let out a rolling chuckle.

"Is that...is it chivalry, though? I was just being help-ful," I said.

"To you it may have been something minor or even enjoyable." Agnes gave a mock shudder. "But to Lachlan? You probably *were* his hero. He loathes paperwork and puts it off constantly. It's a monumental burden you've taken from his shoulders, and that's the truth of it."

"So chivalry. Check." Matthew made a little check mark in the air with his hand. "What's next, then?"

"I mean, I could go volunteer somewhere? Save a kitten?" I asked, but Agnes shook her head.

"Based on this passage, I suspect it's far more nuanced than that. Keep in mind that the Clach na Fìrinn knows all things. It is going to know if you're just showing off to gain its approval. You're being judged in everything you do, and I think the stone will decide if you're pure of heart."

"I can't tell you how much I hate the ambiguity of that," I murmured, leaning over to take the piece of paper from Agnes and read the words there. "A lie will be drowned. Money is not sound. The truth is found when a Knight is not bound."

"Curious." Matthew took the page from me and studied the phrase.

"I copied it from a Gaelic translation, so it might not be exact, but I think this is the thrust of it, no?" Agnes asked.

"I'd agree. I think, Sophie, you're just going to have to be you. I wouldn't think so much about how to be a Knight, and instead take things as they come." Matthew threw back his head and laughed when I looked at him in horror.

"Just...have no plans at all?" My voice squeaked.

"Oh, this is truly going to be delightful to watch. Have I thanked you yet for taking me on this trip with you? I don't know when I've been more entertained. Now...let's get back to the cozy office part. Is that where Lachlan had his way with you?" Matthew steepled his hands in front of his face, and I knew I wasn't getting out of giving full details.

"Yes, and never tell him this...but it was mind-blowing." I leaned forward to gossip as the rain pounded the windows, surrounding the village in its gloomy gray mood.

CHAPTER EIGHTEEN

SOPHIE

"Sorry to wake you." I laughed into the phone.

We'd just returned from the bookshop, Agnes having closed the store for a moment to give us a quick lift home. We hadn't thought to grab an umbrella on the way out, and I was more than grateful to accept her offer of a ride. Now, I huddled in my bedroom while Matthew disappeared to the library and pulled the blanket over my lap as I opened my laptop.

"I know you're smart enough to be aware of different time zones, right? You haven't turned into a flat earther on me, have you?" Lottie's voice immediately soothed me, and I snuggled more deeply into the comforter as I pictured her glaring in annoyance at the phone. Lottie was one of the most cheerful women I'd ever met, aside from when she first woke up. Sleepy Lottie was a

late stage when discovered, and his decline had followed rapidly.

"A little warning might have helped." Okay, so maybe I needed to complain a bit.

"I couldn't. It was a stipulation of Arthur's will. He wanted you to make these discoveries on your own, my love. There are lessons he wanted you to learn about life and who you are. And I have to agree with him. You've followed a very regimented path. Now is the time to stray from that and see what more the world has to offer," Lottie said, and all annoyance I had with her disappeared. Of course Arthur had dictated what she could say to me. He'd rarely missed any details.

"Well, it's been a whirlwind, I'll admit." I spent the next half hour telling her everything I learned about magick, the Stone of Truth, and the people of the town. By the time I'd finished, I had almost forgotten why I'd called.

"You're right. I may have to get on a plane to come see you soon. This all sounds deeply fascinating and likely a good diversion from grieving. And navigating probate. The legalities of death are bland and tedious. I don't like dealing with them, I'll admit."

"I'm happy to look over any paperwork if you need help," I offered. "Actually, speaking of legalities, I do have a question for you regarding Arthur's interests in this town. Did he invest in more than just the castle here?"

"I believe so. Do you need me to check? I'm passing his office right now," Lottie said, and I heard the squeak of hinges through the phone.

"Yes, please. I need to know if David Goodwin of New York is the property manager for any other properties he's acquired. And his contact information. Oh, and who owns those properties now, if that's the case." I opened a document on my computer, ready to type the information as I listened to Lottie rustle through some paperwork.

"Here we go. Neatly labeled. You and Arthur shared the same love of a tidy office, didn't you? Hmm..." I waited for Lottie to continue. "Yes, I can send this all to you. It seems that along with the purchase of the castle estate, there were a dozen or so properties in the town that came as part of the parcel. Making you the owner of several other buildings. It seems a pub, a bookstore, a market...that kind of thing. And, yes, you're correct. David Goodwin has been collecting rent from the tenants there as part of portfolio management for Arthur."

"Can I fire him?" I asked, my heart pounding hard in my chest. It was a bold move, and one I wouldn't normally make, but it felt right.

"Of course you can as these are your properties now. But why? Has he done something wrong?" Lottie's voice held a worried note. "You can contact Harold as well. He'll handle anything you need when it comes to that."

"I'll do so. Yes, he has. See, the town has fallen on hard times due to the Kelpies. People are scared to visit, and tourism has all but dried up. It's becoming a ghost town, and families are suffering. Instead of being understanding, David has been demanding rent and threatening evictions."

"Well, now, that's positively churlish," Lottie exclaimed. She, like Arthur, agreed that exceptions must be made in business.

"I'd like to fire him, make available a stipend for any

families that need it, and provide free rent for at least a year for those in need. Can the finances support that?" I asked.

"Darling, you could not require rent of the entire village for the next twenty years and the trust would well support it. I think it is very noble of you, and a kind and generous deed," Lottie said, and I could hear the smile in her voice. Her approval eased the tension in my shoulders that had stayed with me since I'd left the bookstore. I hated thinking that I had inadvertently contributed to the hardships in this lovely little town.

"And is there a way that this can all be arranged without revealing that it comes from me?" I asked.

"Of course. We can shield it in the business name or a trust. Harold's a master at it. Knowing him, he'll have it set up by the end of the day or tomorrow at the latest."

"Perfect, I'll call him now," I said.

"It's early..." Lottie started. "Ah, well, never mind. He's paid well. Plus, Harold loves doing these things. He may be a tough attorney on the outside, but he's a real softie. This will make his day."

"I love you," I said, standing at the window and looking out to where the rain still pummeled the loch. "I hope you're doing okay. I know it must be lonely without Arthur around."

"I miss him every minute of every day. But, oh, did I love that man. I never wasted a minute of my time with him, either. For that, I'm grateful. His memories will keep my heart warm, child. Don't you worry about me. I'll be just fine. And I'm coming to see you soon. I want to meet this Lachlan of yours."

"He's not...why do you say it like that?" I asked.

"Your voice softened when you spoke about him," Lottie said. "But you can tell me in your own time. That's enough talking for me at this hour, anyway. Love you." With that, she clicked off, and I was left staring at the background screen on my phone, my mind whirling with thoughts about Lachlan. Pushing those aside, I typed in Harold's number.

As Lottie had predicted, Harold had things taken care of by the following afternoon, and I tried to entice Matthew to go to the pub to celebrate. Not that he knew I was celebrating, as I'd kept the information to myself. Matthew demurred, insisting he did *actually* need to work on his book. To my surprise, Lachlan overheard and offered to accompany me to the pub instead. Now, nerves twisted low in my stomach as we left the castle together, as I'd successfully avoided him since he'd, well, since I'd last seen him. As we walked in the chilly evening hours, my brain scrambled for a topic of conversation that didn't involve his mouth on my body. It was still light even though it was almost nine at night. Seizing on that, I pointed at the sky.

"That's how you know we're nearing summer," Lachlan said, nodding to the dim sky. "It stays light later here."

"Does it? I didn't know that." Loch Mirren looked starkly beautiful in the low light, the water rippling softly as a cold wind whipped across the hills. I burrowed more deeply into my sweater, breathing deeply of the soapy scent that still clung to it, and wondered if I would acclimate to the cold soon.

"It can be a touch disconcerting, as the time gets away from you. Then you've gone from having a wee dram to

"If you say so..." Agnes shrugged. "Men always tend to think they satisfy their women but rarely bother to ask."

"I'm more than happy to demonstrate, darling." Graham leaned forward, a sultry smile on his lips. "I'm a hands-on man, as I'm sure you've heard."

Agnes snorted. "Your hand is all you're getting these days from what I hear."

"Keeping tabs on my dating life, are ye then? I knew I'd woo you eventually," Graham said, giving Agnes a cheerful smile.

"I'm too happy to let you get to me this night, Graham. I'll not be taking the bait." Agnes turned to us again and clapped her hands. "I had a call from a lovely solicitor named Harold. It seems he's heard of our troubles and is giving everyone a year of free rent, along with a cushion for any upgrades if any of the properties need sprucing up. For a new boiler or windows and the like. Isn't that fabulous? I was starting to worry I'd have to pack up my shop, but now we've been given a grace period."

"Is that right?" Lachlan's voice caused me to glance over and find him regarding me with a calculating look. "How unusually generous."

"It is. That's wonderful news, Agnes," I said. I hoped that Lachlan wouldn't figure out that I was behind the windfall for the people of the town. I wanted to avoid putting myself in the position of anyone using me for money ever again. Chad had been the last straw in a long line of people who had tried to date or befriend me based on my wealthy family and being here felt like a way for me to shed that. In Loren Brae, I was the Knight. A woman who could help save the town. Money had no stake in why people admired me. I wanted to keep it that way.

"I can't say that it's not a bit odd, but I'll take the reprieve myself," Graham admitted, leaning onto the bar. "While business has been steady, it's much slower than usual this time of year, and I need to save what I earn in the spring and summer to tide me over for the lean winter months."

"I don't care the how or the why of it. I just know that for the first time in months, I can sleep easy tonight without feeling like a beast is breathing at my doorstep." Agnes held her pint up. "To happy windfalls!"

The rest of the pub raised their glasses and shouted their cheers, and a lively song broke out across the room. Soon, Agnes had dragged me from my chair to perform some sort of Scottish swing-dancing and the night disappeared into one of joy and celebration.

It made my heart happy, and I knew that Uncle Arthur would have been proud of my decision to help. While he'd been a pragmatic businessman, he'd also had a heart of gold. Silently, I sent up a little thank-you to him, glad I'd been able to ease some of the tension that clung to Loren Brae.

Now, if I could just master this whole Knight thing, maybe I could send the Kelpies home and bring the town back to its bustling level of tourism that it had once enjoyed.

One thing at a time, I supposed, as I was swept once more into a complicated dance that I was sure I butchered. Letting my cares go for the night, I ordered another pint and smiled at Lachlan easily when he came and looped an arm around my waist.

"The rain has stopped for the moment. Now's our chance to make a break for the castle," Lachlan said. His arm felt too comfortable around my waist, and nerves skittered through me. I wanted a taste of him again.

And I needed to keep him at arm's length.

Love had never been something that came easily to me. It didn't take an expensive therapist for me to know that it stemmed from my parents' abandonment and my difficulty with feeling worthy of love. Nevertheless, I'd gone my whole life without having my heart broken, and I'd like to continue with that streak. Looking up at Lachlan, his handsome face warm with affection and something else I wasn't ready to decipher, I came to a startling realization.

This man could break my heart.

Easing out of his grasp, I pasted a bland smile on my face.

"I could stay for another pint. I don't want to catch my death in the freezing rain, either. But I'm happy to wait and see if Graham can drive me home too, if you're leaving."

There, I'd given him an easy out and put some distance between us. Lachlan's face clouded as he glanced between me and where Graham smiled lazily at a pretty brunette.

"I'll be seeing you home," Lachlan said, hooking an arm through mine. Annoyed at his high-handedness, I pulled my arm loose and glared at him.

"I don't need anyone to see me home. I'm a grown woman who has somehow managed to find her way to and from places without the assistance of some overbearing male for years now." I glared at Lachlan.

"You tell him, Sophie! We women are tougher than we

look." Agnes raised her pint to me from where she rocked lightly on her stool.

"Och, and you've been dealing with the Kelpies your whole life then too?" Lachlan lowered his voice on the last bit, but his words sent a shiver across my skin. I'd forgotten for a moment about the Kelpies, and now that the night had gone dark, I realized that having Lachlan by my side on the cold walk past the loch might be smart.

"At least I've acknowledged them and didn't try to pretend they were fake," I bit out as I swung out the door without saying goodbye. Annoyance rippled through me and the blast of cold on my face did little to stem my mood. I wanted to feel this anger because otherwise I suspected I'd let myself lean too far the other way. And that way led to big emotions and potential heartbreak. No, better to pick a fight and push Lachlan back. He'd likely thank me for it one day.

"I don't know what you're so prickly about, but I'll just let you be," Lachlan said, walking beside me and allowing silence to fill the cool night air. It annoyed me even further that he refused to take the bait. Opening my mouth to argue more, I skidded to a halt as a shriek split the night.

seeing how small Sophie looked next to the massive beasts. But in seconds, they receded peacefully, the water swallowing them back up, and Sophie crossed to me.

My warrior queen, I thought, her face drained of color except for two bright spots on her cheeks, her shoulders hunched inside my old jumper. I wanted to hug her. To take her inside and show her how much she meant to me, already, inexplicably so. And still, I remained frozen, the fear and loss I'd felt as a boy reminding me of what happens when you love someone.

They got taken away.

The little voice in my head finally snapped me out of it, and I crossed my arms in front of my chest, forcing a bravado I didn't feel.

"Well, that was intense, eh?" I aimed for lightness but realized I missed the mark when Sophie just studied me with her wide blue eyes, her teeth buried in that thick lower lip of hers. I wanted to bite her just there too but had to dig my fingers into my palms to stop myself from reaching out to her.

"It was terrifying. I can imagine even more so for you." Sophie's voice was gentle, as though she was soothing a wild horse, and I bristled at her tone. I didn't need to be something else she tamed.

"It wasn't terrifying. It's just a shock to see them. It was foolish of you to go over there. Do you have any idea how quickly you can drown if the water had come down on top of you?" It was better if I went on the defense, I realized.

"And do you have a better suggestion on how I should have handled that?" Sophie arched a brow at me, and I felt her call my manhood into question.

"You should have stayed back and let me handle it," I said, turning to hike toward the castle, furious with myself and with her. "I've been dealing with this for years, not you. It's not your problem to solve."

"Oh, so just get out? You're not one of us? Seems to me I've been exactly what you've been waiting for," Sophie said. At her words, I whirled and stunned myself by reaching for her. I wanted to throttle her.

Instead, I kissed her.

I kissed her until spots danced in front of my eyes and I could barely breathe for wanting her. I kissed her until the memory of the fear I'd felt faded away and a new fear filled me. A fear of losing this incredible woman before me—both tenderhearted and fierce—who looked at me as though she knew all my secrets. I kissed her until nothing else mattered except that I had to fill myself with her taste, her scent, her very essence. Without a second thought, I picked Sophie up and tossed her over my shoulder, making a beeline for the stables, which I knew would be empty at these hours. Kicking the door to the tack room open, I grabbed a clean horse blanket and headed for the hay room. There, I flicked on the rusty overhead light, which barely shined a pall across the floor, and tossed the blanket over some loose hay.

"Lachlan!" Sophie gasped. I slipped her down my body, already hard with need for her, and found her mouth once more. There I lost myself, adrenaline pounding through me, and slipped my hands beneath her jumper to find smooth skin. I needed this woman more than I needed my next breath and, if she said no to me now, I might well and truly lose my mind.

so she lay back on the blanket, and she blinked up at me in surprise.

"Forget who was down there?" I asked, acknowledging the surprise on her face.

"No...I just..." Sophie shook her head and seemed to have some internal battle with herself. "Nobody I've been with before is able to lift me so easily. It's...disconcerting."

"Stop dating weak men," I said, kissing my way up the soft skin of her stomach, and then lapping her hard nipple through the silk of her bra. She gasped, arching into my mouth, and I wet the silk, enjoying how all of her softness shifted beneath me. Sophie was a dream come to life, and I needed to be inside her.

"Sophie." I palmed both her breasts, tweaking her nipples lightly, and she moaned again. "I want to be inside you. But I don't have a condom."

"I'm protected," Sophie said, blinking up at me. "I have an IUD."

I reared back, ripping my shirt over my head and divesting myself of my shoes and jeans faster than anything I'd done in my life, worried she'd change her mind before I could rid myself of this burning need to be inside her. Sliding between her legs, I rubbed my cock against her, feeling how wet she was for me, and played with her while I drew out the anticipation. Remembering her words about the men she dated, I wrapped my arms around her back, and she let out a shriek when I rolled so she was on top of me.

"How did you?" Sophie gasped, slapping a palm down on my chest to steady herself, the other hand brushing her mass of tangled auburn hair from her face.

"I'm strong, Sophie." I laughed up at her, reveling in the sight of her straddling me. Never had I seen a woman more beautiful, her skin flushed pink with desire, her hair in a riotous mass around her head, and her large breasts heaving with each breath.

"I see that." Sophie gasped, steadying herself.

"You are, quite possibly, the most beautiful woman I've ever seen. Just look at you..." I said, adoration in my voice. I traced my hands up her sides, feeling her body twitch under my palms, delighting in the fact that I had this power over her. "Silky skin. Stunning curves. Breasts I could lose myself in for hours. That mouth I've been wanting to bite for days now. You're a goddess, Sophie, a goddamn goddess. And I swear if you don't take me inside you this instant, I'll die."

"Oh." Sophie let out a breath of air and then lifted herself so that I slid inside her warm, wet heat, and I shouted as I bucked up into her, not caring about yesterday or tomorrow because absolution was delivered at this moment. If I never woke again, I'd die the happiest of men at the hands of a warrior goddess the likes of which this world had not seen in ages.

When Sophie rocked us both to completion, her eyes wide in shock, we stared at each other, our chests heaving as we said a thousand things with our eyes.

But none with our words.

Instead, we grinned sheepishly at each other, gathering our clothes hastily like naughty teenagers, and crept from the stables in the darkness. Racing through the rain to the front of the castle, I stole one more kiss from Sophie before she disappeared to her room without another word, and I went to the lounge to pour myself a dram of whisky and stare out at the moody waters of Loch Mirren.

I didn't know what tomorrow would bring, but I did know that everything had changed. If only I knew what to do about it.

CHAPTER TWENTY

Sophie

"Do you have to go?" I worried my bottom lip as Matthew packed his bag. It had been four days since Lachlan had rocked my world in the stables, and I'd busied myself with learning more about my magick and trying to figure out why a second stone—an emerald this time—had shown up in my dirk. If we were going by deeds alone, Matthew thought it was due to my generosity with the townspeople, but I wondered if it had to do with protecting Lachlan from the Kelpies.

The insanely terrifying and intoxicatingly beautiful Kelpies.

At that moment, I'd discovered what I thought might be my magick, and I'd quietly been sneaking away to practice it where the others couldn't weigh in on what I was doing. And if I was correct, I was pretty sure that compulsion was my power. Which, frankly, was astounding to me. For so long, I'd been battling to be heard, and now my gift was my voice.

Talk about revelations, eh?

"Though it kills me to do so, yes, I have to go. I know I'm supposed to be on sabbatical, but they really do need my help," Matthew said, neatly rolling his socks. The professor shouldering his classes at school had been in a car accident and would take a while to recover. Since Matthew was technically able to assist, he'd offered to cut his sabbatical short to help the department out. I'd miss him terribly and was pouting more than just a bit this morning.

"You haven't even seen the Kelpies yet." I played my last card, knowing how desperately Matthew had wanted to see a myth come to life and crossed my fingers, hoping he'd take the bait.

"You have no idea how much this breaks my heart." Matthew leveled a serious look at me. "But I'm a man of honor. They really do need me. And since I'm so enthralled with everything happening here, I can't claim to be working all that hard on my book."

"Well, maybe there are some ideas for a new book. A *better* book," I wheedled, leaning against the bed as he ducked his head into the tall armoire to search for any last items of clothing. Outside, the rain pattered at the window, and a dull gray light filtered into the room.

"Sophie. I love you. I don't want to leave you. I'd stay if I could, but they need me. And this will give me even more freedom to come back once this class is over for the summer. It's only a four-week intensive class so, by the time I finish up, the weather should have warmed, and I can be back on a plane out here. You have a phone. Call me every day and fill me in on the developments with Lachlan."

"Ha! Like anything will develop there. The man is acting like he wasn't just inside me days ago." It rankled the way Lachlan treated me with utmost respect, only consulting me on things relating to the Order. Gone was the banter, the needling, and the frustration he'd directed my way. Instead, I'd been served with polite "customer service" Lachlan, and I had to say—I was deeply annoyed.

"From what it sounds like, the Kelpies have played a huge role in a major personal tragedy in his life. Be gentle, Soph. He's grieving." Matthew rounded the bed and put his arms around my shoulders. I looked up into his warm eyes, needing his support, and my own eyes filled.

"I'm grieving too," I reminded him, not caring if I sounded petulant.

"I know you are. And you will be for a long time. I can't help but wonder if Arthur set this all up so you'd be too distracted to realize how much you miss him." Matthew pulled me into his chest and spoke into my hair.

"I wouldn't put it past him. But even Arthur wasn't powerful enough to engineer the Stone of Truth or pull magickal beings from the loch," I murmured against his chest. "I miss him."

"I know you do. He was one of a kind." Matthew stroked my back. "But you have to be strong and see this through." He pulled back and brought a finger beneath my chin, tilting my face up to his.

"I'm going to," I said.

"This...this right here, Sophie? It's the stuff of fairy tales. And you get to live it. In real life. It's not a movie or a made-up story told to you at bedtime with a cup of cocoa. It's the real deal. You're *magick*. Just think about that for a second. You are well and truly a magickal knight of awesomeness. You get to do that. Right now. Right here. And the hunky man of the castle? He could be yours too. It's all at your doorstep. You don't need me to open the door for you. You've *got* this."

"You're the best." I hugged him fiercely once more, hating that he had to leave but loving him for his amazing pep talk. He'd always been one of my biggest champions, and his words soothed me, even if the truth of them made me nervous. Particularly the hunky man of the castle part. Frankly, I wasn't entirely upset that Lachlan had been giving me a bit of the cold shoulder. Our fire had run so hot the other night that I think I also needed to step away from the flames to cool off. And if I was being honest, I was used to being abandoned, so it felt about par for the course whenever I let myself get close to someone.

Not that we were all that close, I reminded myself. I still didn't know things like what his favorite color was or if he liked mashed potatoes. But I did know he had an unshakeable code of honor, that everyone in the village spoke highly of him, and he had a lightning-quick wit when he decided to use it. And that he hated numbers. I'd spent more time in his office when he wasn't there, digging deeper into the past years' accounts and noting any issues I'd discovered. And then, helpless not to, I'd stayed up late to start working on a brand campaign for MacAlpine Castle. I couldn't help myself, really and, of course, Sir Buster, Lachlan, and Graham would all be heavily featured in my campaign. Because nothing drew tourists more than a cute dog and sexy men in kilts. It would be like shooting fish in a barrel once I started my advertising run. But in the meantime, I still had to delve deeper into the Order of Caledonia.

"Matthew!" Hilda called from downstairs, and Matthew zipped his bag.

"That's my ride. I love you. Remember, nobody puts Baby in a corner, okay?" Matthew said, quoting our favorite line from *Dirty Dancing*. He'd used it through the years when he'd seen my insecurities rise and when I had tried to hide in the background. Giving him a kiss, I waited until he left and then pulled a raincoat over my sweater and wound my way through the long hallways of the castle and to the back entrance, where I came upon Archie having a conversation with Sir Buster.

"We've discussed this, laddie. You still have to go outside to do your business even in the rain," Archie lectured. Sir Buster looked up at him, his teeth bared in a growl, and I laughed despite my sadness at Matthew leaving.

"It looks to be slowing. At least I'm hopeful," I said, and Sir Buster cast wide eyes full of doubt at me.

"Off to work on your driving?" Archie reached for keys hanging from a peg by the door. I'd approached Archie about a car earlier that week, and once he'd realized that I had no clue how to drive a stick shift, he'd taken me out in the pasture in his old farm truck. Once he was confident enough that I understood the basics, he'd given me the go-ahead to take the truck out on my own to practice driving around the long dirt road that hugged the edges of the farm. It was nice being able to learn without pressure, and I'd started to grow a touch more confident with my skills.

Once I was far enough away from the castle, I'd taken to practicing my magick and my sword skills, knowing full well that I'd likely have to face the Kelpies once more.

Not that stabbing a horse made of water would do much, but it was hard to say where the dangers ahead could come from. If someone had told me last month that I'd be a magickal Knight in Scotland battling mythological water horses, I'd have quietly backed away like Homer Simpson disappearing into a bush when his neighbor talked too much. Bending to pat Sir Buster on the head, who tolerated my touch just barely, I raced from the castle to the old truck and hopped inside. The rain had already slowed, but I didn't want to get my leggings too wet. My Amazon order had arrived this week, and I finally had a few pieces of clothing that were more suited to the moody Scottish weather.

After a few failed attempts at starting the truck, I eventually managed to get it in gear and took off across the field, bumping along the muddy road until the castle faded out of sight behind a long stretch of trees. There, with nobody to watch, I spent time starting and stopping the truck, reversing, and shifting gears as I recited all of the rules that Archie had taught me. Once I'd deemed my driving lesson done for the day, I pulled up to a small cluster of trees that hid me from view and jumped out of the truck. Earlier that week, I had cajoled Archie into loading a few bales of hay for me to practice my sword skills on, and I'd placed them in front of the trees. Now, with the rain having disappeared, I lent myself to the task of keeping my skills fresh.

For two hours, I practiced until sweat dripped down my back beneath my T-shirt and my breath came out in little puffs of air. Finally, after I'd well and truly stabbed the last bale of hay, I stepped back and returned the dirk to the front seat of the truck. There I gulped water while I stared down at the blade, wondering how the jewels had fused into the metal and if it had been my standing for Lachlan that had caused the second one to show up. Wasn't courage one of the knightly duties as well? Frustration at having no clear-cut answers made me want to stomp my foot. I liked things that fit into neat boxes, like spreadsheets, and not these random and weird rules of magick. If there were even rules.

I wondered if the Stone of Truth could read my thoughts.

I was curious about the stone, but I knew that trying to see it was a death wish. Instead, I poked at Agnes until she'd told me more of the history behind it. How it had passed briefly through certain famous inventors' hands, and how their brush with it had enhanced modern-day society. The problem was, if the stone ever fell into the wrong hands—like those of a ruler like Hitler—it would be catastrophic to the world. Not that Hitler hadn't already been catastrophic, but the heights of power that someone with the stone could achieve were unimaginable. Agnes assured me that protecting the stone from discovery was one of the greatest gifts I could give to humanity. That alone had bolstered me, providing me with the necessary motivation to discover more about my magick, and I'd been serious with my training ever since.

Now, I reached into the car and brought out a bag of treats for the crows. Unknown to anyone, they were also helping me with my magick.

Already, they waited, lining the branches of the trees above me, their heads cocked as in question. I stepped in front of the truck and leaned back against it, studying the line of crows that waited patiently for me to speak.

"Larry. Come down to me." I spoke from my core, pulling the thread of power I felt there, and the bird I'd nicknamed Larry dove from the branch and landed at my feet. "Turn in a circle." Larry dutifully turned in a circle, his wings flapping out awkwardly as he hopped around.

I repeated the exercise with Moe and Curly, having named the three crows after Arthur's favorite slapstick comedians. Each day I'd command them to do something different, as I knew that crows were highly intelligent. Already they'd taken to leaving gifts around the hay bales, shiny bits and bobs they found on their wanders and, just this morning, I'd found a coin on the ledge outside my bedroom window.

I was learning that if I used my voice in a particular manner, the crows would answer to me. I was certain that was what had happened the other night when I'd commanded the Kelpies to leave us alone. Maybe my magick was a play on the whole idea that the pen was mightier than the sword, just that my words weren't written.

"What are you doing?"

I jumped, scattering the birdseed I'd brought for the crows, and turned to see Lachlan looking far too handsome bundled into a green canvas coat with flannel lining, worn jeans, and sturdy boots. I wanted to climb him like a tree.

Instead, I turned back to where the crows pecked at the

birdseed, shooting curious glances at Lachlan as he rounded the front of the truck.

"You scared me," I said, a fine trembling starting through my body.

"I'm sorry, I should have called out to you. I suppose you could have thrown your dirk at me." Lachlan studied the torn bales of hay. "Practicing?"

"Yes, I felt it best to stay strong with my sword skills." I shifted, unsure of our path forward or what to say to him. This man had been inside me days ago, and now I could barely bring myself to look him in the eyes.

"You're already excellent. One of the best swordswomen I've seen. What's with the birds? Making friends?" Lachlan asked. His hand strayed unconsciously to his neck, and I was reminded of the coin he wore for his mother. The same coin the birds had given her. Suspicion worked through me.

"Yes, I am. I'm, um..." Shyness crept in.

"It's okay if you talk to birds," Lachlan said, his voice going soft as he edged closer to me. "I like that."

"I am. I do," I sputtered. "I've been working on compulsion actually. I think it's what my power is. The birds are cool about it, and I give them plenty of rewards once we've worked through it."

"Is that right?" Lachlan rocked back on his heels, his eyes going to the birds once more. "Do they like you?"

"They do. They brought me a gift. Well, many gifts. But this was on my window ledge this morning." I dug in my pocket and handed him the coin, my heart stuttering in my chest as his eyes rounded.

"It's..." Lachlan's voice trailed off as he turned the coin over and cleared his throat. "It's the same..."

"As the one you wear for your mother?" I whispered.

"Aye. And the year she died," Lachlan murmured, looking closely at the date. When his tortured eyes lifted from the coin to mine, my heart cracked open. "I can't stay away from you, Sophie. I'm not sure I even want to. But I don't know how to do this, to love you. I'm so scared to lose someone again."

There it was, the truth laid bare, scattered across the dirt like the birdseed I tossed to the crows. Was his truth an offering worthy of my taking?

"Everybody leaves me," I rushed out before I lost my nerve. "Starting with my parents walking away from me like I was nothing to them up to my most recent boyfriend. Nobody stays."

We stared at each other, our vulnerabilities circling the other's, the crows having stopped eating to watch us. I wondered if they understood our words or merely sensed the tension in the air.

"I can't promise that I'll stay..." Lachlan said, his voice cracking.

"And I can't promise that I won't leave," I admitted. Though at this moment, I wanted nothing more than to stay. To stay here in this wild and fierce land, where magick coiled itself around the Scottish landscape, creeping its way into legends and stories told at the pub, like the wisteria that climbed up Lottie's garden shed.

"So what do we do?" Lachlan took a step closer to me, and I felt it, as though a chain connected us, every small movement of his rocking my core.

I stared at him, my mind going to Arthur and his infectious joy for love. He'd never hesitated to love, jumping in fully clothed and eyes wide open, and no matter how many times he'd been burned, he'd always kept his head above water.

"Love isn't meant to be tidy, Sophie. It's messy and uncertain. But oh, my sweet Sophie, it's always, always worth it. Never close your heart to love that is offered. You can't possibly know the sweetness of the path you'll walk together." Arthur's words echoed in my mind, spoken to me in various iterations through the years. But he'd always told me to take a chance. Maybe it was time for me to finally listen to his advice.

"I think we have to take a chance," I whispered. My words hung suspended in the air between us, and even the crows stilled as though waiting for Lachlan's answer. He turned the coin over in his palm, studying it, before holding it out to me.

"What are the odds?" Lachlan mused, his lips pursed. "If I was a betting man, I'd say this is our lucky coin."

"Our?" I asked, hope filling me. *Maybe this time.*

"Ours," Lachlan said, stepping forward to take me into his arms. "I want to be with you, Sophie. It terrifies me, I won't lie. I *can't* lie about that. If you're patient with me, I think we can learn, together, how to trust in love again."

Lachlan claimed my lips in the softest of kisses, drawing out the moment, as warmth flooded through me. Unlike the flames that had consumed us the other night, this warmth comforted, as though to promise me that I'd never feel cold again.

When the crows squawked in unison, a raucous

cacophony, we pulled apart and laughed, looking to where they'd fluttered to a branch.

My heart stilled.

Beneath the branch, a horse, no, a *unicorn*, hoofed the ground, blowing out a soft breath. She nickered softly, shaking her glorious mane of cascading hair, her horn a stunning pearlescent white. She bowed her head to us, stamping her hoof into the ground as though giving us her stamp of approval as her horn lit with an effervescent light. In seconds, she turned and thundered back into the forest. I remained frozen, tears glazing my eyes, as love for this beautiful and mysterious land overwhelmed me.

"I think she approves," Lachlan said softly at my ear, pulling me close to him. Still, I stared into the forest, hoping for one more glimpse, and briefly debated trying to use compulsion to force the unicorn back to me. But, no, I realized that would be wrong. Compulsion shouldn't be used on something so wild and free. She'd given us a gift this day, blessing us with her presence, and I realized now what Arthur had meant about taking risks.

Without them, you'd never see the unicorn.

CHAPTER TWENTY-ONE

LACHLAN

The next few weeks passed in an almost blissful and peaceful manner. I winced at the thought, worried that even thinking about how peaceful it had been might ruin the streak of luck we'd had of late. It was as though everything was falling into place, and nobody, myself included, would comment on it lest we jinx the powers that be and bring doom back to Loren Brae.

As we neared summer, the weather began to warm, and the days grew lighter. Sophie and I had fallen into an easy pattern of spending our days buried in our own tasks, and our nights buried in each other. I couldn't get enough of her, and I kept waiting for this initial first rush of lust to wear off. The heady intoxication that came with new love was addictive, yet I couldn't help but worry what was around the corner. What would happen when the newness

out at where the car park had begun to fill up. As mutually understood between men, we didn't meet each other's eyes as we spoke of our feelings. "When you're used to rough seas, calm sailing must feel like a warning."

"Aye..." I trailed off, struck by his words. Was it possible that I was so used to living in my own trauma that any sense of normalcy seemed foreign to me? Could it be something so simple as that? "Since when did you become a bloody therapist?"

"Och, and it's a bartender's job, isn't it then? You can't think I'm just slinging pints and wooing pretty ladies all day, can ye?" Graham demanded, putting on an affronted look.

"And here was me thinking you were nothing more than a glorified waiter," I poked at him, banter restoring our balance.

"Better than a pretty boy trussed up like a supermodel to sell tickets to the castle. At least I know how to work hard." Graham nodded to where Sophie approached, camera in hand. "Your photo shoot awaits, mi' lord."

"Fecking eejit," I muttered, but low enough so that Sophie didn't hear as she smiled widely up at me.

"You both look amazing," Sophie squealed, and helpless not to, I bent to kiss her. Her lips tasted like the mint tea she favored, and I had to stop myself from thinking of how cuddly she'd been in bed that morning or I was sure to embarrass myself in front of the tourists that had begun to queue. "I can't wait to take your photos. I've two particular spots in mind, if you both want to follow me?"

"Both?" Graham piped up, his brows lowering.

"You didn't think you were getting out of this, did you,

Graham? You're positively the face of the village, right? Everybody goes to the Tipsy Thistle after they tour the castle, and you're quite the draw. Come on, then." Sophie waved to us, already turning the corner of the castle, and Graham turned to me with an aggrieved look.

"Don't start with me." I held up a hand and laughed. "Looks like you're the cover model now, boyo."

Graham muttered a few less than polite words under his breath and then sighed, admitting defeat. Nobody could say no to Sophie once she got an idea stuck in her head.

"Want to get out of here for a couple of days? I've been invited to tour a few distilleries that want me to stock their whisky. We could even maybe get a round of golf in if the weather holds," Graham said. "Maybe being away will give you a little time to clear your head and settle into getting comfortable with being in a real relationship. Spaces in your togetherness and all that."

A relationship.

It struck me then that I'd never truly let myself be in a real relationship before. No wonder I was on tenterhooks the whole time. Between fear of losing Sophie, and I guess fear of losing myself, I couldn't quite settle into contentment.

Maybe a lads' holiday was exactly what I needed.

"You know what? That sounds perfect. When are you going?" I asked as we rounded the castle to find Sophie holding a treat in the air for Sir Buster, who sat dutifully in his kilt on the steps in front of the majestic front doors.

"Tomorrow. Think she'll let you go?" Graham asked, needling me a bit.

"Of course. I can make my own decisions." I shot

Graham a nasty look, and he threw his head back and laughed. Turning, I saw Sophie had her camera trained on us and pasted a smile on my face.

"What's that grumpy look for, Lachlan?" Sophie asked, tugging on the strap that held the camera around her neck.

"Graham thinks you won't let me go with him to visit some distilleries for a couple of nights," I said, neatly throwing Graham under the bus.

"Och, now, I didn't say it quite like that..." Graham protested, raising his hands in the air.

"I don't have a say in what Lachlan does." Sophie narrowed her eyes at Graham. "He's free to go wherever he wants."

Why did that sound like a threat? I waited to see what Graham would say, as navigating this was new territory for me.

"Och, I know you're a fine lass, Sophie. But not all women let their men off on lads' holidays is all. Some get weird about it."

"What are your plans?" Sophie scrunched up her nose, and I realized she was considering whether she was supposed to get upset or not.

"I want to visit a couple of distilleries that are asking for me to stock the pub with their bottles. And maybe a round of golf if the weather suits," Graham said.

"I really don't see why that would be an issue." Sophie shrugged and then stilled, her eyes darting out to the loch. "Oh, well, maybe I do."

"The Kelpies have been quiet," I murmured, wrapping an arm around her waist for a moment. "It's likely a good time for me to go."

"That's true. Things have much improved, haven't they? I think you should go. It'll give me time to do a deep delve into the accounts. I'm almost ready to launch our new advertising campaign, once I get my images and branding down, so this will be a perfect time for me to work on things."

"I thought the accounts were doing better?" I frowned down at Sophie.

"They are, but you're not in the clear yet. There are still some debts to be paid, and we have to repair the roof this year. I'd like to make a list of renovations and upkeep, and then prioritize them to see what can fit in the budget this year and what can wait for another time." Sophie's eyes gleamed, as though diving into spreadsheets was the most exciting thing in the world.

"I'll admit, I haven't been able to make many big improvements the last few years. We've been suffering, and that's the truth of it. We dearly need a good high season, or I'm not sure what next year will bring for the castle, or Loren Brae." Worry filled me as I looked back out to the loch, my eyes landing on the island where the Stone of Truth supposedly sat. You'd think our efforts to protect the stone would give us a miraculous windfall of luck, and instead we still struggled. I hated thinking about money and the constant burden that all our people now shouldered.

Eased a bit, by Sophie. Of that much, I was sure. I'd taken the time to look into the purchase agreement for the castle and had learned that her uncle had also gained many properties with the agreement. Somehow, Sophie had managed to arrange free rent for the year for those properties and was determined to keep that fact secret. I respected

a stack of folders. Soon, I was in my happy place, running numbers, making notes, and organizing files. An hour later, I winced as I came across the most recent bank statement.

Lachlan hadn't been lying when he said the castle was in dire straits. I hoped, with the terms of the trust, to be able to change that around this year. I knew that Arthur had stipulated that in the first year I could use some of the money for necessary improvements in the castle, and I planned to be judicious in where I would choose to use that. First, because I didn't want to fall into the role of being the sugar mama who came in and took care of everything and, secondly, because I still needed time to see how things ran around here and decide where the money would be put to best use. Even though I now owned the castle and could paint it pink and decorate it in velvet leopard print furniture if I wanted to, I respected the heritage enough to want to make sensible changes. To be honest, the castle didn't belong to me even if I *was* the owner. It belonged to the people of Loren Brae and, as their Knight, I was meant to be in service to them.

At that thought, I kicked back in my chair for a moment, steepling my fingers as I stared out of the small arched window in front of Lachlan's desk that overlooked Loch Mirren. It was a blustery day, though no rain fell, and the surface of the water looked jagged like someone had roughed it up with sandpaper. The Order of Caledonia weighed heavily on my mind, as a third jewel had yet to appear in my dirk, and I wondered how else I could be of service to Loren Brae. Being a knight was not all it was cracked up to be, I realized, particularly when we weren't in times of war like the olden days. So could I fight a modern-day battle? It was what I hoped I was doing with my tourism campaign that I planned to launch once I got the images back from my graphic designer.

I was meant to notify the next of the Order.

Hilda had informed me of that particular fact earlier this week, telling me that she'd started a list of potential candidates for me to recruit. It made me laugh at the time, but now my stomach swam with nerves. How could I, Sophie MacKnight, recruit someone to stand for the Order of Caledonia when I hadn't yet been able to complete my own rite of passage? Sure, the Kelpies had been quiet of late but, as Archie had warned me, that didn't mean they were satisfied. The Stone of Truth needed constant protection, and it appeared that once challenges had been met, the next of the Order would need to start theirs. And on it went, until the Stone was once more fully protected, though how it was keeping track, I did not know.

And maybe I didn't need to know. Just because I didn't understand something didn't make it any less real, I'd come to learn. The day the unicorn had appeared before Lachlan and me had been one of the most thrilling and magickal moments of my life. Though my practical mind wanted to dissect it and try to find a reason for the existence of this unicorn, my heart begged me to stop.

Just stop.

Some things needed to be accepted for what they were. Unequivocally and without explanation. The unicorn was a reminder to me that love was much the same. I couldn't shove it into a neat little box on a spreadsheet and mark it off my to-do list. Love wasn't something to be accomplished, it was an ongoing living and breathing challenge. And one I was ready to accept with Lachlan, if he'd let me.

Shaking my head as my thoughts drifted back to Lachlan, once again, I opened the last manila envelope I'd found buried in the back of the bottom drawer. Humming, I scanned the contents, flipping rapidly through the pages, and then my hands stilled when I saw my name.

Sophie MacKnight.

Five Million Pounds.

Six months at MacAlpine Castle.

The words blurred before my eyes, and my chest hitched as my breath caught, and I pushed myself back from the desk to take a moment to steady my breathing. Once I'd calmed myself, I forced myself to read the contract in whole. Then I read it again, just to make sure I wasn't misinterpreting anything or letting my emotions cloud my judgment.

My lips thinned as I pressed them tightly together, as anger coiled low in my stomach. *He'd known.*

Despite all his bluster and initial anger, Lachlan had known that I was coming.

The sale of MacAlpine Castle had included a clause that upon Arthur's death, if the caretakers of the castle could convince one Sophie MacKnight to stay at the castle of her own free will for at least six months, then five million pounds would be put into a trust for the caretakers to use for castle upkeep.

And he knew he'd have to find a way to get me to stay...

And what better way to do that than to make me fall in love? I tasted bitterness on my tongue, like I'd bitten into black licorice candy, and I rose from the desk, my fists clenched. I needed to rage—to throw something—but I didn't know what. I stared blindly out the window at Loch Mirren, as anger gave way to sadness, and then, finally, to acceptance.

I wasn't one to rage. I didn't say a word when my parents left me. Not even when my mother didn't choose me when Harold had read the will. Why would I rage now when I understood that Lachlan, like everyone else, had just been using me for my money. I couldn't blame him, not really. He was loyal to this castle, his only home and the place where he'd lost his mother. Loren Brae was his life, his first love, and I knew, without a doubt, that he'd do anything for his people.

I just refused to be his sacrifice.

I had fallen in love with this castle and these people, and I had wanted to be here to see all my branding dreams become reality. Had wanted to believe that what I saw in Lachlan could last. But despite Loren Brae's enthusiastic welcome, once again I was only wanted for what I could give and do.

It isn't me they truly want. Just like my parents.

And if I stayed and continued to be the pawn, my heart would break into more pieces than I could recover.

My heart is already too fragile for more loss.

It's time to go.

Gathering my strength, I made up my mind and rushed to my apartment.

There, I packed my bag quickly, glad that I'd been prudent with my shopping, and returned to the office once I'd finished. Digging out a notebook, I dashed off a note, and then flipped my checkbook open, writing out the full amount that Lachlan would have been given if I'd lasted the whole six months.

I wasn't going to be the reason that MacAlpine Castle wouldn't get the money it needed, but I also couldn't stay. I would compose an email to Harold asking him to draft the documents to transfer the deed to Hilda for the price of one whole pound. With that and the five million pounds, they'd be set for a long time.

As for me?

I'd have to find my own way. But it wasn't here, in this place, with this man who had knowingly used me for my money. I'd just have to learn to get better at recognizing red flags. A hot man in a kilt did not a partner make, I reminded myself, as I rolled my suitcase down the hallway.

"Moooooooooooooo."

The most plaintive moo that I'd ever heard stopped me in my tracks, and I turned to see Clyde behind me in the hallway, his big stocky head lifted to the sky, wailing his heart out.

"Clyde, I'm sorry. I can't stay. Not like this," I told him, waving my hand in the air.

"Moooooooooooooo."

Another heartbreaking wail brought tears to my eyes, and I shook my head, turning away and hurrying down the corridor. I refused to cry over Lachlan, but damn if a ghost coo wasn't about to make me lose my shit. Racing to the back stairs, I grabbed the truck keys from the hook by the door and ran across the lot, tossing my suitcase in the back seat of the pickup. I hoped Archie would forgive me for stealing his ride, but I figured with this new windfall he could buy a new and improved truck. Plus, once I got to the airport, I'd leave the keys under the seat and let him know where I'd parked.

Resolved, I only stalled twice before rocketing down the drive, leaving my heart and MacAlpine Castle in the rearview mirror.

CHAPTER TWENTY-THREE

LACHLAN

I was a goner.

Well and truly gone, as Graham delighted in reminding me on the golf course the next day, as once again I brought up something Sophie had done to make me laugh. He wasn't far wrong, I realized. Even as we'd driven away from the castle, I'd felt like I was leaving a piece of me behind and hated that Sophie wasn't with me to tour the distilleries. Which was silly, really, the woman didn't even *like* whisky.

How had I fallen for a woman who didn't like whisky?

And fallen I think I had. We'd danced around the word "love" with each other, neither of us saying it, and yet, here I was. Well and truly in love with Sophie. I admired her resilience, her intelligence, and her willingness to take risks. She'd crossed an ocean while battling grief and bravely taken on a challenge that many would have run screaming from. On top of that, she'd taken a chance on me—a well-documented flight risk—and had made my days brighter for it. She was one in a million and, when I got home, I planned to tell her just that.

"Och, you're just jealous, ye bastard," I said, lining up my shot. We'd lucked out with some fair weather thus far, though I noted the presence of darkening clouds hovering on the horizon.

"Might be," Graham admitted, his eyes narrowing as the ringer went off on my mobile phone in my golf bag. "I thought we said no phones."

"I'm sorry. I was certain I'd turned the ringer off. I never use the damn thing anyway," I said. It was true too, though I'd found myself checking it since I left, wondering why I hadn't had a text from Sophie. Not that I'd sent her one, but usually she'd forward me a funny picture of Sir Buster or a cute note. I did my best to respond, but I hated typing on the phone. Still, I saved every one of her notes, sometimes re-reading them to bring a smile to my face.

Yeesh, I *was* besotted, wasn't I?

Digging in my bag, I pulled out the phone and went to turn it off when I saw it was Hilda calling. Answering, I waved away Graham's protest.

"Hilda. What's up? Everything okay?"

"No, it's not okay," Hilda said, her voice dead serious, and I straightened, motioning to Graham to come over.

"What's wrong?" I stilled.

Graham could be a pain in the arse at times, but when he heard my tone, he picked up our balls and hoisted his bag onto his shoulder, already moving toward the club-

loopy signature. My brain, quite simply, could not compute what I was seeing.

"There's a note." Hilda handed me a piece of paper.

Lachlan,

I'm worthy of more than this. Even you must know that. Especially you.

However, I'm willing to take the blame. I should have acknowledged

the red flags when I saw them. Mea culpa and all that. Here's a check for the full

amount. I release you from the clause, and you're no longer indebted

to take one for the team in order to save the village. Your honor, though

skewed, is admirable. Your people deserve you. But you do not deserve

my love. Sophie.

My heart cracked open, and dots danced in front of my eyes. I had to steady myself on the side of the table, my hands digging into the wood so hard that my knuckles cracked.

"I don't understand," I gasped.

"I do."

I whirled at Archie's voice. "What did you do?"

"*I* didn't do anything. But I read the contract that Sophie found on your desk. You must have never opened your mail." Archie crossed the room and poured himself a dram. I noticed his hand was shaking, and I wondered if it was from fear or anger.

"Explain," I ordered, feeling close to flipping the table if someone didn't tell me what the hell was going on.

"There was a clause in the sale of the castle that if Sophie stayed for at least six months, here at the castle of her own free will, then the caretakers would be awarded five million pounds to use to care for the needs of the castle and the town," Hilda said.

My heart skipped a beat.

Time slowed, as I imagined Sophie happily digging through the books in my office, content to linger over spreadsheets, discovering this.

And I hadn't been there to tell her I hadn't known about it.

I hadn't told her I loved her before I'd left either.

Instead, I'd given her the equivalent of a pat on the head and went on my merry way.

Now, she was somewhere in Scotland, convinced that another man was just using her for her money.

I stood, frozen, as sadness mixed with rage in my gut.

But she'd left me anyway, just like I'd thought she would, hadn't she? Instead of asking me about this paperwork, which I could have readily told her that I had no knowledge of and would have happily torn up in her face, she'd judged me and found me wanting. Sophie MacKnight was a coward, I realized, and my lip curled with anger. She honestly thought that I would participate in something like this? The same man who wouldn't let her pay for dinner and refused to let her spend money on unnecessary improvements to the castle? How could I love a woman who clearly didn't know me at all?

And it seemed I didn't know her either.

"Lachlan!" Graham slapped a hand on my shoulder, and I realized that he'd been calling my name for a while now as I'd stood frozen, my thoughts tumbling over each other in rapid succession. When I raised my eyes to his, what he saw there caused his face to pale. "Man, stay with me. We've got bigger problems. The Kelpies."

I turned to see the Kelpies forming by the island—in broad daylight—and I knew that Loren Brae was in trouble. Racing from the room, I grabbed a sword that I'd placed by the door and ran, full speed, down the drive to the edge of the loch. Once there, I saw people screaming and running for their houses, doors being slammed, and on the wind, one tiny, furious howl carried to me.

My blood chilled as I turned to see Sir Buster, his furious body paddling rapidly in the cold waters of the loch. Without another thought, I dove in after him.

CHAPTER TWENTY-FOUR

SOPHIE

I didn't make it far.

It seemed that driving the truck on a single road with no traffic was much easier than navigating things like roundabouts and driving on the opposite side of the road. I'd barely made it to the next town over before I'd found a small B&B willing to take me in on a moment's notice. I'd fallen into bed, the adrenaline rush from the drive and the overwhelm from my discovery sending me into an exhausted sleep that saw me well into late morning. When I'd awoken, blinking in confusion at my surroundings, I peeled myself from the bed at the gentle knocking on my door.

"It's time for checkout," the woman had informed me with a polite smile on her face.

"Can I book another night? And do you have Wi-Fi?"

I'd paid for another night on the spot and given her extra to deliver a simple lunch of soup and bread. Frankly, it was all I could stomach, as I tried to work through the pain that currently was immobilizing.

I didn't want to leave Lachlan.

I didn't want to leave Scotland.

I loved Loren Brae.

I felt like a different person there. I didn't want to have to go, but how could I stay, knowing what I now knew? Torn, I'd spent the last hour looking up flights and trying to decide what to do.

If I left, I couldn't go back to my job for at least a year. I'd even called Harold to read me the terms of the will again, and they were exacting and very clear. No job for one year. No thirty million dollars if I left MacAlpine Castle.

Not that I really cared that much about the money, but I also wasn't stupid. It was the kind of money that I could really make a difference with, and I shouldn't make whatever my next decision was lightly. Feeling trapped, I paced my room, stopping when my phone rang.

Seeing Lachlan's name on the screen, with a little heart emoji after it, felt like a knife in my gut. I stared at the screen, immobilized, until my voicemail finally picked up. Dropping to the bed, I buried my face in my hands.

I didn't know what to do.

Was this what Arthur had sent me here for? I felt like he'd been cagey in his dealings and now I wasn't sure what to think. He'd already set me up to teach me a lesson about my mother, and now was this his sneaky way of teaching me about my own worth? Even for Arthur, this seemed a step too far.

Two hours later, I was no closer to a decision, though I'd all but worn a path in the rug on the floor with my pacing. True to form, I'd opened a spreadsheet on my computer and had started a pros and cons list to try to help me make my decision. When my phone rang again, my heart leaped.

Agnes's name flashed across the screen and this time I did pick up.

"Where are you?" Agnes shouted, and my heart jumped into my throat.

"What...what do you mean? What's going on?" I tried to play it cool, but already tears filled my eyes.

"You can't just leave us, Sophie," Agnes said, and I stilled when I heard the shriek of the Kelpies in the background. "You can leave Lachlan if you want, but you can't leave your friends."

"Oh God, oh no...I didn't think..." My pulse picked up and I scrambled across the room, the phone clutched to my ear, shoving my laptop into my bag.

"We need you, Sophie. We're in trouble," Agnes's voice panted. "What do we do?"

"I don't know...I don't know. I'm coming. I promise. I'm not far." I burst from the room at a dead run, grateful that I hadn't bothered to bring my luggage in the night before, just my tote bag with my computer and important documents. Since I'd already paid for the room, I didn't care about leaving without checking out. Once in the truck, I fumbled with the key and stared at the wheel.

"Agnes?"

"Sophie, don't abandon us. Please. I'm scared to go

outside," Agnes whispered into the phone. It was quiet now, and I didn't know if that was a good or bad thing.

"Don't move. I'm on my way."

Hanging up the phone, I pulled my dirk from my purse and laid it on the seat next to me before starting the engine.

"Don't mess with me." I slapped my hand on the steering wheel and, shifting into reverse, I almost cried again when the car moved without stalling. Turning, I shifted into first and roared from the parking lot, slamming forward in my seat when I forgot to shift to the next gear in time. Pulling myself together, I kept my eyes trained on the road, slammed on the gas, and raced toward Loren Brae. I only hoped I wasn't too late to help.

"Stupid, stupid, stupid," I muttered the whole time. I'd been so caught up in my own feelings that I'd forgotten I was the only one who could drive the Kelpies away from the town. Lachlan wasn't there to help, not that I'm sure he even could, but at the very least he'd offered a soothing presence to the people.

What were the Kelpies doing out during the day? That had to be unusual. It was only late afternoon, and I'd only ever heard them at night. Sweat dripped down the back of my neck under my sweater, and I drummed my fingers on the steering wheel, all but bouncing in my seat as I took the final hill into Loren Brae thirty minutes later, hoping I wasn't about to see mass destruction before me.

Instead, I saw something worse.

Lachlan diving into the icy cold waters of Loch Mirren.

My eyes widened as I slammed the truck to a shuddering halt, stalling as I forgot to downshift, the car shaking to a stop. I was out of the car and running before it had stopped moving, the dirk in my hand, as the Kelpies raced across the loch to where Lachlan had disappeared into the water.

"Lachlan!" I screamed. Terror filled me as the Kelpies arrived, rearing high into the air, as Lachlan surfaced with something in his arms.

Sir Buster.

My heart stilled as I realized what was happening, and I held my dirk to the sky, pointing at the Kelpies.

"Stand down! Retreat! You shall not pass!" I screamed anything that I could think of, pulling at the power I felt deep in my gut, forcing the Kelpies back. It was different this time, from when I'd seen them before, as now they challenged me. Their power pushed at me, like those waves that had battered me on the beach in Mexico, and I was forced a step backward. I continued to scream my commands into the shrieking wind, and still they pushed forward, drawing close to where Lachlan swam awkwardly with one arm. I lifted my chin.

And I found my voice.

"Back off. You will not hurt them. I command you to return to your island. Immediately." I spoke the words evenly, with the complete and utter assurance that the Kelpies would obey my command. They paused their thrashing, tilting their heads to study me, before instantly heeding my orders. They retreated, dissipating evenly into the water with barely a ripple, as Lachlan reached the shore and clambered out of the water, holding Sir Buster close to him.

"Lachlan. Oh no, is he okay? Are you okay?" I ran over to Lachlan and reached for him, but the look on his face

teeth at the vet, I couldn't help but smile. We were back to normal, it seemed.

"He's doing great. Just easy on the food for tonight and keep him cozy. He's a lucky dog. I called Hilda at the castle to tell her he was safe." The vet glanced around and then back to me and lowered his voice. "That was really scary today, wasn't it? I don't even know what to think. Is that... what's normal here?" The vet had only just moved to town six months ago, and we'd greatly needed his assistance. Now, I hoped seeing the Kelpies wouldn't send him screaming for the hills.

"It's not, no. But I think we'll have that under control moving forward." I cleared my throat. "At least we're working on it."

"Good to hear. No charge today. What with taking care of...that." The vet nodded his head at the door while he smoothly removed the tube from Sir Buster's leg and wrapped it quickly with some gauze. "There now, wee man. You live to fight another day."

Sir Buster growled at him, and I laughed, scooping him gently into my arms. Only then did I realize that I'd been sitting there in my dripping wet clothes and had left a puddle all over the examining room.

"Och, I'm sorry," I said, glancing down at myself.

"No bother. It's not the worst fluids we've had to clean up here. Unless you've pissed yourself?" The vet laughed at my look and waved me on.

I left the office, my eyes going to where the truck had been and finding it gone. I hoped that Sophie had returned to the castle, but I'd have to track her down after I found a change of clothes.

And a new mobile phone, I realized, patting my pockets. I'd jumped into the water without hesitating, which meant my mobile phone was well and truly saturated.

I'd deal with that later. First, I needed dry clothes and to find Sophie.

The castle was empty on my arrival back, which was odd, until I saw a note on the table that Graham had taken everyone to the pub to hunker down. It made sense, as the pub was a central spot in town where people would gather in times of good and bad. And, well, with Kelpies raging across the loch, I could see why the people would want to get together. Bringing Sir Buster with me to my room, I placed him on the bed and wrapped him in a fleece blanket before having a quick shower and changing into a clean pair of jeans, a thick flannel shirt, and my other pair of boots. Once done, I tugged a soft knit cap over my still-wet hair and went to check on Sir Buster. Kneeling by the bed, I whispered to where he snored softly.

"Hey, buddy."

His warm brown eyes flickered open and still he didn't growl at me. Maybe we'd turned a corner, finally.

"I'm going to the pub. And I think you should come with me. What do you say? Fancy a pint?" As though he understood me, Sir Buster stood and stretched on his little legs before trotting to the side of the bed and waiting for me to pick him up. Perhaps it was a miracle. And I was glad for it. I'm sure in a day or two he'd be back to sniping at me in his usually gloriously grumpy self, but for today I'd welcome his cuddles.

I spoke softly to him the whole walk to the pub, soothing him when he began to tremble as we walked past

Loch Mirren, promising him I'd always be there for him. By the time I'd reached the door of Tipsy Thistle, I had to take a moment to blink the tears from my eyes. I guess I wasn't the only one still reeling from a near-brush with death. Taking a deep breath, I released it, and then opened the door, the voices and the warmth reaching out to me like a hug.

"Sir Buster!" Hilda squealed, yes, *squealed*, as I moved into the main part of the pub and the dog was snatched from my arms by a distraught Hilda. Sir Buster, equally excited, licked Hilda's face like crazy, and I caught Archie dashing the back of his palm across his face before reaching out to scratch Sir Buster's fur.

"I'm safe too," I grumbled, and Hilda just nodded before continuing her adulation of the dog.

"Lachlan!" Agnes squealed, a perfect imitation of Hilda, and threw her arms around me, pretending to lick my face in excitement.

"Och, I get no recognition around here. That's the truth of it," I complained.

"I'll get ye a pint, if that'll do you?" Graham asked with a smile, and I sighed, defeated. The dog would always win where the women were concerned. Speaking of women, I looked around the room, searching for Sophie.

"Have you seen Sophie?" I asked Agnes as she settled onto the stool next to me.

"Aye," Agnes said, tucking one of her wayward curls behind her ears.

"Annnnd?" I raised both eyebrows at her, waiting for her to elaborate. Agnes just shrugged and Graham shook his head.

"See, Lachlan? This is why you shouldn't get involved with women. They either talk back or spin nonsense your way."

"Unlike your hand, right, Graham?" Agnes shot back and everyone in the pub laughed, used to their banter.

Graham opened his mouth to retort, but I raised my hand to stop him. Sophie had entered from a back room, her eyes wide and uncertain, two spots of bright pink on her pale cheeks. I stood and moved to stand in front of her as the entire pub went silent. Someone even killed the music.

"Lachlan—"

"Sophie. Before you say anything...just listen—"

"Och, just like a man," Agnes grumbled in the background.

"We have to cut women off or we'd never get a word in edgewise," Graham complained.

"Maybe if you listened once in a while, we wouldn't have to repeat ourselves twenty times," Agnes shot back.

"Guys!" I shouted, snapping my fingers. "Do you mind if I declare my love here?"

Sophie's mouth rounded into a perfect O.

"Fine, fine. Get on with it then," Graham said. I made a note to kill him later.

"Sophie, I'm sorry for what you saw...and for the way it made you feel. I didn't know about it, I promise you that. I'm not a liar, and I never would have used you in such a manner. But I understand that others have been careless with your heart. I understand why you left. You were scared. Just like I was scared. I was too scared to love you and lose you, so it was easier to keep you at arm's length.

Even when we took a chance on each other, I was still waiting for you to leave. Convinced that one day you would. And now I realize that's no way to live. My mother..." My voice cracked, and Sophie reached for me, but I stepped back, needing to finish this. "My mother would not have wanted me to live this way. To live in fear. Of love. Of the Kelpies. Of what the Order of Caledonia means for protecting our town. I won't always know how to protect you, Sophie. And I hate that. But I'm telling you here, in front of everyone, that I will love you until my last breath, I will spend my life protecting you any way that I can, and hell, I'll even let you continue to save me if needed."

A laugh rose at that.

"I'm not too proud to admit that I need some help sometimes. And I do need your help. Not your money, Sophie. *You*. I love the castle. I love Loren Brae. And I love you. Will you stay and help me?"

The only sound that filled the room was Sir Buster's tiny snores from where he'd nestled into the crook of Hilda's arms and instantly fallen asleep. I waited, my future on hold, as Sophie studied me with those wide all-seeing eyes.

"I learned something about myself today too," Sophie said, and the room seemed to collectively hold its breath, myself included. "I learned that I have a voice. One that matters. And that love is worth fighting for. And that I love this town. I love grumpy Sir Buster, and Clyde with his coo jokes, and how kind everyone is here. I love the wildness of this land and the beauty to be found around every corner. And, Lachlan, I love *me*. And I love the *me* that you see me as. I don't want to stop being that woman. If you'll accept me, after I made awful judgments about you today, I promise to love you unreservedly for all of my days. I want to stay."

My lips were already on hers before her last words were out, and I was lost in her kiss as the pub erupted in cheers.

"Stay and fight!" Agnes crowed, and the pub took up the chant.

"Stay and fight! Stay and fight!"

Pulling away, I wrapped my arm around Sophie and joined the chant, and Sophie raised her hand, gasping at the dirk she held.

"Look!" Sophie shouted, and Agnes sprang from her seat, rushing to our side. There, next to the two stones before it, glimmered a beautiful blood-red ruby.

"The final stone! Och, Sophie! Courage! It's the courage to stay and overcome your fears. You did it," Agnes crowed and cheers erupted once more around the pub.

Sophie blinked up at me, tears filling her eyes.

"I did it, Lachlan, I'm your Knight."

"And you can ride me anytime, darling," I whispered the last part in her ear, loving the way her skin flushed at my words.

Was I a bit crass? Yes, but it had been a long day. I'd gone from thinking I'd lost the woman I loved, to almost losing my dog's and my life, to finding my love again.

Maybe, just this once, my crudeness could be forgiven.

EPILOGUE

SOPHIE

"Is that the best you got?" I raised my voice and stuck a hand on my hip, rolling my eyes dramatically.

The crowd laughed, as I'd wanted them to, while Lachlan made a great show of standing from where he knelt in front of me in the grass.

"Och, I'm only getting started, lassie. It'll be a cold day in hell before I let a woman best me," Lachlan thundered, advancing with his sword.

I smiled sweetly at him, easily dodging his attempts, knowing that would only annoy him further.

Was it wrong of me to use our fake swordplay as foreplay? Probably. But the combination of Lachlan all done up in his kilt, plus my ability to needle him when we faced off during the broadswords exhibition, got me excited. We'd already had more than one hasty session tucked away in a closet after a match before Lachlan had smoothed his hair, straightened his collar, and returned to leading tourists through the castle.

I had to admit, kilts were convenient for a quick rendezvous.

And, yes, what they say is true about kilts.

My ad campaign had started two months ago, and it was hitting the sweet spot with the European and American markets. Though both Lachlan and Graham had griped at the images of them that had graced the cover of one of the local Scottish magazines, I noticed that Graham didn't seem to have a problem displaying that same edition in his pub for his guests to read over a pint.

I'd added the swords demonstration to the weekend tours, as it was too much work to host a Highland Games each weekend. Not only did the banter and swordplay entertain the crowd, but it also kept my skills sharp. The Kelpies had been quiet since I'd passed my last challenge, but Archie had warned me that we were far from completing the Order of Caledonia.

I gasped as Lachlan tapped my side with his sword, tearing my thoughts away from the Order and back to the current fight on hand.

"Och, the lass is dreaming," Lachlan crowed, delighted he'd gotten one by me. Furrowing my brow, I raised my sword and advanced, putting him on his back foot. While he was a fair opponent, it was clear that Lachlan had never had the training I had been given. All those lessons with Uncle Arthur had paid off, and now I made short work of Lachlan, leaving him gasping on the ground once more. Raising my hands in the air, I bowed to the crowd's thunderous applause before turning to give Lachlan a smacking kiss.

He held me close, turning his mouth to my ear.

"That last hit was a touch too near my jewels, darling," Lachlan said.

"That's for the bruise you gave me last night," I replied, smiling widely at him like we weren't discussing our naughty bedroom antics.

"But your bum is just so biteable." Lachlan's eyes gleamed, and he leaned closer. "Should we meet...say in fifteen minutes?"

"Rain check on that, my love. Lottie's just arrived." I'd seen her on the edge of the crowd, her floral headband and bright pink sweater making her stand out. She'd made good on her promise to visit, first making sure that Sarah, her chef, was more than happy to enjoy a few weeks at the house watching over the dogs. Once they were seen to, Lottie had been on a plane to visit. Now, I left Lachlan after one more kiss and raced across the grass to where she stood, her arms wide open for a hug.

"Lottie!" I gasped, tears welling into my eyes, and she pulled me tight. We rocked back and forth, like an erratic metronome, laughing and crying at the same time. "I'm so glad you're here."

"I couldn't stay away a moment longer. I had to see this place for myself and meet your young man." Lottie pulled back and pursed her lips, her shrewd eyes scanning my face. Despite her creative spirit and penchant for oddities, Lottie was no space cadet. Her intelligence had been an equal match for Arthur's and had been one of the traits that Arthur loved most about Lottie. If I'd been unhappy or stressed, she would have read it in an instant and jumped into action. Instead, a relieved smile spread across her face and then her gaze flitted over my shoulder. "Oh, my."

I knew she had to be looking at Lachlan. It was the same reaction I'd had when I'd first seen him as well.

"Yes, I know," I sighed. "He's just too good, right?"

"Finally, you've picked a man worthy of you," Lottie decided, her gaze still on where Lachlan posed for photos with a tourist. "If I was thirty years younger, I'd buy a ticket for his ride."

"Lottie!" I gasped.

"I'm old, Sophie, but not dead. I've eyes in my head, don't I?" Lottie threaded her arm through mine. "Now, introduce me and I'll try not to giggle and blush."

"I don't think you've blushed a day in your life," I snorted. Tugging her through the crowd, I waited while Lachlan finished and then turned to us, a smile on his handsome face.

"You must be the infamous Lottie," Lachlan said, the Highlands whispering through his voice, and Lottie turned to me, her eyebrows raised.

"Maybe I will giggle, just a bit…" she said.

"It's the accent. It gets you every time, I swear." I laughed. "Lachlan, this is Lottie. I'm so excited she's here. I can't wait to show her the castle. Can she join your tour? I'll pay the fee, I promise."

"There's no fee for family, lass." Lachlan threaded his arm through Lottie's, who looked like a cat who'd just lapped a bowl of cream, and dragged her away. I waved, not following, as I had other duties to attend to before we met with Agnes in an hour. Hurrying across the lawn, I gathered up the swords and returned them to the storage closet by the stables and stopped to poke my head in by Archie's workshop.

"Lottie's just arrived, and she's on tour with Lachlan."

"Aye, that's grand. I'll be in at half past. I'm just finishing up here." Archie didn't look up from where he hammered a nail into a shelving unit. "Sir Buster's with Hilda around front."

"Perfect. We have record numbers so far today. I think the ad campaign is working."

"It was bloody brilliant, it was. It's about time those two loafers did some work around here," Archie griped.

"Lachlan pretends to hate it, as does Graham, but I think their egos have inflated quite a bit. Collateral damage, I suppose, but well worth it. I don't mind taking them down a peg or two when they get too big for their britches," I said with a smile.

"Och, that's the Scottish way, lass." Archie grinned.

An hour later, we were gathered in the library, Lachlan having passed his tour duties off to some of the staff we'd been able to hire back. He'd kept his kilt on, likely to drive me mad, and now I was torn between paying attention to Agnes and where his hand toyed lightly at my knee.

Hilda and Lottie sat next to each other, both sipping on a cup of tea. The two had sized each other up and had become instant best friends. Already, Hilda was talking about where they could set up an artist studio for Lottie to paint, and Lottie was asking how she could help around the castle. Sir Buster had also taken to Lottie immediately, and eschewing his usual growly greeting, he now clambered at her leg for more attention. Lottie bent and before I could warn her, she absentmindedly picked Sir Buster up and put him on her lap while continuing her conversation with Hilda.

"Unbelievable," Lachlan muttered. After his traumatic rescue, Sir Buster had been kind to Lachlan for about a week before falling back into his usual grumbly routine with him. It seemed to suit the both of them just fine.

"Lottie, are you up to speed on what we're here to talk about today?" Agnes asked, sounding more formal than she looked in her faded jeans with rips in the knees and Ramone's T-shirt.

"Mostly, though I'd like clarification on what comprises the Order of Caledonia. Are we looking to recruit another Knight then?" Lottie asked, snapping to attention as she stroked Sir Buster's back.

"No, that role has been filled." Agnes shook her head. "It's an interesting thing, the way this Order was designed. From what I've been able to translate, it seems the Order is meant to be filled with people who embody the roles that you would find in a traditional medieval castle or village. The Stone of Truth seems to think that a holistic approach to fulfilling the Order is the wisest one, where differing viewpoints and talents will make a complete and well-functioning group. Until the Order is complete, we will still be under threat of the Kelpies, as well as any other ways that the Stone feels it needs to protect itself."

"The Stone likes diversification." Lottie nodded. "I can understand that. It's like when an entire boardroom is full of men who are designing a product for a woman. It makes no sense."

"Exactly," Hilda said. "Remember when they came out with those pens designed just for women? Silly."

"Well, I, for one, had never been able to write until a man designed a pen for me. Thank goodness. I was saved," Lottie quipped, and we all laughed.

"In the interests of diversification, I made a list of past members of the Order, and some of the varying roles they filled. Then, from there, I started tracing down the line to see if any of their descendants were around." Agnes held up a spreadsheet, and my heart did a little dance in my chest.

"Oh, spreadsheets. Gimme," I exclaimed, and Agnes passed it over so I could scan the papers. I had to hand it to her, she'd done an extensive amount of research. "Agnes, you should have asked for help with this. I would have been happy to give you my time. This is a lot of work."

"I don't mind it. You've had other things on your mind." Agnes laughed. "It's not like I'm dating anyone either. My free time is dedicated to the cause."

"We can change that," Hilda piped up and Lottie leaned forward, a gleam in her eyes.

"Back off, matchmakers." Agnes held out a hand. "We are not here to discuss my love life."

"Or lack thereof." Lachlan smiled sweetly.

"It's not like you had a shining dating history either." I elbowed Lachlan and Agnes laughed. "Okay, so, it looks like you've narrowed in on someone."

"I have. I think." Agnes nodded, catching my eye.

I studied the sheet, seeing how she'd traced the lineage, and where she'd landed.

"A baker? Or a chef? The cook?" I guessed.

"Aye," Agnes said. "Arguably one of the most important

roles in a castle and village, those who provided the food and managed the food supplies were vitally important."

"That makes sense," Lachlan said, leaning back to throw an arm around my shoulder. "I've always admired anyone who has that skill. I'm content to open a cold can of beans and eat it straight from the can."

"Of course the chefs are the most important," Lottie piped in, nodding along to the conversation. "A good one always adds a key ingredient to every dish."

"What's that?" I asked.

"Love," Lottie said, turning to me with a wide smile. "Love is always the best ingredient." For such a long time, I would have mocked Lottie for that comment. But I now knew her words to true. Love had been the missing ingredient in my life because I'd steered clear of it. Feared the rejection that could come with it. But here in Loren Brae, I had grabbed hold of love with arms open wide, and my life was all the better for it.

Kelpies and all.

Can't get enough of Sophie and Lachlan? Sign up to my newsletter to get, Lady Lola, a short story that will make you smile and swoon. Could Sir Buster be getting a friend and a new addition to the family?
www.triciaomalley.com/free

WHO WILL the next member of the Order of Caledonia be? Read on for a sneak peek into the next book in the Enchanted Highlands series: Wild Scottish Love.

WILD SCOTTISH LOVE

BOOK 2 IN THE ENCHANTED HIGHLANDS SERIES

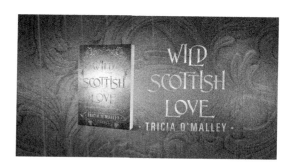

LIA

"Grasshoppers?"

An alarm sounded in my head as, Damien, the new owner of Suzette's, a fine-dining restaurant tucked in the cozy North End of Boston, dropped a box on my spotless prep table. As head chef, *I* should have been the one ordering the ingredients for the menu, not Damien.

At least that was the way things had been when Suzette

had been alive. Now I was shouldered with dealing with her sleaze of a son who couldn't leave well enough alone. Suzette's was one of the hottest restaurants in Boston, thanks to my inventive themed surprise menus, and Damien had taken his new role as an opportunity to strut his authority around the restaurant. Every night, like cock of the walk, he'd stroll through the dining room and publicly find fault with something, often sending one of the servers into tears. We'd all been on edge for months now, and I knew that more than one of the staff were actively looking for other jobs.

It was hard enough to grieve the loss of Suzette, a kind woman who had shared my dream of building a restaurant that was both cozy and innovative, without having to also navigate a new boss who never bothered to learn anything about the service industry. Even worse? I woke up each night, drenched in sweat, panic gripping me that the one goal that I'd devoted my entire life to was slipping from my grasp.

"Yeah, it's all the rage," Damien said, picking up my custom chef's knife. The knife had been a gift from Suzette when Boston Magazine had run a feature article labeling me as the hot up-and-coming chef in Boston's elite culinary scene, and it had been designed to perfectly balance in my palm. I cared for that knife like it was my baby, and seeing Damien's greasy fingers on it made my lip curl in disgust. The bright side? He likely had no clue how sharp it was, so there was hope he'd maim himself shortly and I'd be left to get on with my menu for the night.

"Damien...be careful..." I trailed off as he slit the tape at the top of the box, narrowly missing the tip of his finger, and I took a deep breath in an effort to control my temper. He needed to get out of my kitchen, *now*, and take his insects with him.

"I ordered these specially from Brazil. Overnighted them. They're incredibly expensive, so you'll need to make them a Chef's Special. I hear they're salty, like potato chips." Damien said, pausing to wipe the back of the hand holding the knife against his perpetually sweaty forehead. My heart skipped a beat as the tip of my knife just missed his eyes, because while I did enjoy a good maiming, even I would turn squeamish if he popped his eyeball out.

What happened next was like when a sports team wins a big championship, and the celebratory cannons explode confetti across the arena – except replace confetti with grasshoppers.

Live grasshoppers.

While typically I have good reflexes – an important trait in any kitchen – my brain quite simply could not process the catastrophe I was witnessing. Hundreds, no, *thousands*, of grasshoppers pinged around the kitchen, bounced off walls, and landed on any available surface.

"They were supposed to be *dried*, not alive," Damien shrieked, waving his hands in the air, and I narrowly dodged the knife he threw when a grasshopper landed in his open mouth. My breath caught as the knife clattered to the floor while Damien gagged on the grasshopper.

"You *idiot*! You almost killed me." I was also shrieking at this point, but not from fear. Oh no, the last few weeks of buried rage surfaced, as though someone had dropped a match on spilled gasoline, and now I let the inferno engulf me. Crouching, I snatched my knife off the floor and returned it to its case, before slamming the lid closed on the grasshopper box. Not like there were all that many insects still in the box. It was hard to put a bomb back together after it detonated, wasn't it?

"Idiot? You can't talk to me like that. Don't forget who signs your paychecks, doll," Damien had the gall to say to me with a grasshopper perched on his head.

"Look at what you've done," I seethed, holding my hands out to protect my face from grasshoppers that bounced around the room like someone had tossed a bucket of superballs into the kitchen. "Everything has gone to shit since Suzette died. You keep coming in here and screwing things up. You're ruining a good thing, Damien, and I for one, am not interested in sticking around to watch you destroy Suzette's legacy. You should be ashamed of yourself. Your poor mother would be devastated at what you're turning her dream into."

"My mother didn't know what was cool. This place is old and boring. At least I'm here to make it fresh." Damien smashed his hand onto the prep table, squashing a few grasshoppers, as I gaped at him in surprise.

"This? *This* is your idea of fresh?" I swept my arms out and ducked as several grasshoppers flew past. Technically speaking, he wasn't wrong. When the food was still moving, it was about as fresh as it could be. "It's stupid is what it is. And I'm not sticking around to clean up your mess."

I made to move past him, taking my knife with me, and he shouldered his way into the hallway to block me.

"If you leave, you're fired, Lia."

"That's kind of the point, isn't it?" I needed to get out of this insectarium immediately. There weren't enough showers I could take to rid me of the creepy crawly feeling of grasshoppers in my hair. My pulse kicked up when Damien leaned close, his breath heavy with stale cigar.

"You think you can make a name for yourself without me? I'll blackball you in this town faster than you turn men off with your ginger hair and bad attitude."

"Excuse me?" I couldn't think straight, not between the rage that twisted my gut into knots and the sizeable number of insects that were currently doing their best to vacate the kitchen through any means possible.

"Screw it. I never liked this restaurant anyway," Damien crossed his arms over his chest, and huffed out a breath. "I think I'll make it a club. Lots of hot young women in here dancing each night. Yeah, it's gonna be slick as hell."

I gaped at him, honestly at a loss for words, as I thought about the beautiful restaurant that I'd devoted years of my life to.

"I *hate* you. You're gross and it makes me sick what you're doing to this place," I said, not caring if I burned any bridges. I didn't want to work with someone like Damien anyway. He was as dishonorable as the day was long, and I'd rather start my own gig than have to take orders from a sleaze like him.

"Maybe, but I don't care what you think, doll." Damien winked at me. My lip curled in disgust. Being called 'doll' was a pet peeve of mine. "Gingers aren't my type anyway. I like them rail-thin with the big titties."

He was slime. Repulsive slime, and I...I had to go. Right now. Before I did something stupid like burn the restaurant down, so I didn't have to watch him ruin it. At this point, that might be the best option anyway what with the grasshoppers taking up residence.

"Eat shit, Damien. I quit." I went to move past him, and Damien put his arms out, stopping me in my tracks.

"It's Saturday night. We've got a packed house." Damien didn't budge.

"Get out of my way," I said, stepping forward. "If you think that I'll stay and clean this up, you're out of your damn mind."

"You *will* stay. And you *will* cook. Because that's your job." As soon as Damien put his hands on my shoulders and shoved me backward, I did what I'd been dying to do for years now. I brought my knee solidly up between his legs just like my brothers had taught me to. With a pained grunt, Damien crumpled to the floor, a soft keening noise coming from his lips, like a balloon letting out air.

"Big tree falls hard," I mumbled.

"Lia! What's going on?" Savannah, the head bartender, came upstairs with a case of beer in her arms which she immediately dropped upon seeing the grasshoppers. The smash of glass was beyond satisfying as I stepped neatly over Damien.

"Damien's turning the place into a club. Oh, and he wants to feed people grasshoppers." Other servers were walking in the door for their shift, and at my words, they scattered back outside. "I'm leaving."

"I'm with you. I knew this place would go to hell with him in charge," Savannah said, reaching behind the bar to grab her purse. As one, the waitstaff and I pivoted and left Damien, curled on the floor and covered in grasshoppers, screaming after us.

"Screw that guy. Want to go get drunk?" Savannah asked, looking around the North End. "I think this is the first Saturday night I've had free in ages."

"Yes, yes, I do." I mean, I didn't, not really. I wanted to go home and shower for weeks on end to rid myself of the creepy crawly feeling of grasshoppers in my hair. But I'd just quit the single most important thing that I'd done in my life, and alcohol was needed.

Savannah hooked my arm, pulling me down the street, and before I knew it, we were ensconced in a proper Boston dive bar, yelling at the Sox on the brightly lit screens and eating delicious fried food. By the time I staggered into my building, I was well and truly numbed from the shock of quitting my job.

There, I plopped down onto my tiny loveseat in my tiny utilitarian apartment and looked around at my bare walls. There was no cat to greet me, no houseplant to water, only a pile of unfolded laundry on the small breakfast bar. My life, quite literally, had been at the restaurant. Suzette's. My home. My baby. My everything. But it had never really been mine, had it? I'd been running my whole life, away from the little girl who wore hand-me-downs, and now fear dredged low in my stomach as the debt I accrued from attending culinary school loomed in my mind.

My phone pinged with a text message.

Carlo: What's up with the picture of you and Savannah at the bar tonight and her saying you guys quit?

I rolled my eyes at the text from my brother, Carlo. He was the most protective of my brothers and knew how seriously I took my job.

Me: I wish she wouldn't have posted that until I was

ready to share. But yes, I quit. Or Damien let me go. Either way, I'm done. He wants to feed people grasshoppers and turn the restaurant into a club.

Carlo: Grasshoppers? What the hell? I hate him. I've always hated him. Stupid move on his part. Might as well sell the restaurant. He'll make more money than trying to run it himself.

Me: He's ruined everything.

Carlo: Come home. Ma will cook Sunday dinner for you. You haven't been home in months.

Me: I need to sleep. And take a moment to process this. Will call you tomorrow.

Carlo: You'd better be at dinner or I'm telling Ma you got fired.

Me: Dick move.

Carlo: Love you. See you tomorrow.

I sent him a photo of me flipping him off and then sighed and dropped back onto the cushions. I loved my family, loud and overbearing though they were. With four brothers, an Italian mother, and a Scottish father, my childhood had been chaotic even on a good day. And there had been more good days than bad, even though we'd been dirt poor, and my parents had barely been able to make ends meet. However, what I'd lacked in material goods, I'd more than made up for in love. We were a tightly connected bunch, sometimes too tightly, judging from my brother's midnight text message.

I couldn't move back home.

Leaving my small town to live in Boston had been an opportunity to make something of myself. Suzette had taken a chance on me, a naive and tender-hearted girl fresh from high school, and she'd been pivotal in providing me with an environment in which to flourish. I never, ever, asked anyone for help, and I'd been determined to prove myself to Suzette after she'd taken a chance on me. Through several long years of culinary school, and late nights at the restaurant, I'd worked my way up from dishwasher to head chef at Suzette's. When the article in Boston Magazine had come out, my mother had spent almost her entire paycheck on buying multiple copies to give to everyone she knew. I'd *had* every intention of framing that article myself. My blank walls now mocked me.

Blinking down at my phone, I noticed my voicemail indicator. I hadn't heard the ring in the loud bar, and now I stared at the UK number with a shiver of anticipation. *That was odd*. Punching in my code, I pulled up my voicemail.

"Hi, Lia, my name is Sophie, and I'm calling from MacAlpine Castle in Scotland. We've heard talk of your legendary prowess in the kitchen and are hoping to lure you to Scotland to work for us in our restaurant. What do you say? Fancy a chef's job in an honest-to-goodness castle? You'll have free rein with the menu of course. Please let us know. It's quite urgent, but we'll move on to the next name on our list if you're not interested. You're our top choice, naturally." She rattled off her contact information. Surprise had me dropping my phone and I stood up to pace my small living room. Seven steps forward. Seven steps back.

Scotland.

The thought alone made me smile. *Oh, what incredible timing*. It wasn't that unusual for other restaurants to try and ply me away from Suzette's, but I'd never had an offer from someplace as far away as Scotland. Maybe...well, just maybe. Nerves skittered through my stomach. Glancing around at my empty apartment once more, I took a deep breath and picked up my phone.

Fall in love with the much-anticipated second book in the Enchanted Highlands series.

Order Wild Scottish Love today!

AFTERWORD

Dear Reader,

What can I say? I fell in love with this story when the first hints of it teased my mind during our re-routed honeymoon. After our wedding in Scotland last summer, we were meant to tour Europe, but Covid derailed our plans. Instead, we found a darling isolated cottage in the wilds of Scotland and off we went to rest up and learn how to use an outdoor wood-burning hot tub. A town close to us, Inveraray, provided an amazing backdrop for inspiration for this story. It hosts a massive castle, a lovely loch, and a darling village that just begged for a visit from my characters. So, I waved my magic wand, added some magick, and ta-da – Wild Scottish Knight was born. I suppose I'm extra sentimental about this book because even though Covid derailed our honeymoon plans, we still ended up having the perfect time tucked away in our little cottage in the woods. In sickness and in health and all that...

Cottage Honeymoon

I'd also like to thank my lovely sister-in-law, Gillian, for allowing me to write Sir Buster into the story. Buster was their much-loved chihuahua who they lost a week after our wedding. This is my way to honor his memory and remind people that telling stories about those we love, animal and human alike, is the best way to keep everyone's light alive. Safe home will you go, Sir Buster!

Sir Buster

Thank you all for joining me on this journey, and a special thanks to the Scotsman, my soulmate and most-patient-man ever. Thank you for putting up with all my quirks and frustrations as I continue to create these stories that pester my brain. Love you forever.

XX,

Tricia

ALSO BY TRICIA O'MALLEY

THE ISLE OF DESTINY SERIES

Stone Song

Sword Song

Spear Song

Sphere Song

A completed series in Kindle Unlimited.

Available in audio, e-book & paperback!

"Love this series. I will read this multiple times. Keeps you on the edge of your seat. It has action, excitement and romance all in one series."

- Amazon Review

"Not my usual genre but couldn't resist the Florida Keys setting. I was hooked from the first page. A fun read with just the right amount of crazy! Will definitely follow this series."- Amazon Review

A completed series in Kindle Unlimited.

Available in audio, e-book & paperback!

"I have read thousands of books and a fair percentage have been romances. Until I read Wild Irish Heart, I never had a book actually make me believe in love."- Amazon Review

A completed series in Kindle Unlimited.

Available in audio, e-book & paperback!

STAND ALONE NOVELS

Ms. Bitch

"Ms. Bitch is sunshine in a book! An uplifting story of fighting your way through heartbreak and making your own version of happily-ever-after."

~Ann Charles, USA Today Bestselling Author

Starting Over Scottish

Grumpy. Meet Sunshine.

She's American. He's Scottish. She's looking for a fresh start. He's returning to rediscover his roots.

One Way Ticket

A funny and captivating beach read where booking a one-way ticket to paradise means starting over, letting go, and taking a chance on love...one more time

10 out of 10 - The BookLife Prize

CONTACT ME

I hope my books have added a little magick into your life. If you have a moment to add some to my day, you can help by telling your friends and leaving a review. Word-of-mouth is the most powerful way to share my stories. Thank you.

Love books? What about fun giveaways? Nope? Okay, can I entice you with underwater photos and cute dogs? Let's stay friends! Sign up for my newsletter and contact me at my website.

www.triciaomalley.com

Or find me on Facebook and Instagram.
@triciaomalleyauthor

Printed in Great Britain
by Amazon